FELLOW

By David Fettes

Copyright © 2016 David Fettes

All rights reserved.

ISBN: 1530339669
ISBN-13: 9781530339662

Fellow

For my Father

Who knew the Boy

But not the Man

FOREWORD

The landscape of our lives is shaped and formed by the events to which we are exposed. We each, unavoidably, endure an upbringing; an education; relationships. Our own personal history. Each of these forces brings to us the Low and High pressure weather systems of life's moments, moments that can either depress or enthral us. Some are neutral, requiring no reactive emotional response. Others form us, both positively and negatively influencing and controlling our future responses to the daily encounters of life. The nurture by which we are simultaneously delighted and damaged. Life is a potter and we are thrown on its wheel, to be shaped and sculpted before we are fired in the furnace of experience to become the finished article the world sees, set in our ways and seemingly unchangeable.

The nature we enter the world with at birth, our factory installed motherboard, is moulded over time by how we perceive we are treated. We are shaped by how we feel we are regarded and judged. For the fortunate few whose nature is resilient granite, their emotional topography remains intact as their self belief and sense of self worth rebuts the storms that break over them. Too often this resilience does not endear them to their companions, who instead envy their fortitude and independence of thought without being able to emulate it. For the soft sandstone based majority, their topography is weathered and eroded, their nature irreparably changed, their innate essence washed away. We each react to what we see and experience in our own idiosyncratic way. We rarely have the insight to understand why we are angered or pleased, fearful of or excited by the incidents and people we come upon as we follow our particular path on the journey to our grave.

Are we ever a finished product or are we only ever destined to be a work in progress? Ever a continuum of change, of learning. Ever adapting and evolving. Do we have any control over our emotions and reactions? Can we change ourselves? The pheromones we exude are installed in us in our formative years. They repel and attract, as we too are repelled and attracted, our subconscious selves forming attachments and dislikes that have their genesis in our reconstituted nature. Our responses and emotions seem to be guided by an interior force over which we believe we have no control, and so we are often irritated by our response to circumstances, to words, to people. We promise ourselves we will change and be different next time. But when next time happens it reawakens our instinctive feelings, and the cycle of self criticism is repeated.

    Like all of us, Ben's story started its development from the moment of his birth. It shaped his way of dealing with his life and the pressures it brought, the responsibilities he acquired. The little boy could have been a different man, but he didn't know how to be. Do any of us? The amygdala of our being is an overwhelming force, so often out of our control, dominating our reactions. We are enslaved by it, subjugated by its often irresistible but instinctive influence. Subtle changes in Ben's early life could have brought about a different outcome. A redesigned nature in the womb would have made a different man, better able to resist the negative influences of his nurture. But like all of us, Ben only had one life. There are no second chances. Some of us are fortunate enough to learn the power of choice. Some of us discover the ability to wrest back control of our very self, of our thoughts, enabling us to bring about the change in our thinking that empowers us to dictate different outcomes for ourselves, outcomes that suit our objectives better and leave less to the often unwelcome consequences of reactive behaviour. Is this what they call wisdom? Some may call it experience but experience doesn't necessarily change the way we behave or alter our behavioural patterns. Choice does that.

We each only have one story, one history. This is Ben's. Do you think he might have wanted it to be different? How many of us would like a different story, a different outcome? And how much of our present do we lose in the time we invest in regretting our past, even as we waste time wishing for a future that can only exist if we make the changes in ourselves that so many say are impossible to make?

There is only ever the present. The past is unchangeable history and the future is always unknown. Today is yesterday's tomorrow, and today's tomorrow may be too late.

CHAPTER 1

June 1957

Sometimes it's the little details we remember rather than the grand landscape. Those tiny, inconsequential events that can forever define a moment. Buried deep in our subconscious, the oubliette in which we believe they can no longer harm us, they nevertheless lurk beneath the surface of our consciousness waiting for the catalyst that awakens them, the Lazerine moment of resurrection that exhumes them from the tomb where we thought we had interred them. The sound of a church clock's chimes, or the syncopated beat of a drum. The sight of a badly painted fingernail or a highly polished shoe. The scent of someone's perfume in the street. Ben remembered a girl who walked past him in the street. He immediately succumbed to an irresistible urge to turn and follow her for a short while, breathing in her perfume as it flowed behind her, like Isadora Duncan's gossamer scarf, waiting to wrap and entrap. The girl didn't know of course.

L'Air du Temps. It drifted behind her, an ethereal trail for him to follow. As he walked a few yards behind her his mind flooded with memories of a girl he once knew. He was back with her, walking through a field of wild flowers, her soft hand in his, their fingers interlocked, her floral cotton dress billowing in the light summer breeze. The scent of her perfume mingled with that of the flowers and grasses in a pastoral and feminine overload.

An earlier more astringent memory for Ben was his eight year old self, feet dangling in the air as he sat on the hard chair in front of the headmaster's desk. He was flanked by his parents as the headmaster interviewed them about their proposal and desire that Ben should attend his boarding school. The chair Ben was perched on had never been designed for a small person. Sitting on it, Ben swung his feet backwards and forwards until his mother put her hand on his knee, frowning down, irritated at his fidgeting. He immediately replaced the pendulum like swinging of his feet with shaking his bare thighs, like a Bengali babu. The inevitable touch of his mother's hand again stilled his restless limbs

The headmaster's office was a large wood panelled room, with mullioned and leaded windows that looked out across a large playing field. A desultory game of cricket was being played in the afternoon sunshine. It was being umpired by a stooped, elderly man with unkempt white hair. He was festooned in sweaters and had a boy's cap perched on top of his head. It looked like a doily on a bed of thick lichen. Foraging swallows swooped between the players in the outfield, some of whom clearly thought that just turning up was sufficient commitment to the game. Ben could see one of the boys lounging on the grass, far out by the boundary, preoccupied with making a daisy chain, blissfully oblivious of the game and obviously confident the ball was unlikely to come anywhere near him. Even Ben's young self could sense the quintessential Englishness of the scene, its timeless glance back to a pre-war world and its old fashioned values.

Two deep leather armchairs sat side by side in the bay window of the room, overlooking this Albion vista. A small coffee table stood between the armchairs and on it was a folded newspaper, the half completed crossword showing. A pencil lay diagonally across the paper. Next to the paper was an ashtray with a smouldering pipe resting in it. The paraphernalia of a gentleman's relaxation. The scent of tobacco, dust and leather filled the room. A musty, male scent, devoid of any softening feminine traces. A glass fronted bookcase lined one wall. In it were mould-stained leather books and a few silver trophies, each engraved with the names of past champions. A couple of battered filing cabinets were pushed into the corner behind the door and in front of them stood a wooden carver chair with one armrest missing. Two antique looking cricket bats leaned against the solitary armrest and a wooden bowl full of well beaten cricket balls sat on the chair's seat.

Ben suddenly awoke from his reverie as he gazed out of the window, becoming aware the conversation had turned to the subject of his last school report and its litany of rather indifferent exam results. The headmaster was leaning forward, his elbows and forearms on his leather-topped desk. To his left was a large black telephone and a neat pile of papers and letters. A silver inkwell formed a defensive palisade at the front of the desk. Ben stared in fascination at the man's thick-fingered hands with their simian sward of black hair.

"So Ben, not a particularly impressive record is it?" said the headmaster.

It occurred to Ben that the comment in his last report from one of the teachers that *Your son has a wonderful brain. Unfortunately there's nothing in it. He does his work entirely to his own satisfaction,'* was not the ringing endorsement he was supposed to aspire to.

"No sir," he replied, conscious that he didn't have much evidence to support any disagreement with the obvious.

"What's your favourite subject?"

The unexpected question aimed directly at him flummoxed Ben. He had not really expected to have to become involved in the conversation or interview. His mother had told him in the car on the way to the school to say nothing, and in particular not to mention he had already been to four different schools, so he had assumed his parents would handle the negotiations and details. He felt the colour come up into his cheeks as his mind went blank in the oppressive silence in the room. Aware that he had to answer he said the first thing that came into his head.

"Cricket sir," he blurted.

"Aha, a sportsman are you? I was thinking something a bit more academic, perhaps a bit more cerebral." The headmaster's brow furrowed slightly as he turned to Ben's parents, leaving him to wonder why the man had brought up the subject of cereals. Not wishing to look any more of a fool than the one he already felt, he said nothing and glanced at his father for support.

"I think it would be a good idea if I had a chat alone with Ben, so we can get to know each other a bit better," the headmaster said. "I pride myself on knowing the boys here intimately and I like to let them express themselves independently in open conversation with me, man to man. Why don't you both take a look around the school. I see there's a cricket match on so you can see some of our facilities in action. You can get an idea of how we'll indulge Ben in his favourite subject if he is accepted to St Nicholas's. I shall get someone to take you."

The headmaster got up and went to the door, opening it and leaning his head and shoulders out into the corridor. An elderly man was walking past.

"Ah, Smithers, could you pop in please" he said, stepping back into the office. His air of command was self evident, a sense of entitlement and control that brooked no disagreement. The man followed him in.

"This is Mr. Smithers" said the headmaster, introducing the man to Ben's parents. "How long have you been at St Nicholas's Smithers?"

"Forty seven years, headmaster," he replied.

He stood by the open door, slightly stooped and dressed in ill fitting clothes. A well worn corduroy jacket with leather patches on the elbows hung off his thin shoulders. Pens and pencils sprouted from the jacket's top pocket like a shambolic flower arrangement. A few blades of dried grass were protruding from one of the turn-ups of his baggy trousers. Perhaps there was a a field mouse's nest in there, Ben thought.

"Mr Smithers is our longest serving member of staff" said the headmaster. Turning to the elderly man and waving to Ben's parents, he said

"Please show these good people around the school while this young man and I get to know each other better. Take in the new hall, I think, and some of the playing fields. I'm sure they would like to know where their son will pursue his favourite subject. Take your time, there's no hurry," he said turning to Ben's parents.

The sarcasm in his comment appeared to escape Ben's parents' notice as they were ushered out of the room. He imagined his father's failing health was eroding his resistance and will to struggle with anything beyond where the next breath was going to come from, or he would surely have reacted to it. As for his mother, Ben felt she would marry the headmaster if it meant ingratiating herself with him. Even at that young age, Ben could sense her fears and concerns for him. They were ostensibly for him, but he wondered if there was an element that related to the preservation of her own self-esteem. Perhaps her paramount need was to avoid being the subject of the phatic conversation of the cocktail set at home, as they picked over the bones of the corpse of her son's arid educational achievements and compared them with the obese and stellar accomplishments of their own obnoxiously perfect children.

The headmaster turned to face Ben as he closed the door behind his departing parents, his demeanour chillingly changed. This was a different man to the affable figurehead who had greeted them when they had been ushered into the study. He stood staring down at Ben in menacing silence, hands behind his back and feet apart as he swayed slightly, back and forth, rising up on the balls of his feet. His face betrayed no emotion as he watched the boy before him. Ben shifted uncomfortably on the chair, gripping its front edge with hands slightly damp with nervous sweat, his stomach tightening and churning in fear.

"Now young man, these exam results of yours aren't so good, are they?" the headmaster said.

"No," Ben replied.

"No Sir," the headmaster said, without trace of humour, or soft edge to his modulated tones.

"No sir."

"Better but I shouldn't have to remind you. We'll have to do something about that. And your reports. I have seen copies of all of them. A bit thin on achievement I think. Not much in them that we could be proud of, is there?"

"No sir."

"Well, what to do, what to do? That's the question. What do you think we should do about it?"

The headmaster had moved over to the bay window and was looking down on the drive, hands resting in each other behind his back as he spoke. Ben didn't know whether an answer to his questions was needed or expected, and as he could think of nothing to say he remained silent.

"You know your parents spend a lot of money on your education, don't you?" the man said, still looking out over the playing fields below.

"Yes. Yes sir," Ben replied, quickly correcting himself. He was oblivious of the fact his parents had spent anything on his education, nor that they were intending to do so, but felt it wise to agree with everything this suddenly frigidly cold man was saying.

"It's hardly a demonstration of gratitude to produce the results you have, and to put in as little effort into your work as you seem to do. Not after all they have sacrificed for you. So, I think we should have a little punishment, don't you?"

His words, and their unemotional delivery chilled Ben, his blood running cold in his body. Time slowed and it was as though he was looking at the world through an opaque window at the end of a long tube. The headmaster's voice faded, as though he was speaking from another room and down a long, echoing tunnel. Ben's stomach tightened again with the fear now holding him in its iron grip.

"And we'll keep this between ourselves," the headmaster continued, speaking over his shoulder. "Your parents already have enough to be ashamed about because of you. We don't want them to have to add to that the ignominy of knowing you have had to be reprimanded, do we? It would be an embarrassment too far, don't you agree?"

Ben had not the slightest idea what ignominy meant but whatever it was, it didn't sound good. The headmaster turned and looked down on him across the room. He was silhouetted against the window, so it was impossible to see any expression in his face.

"Do you agree I said?"

"Yes sir" Ben replied.

Ben was still trying to absorb the intent behind these seemingly rhetorical questions, but again felt agreement was his only option in the face of this kangaroo court of one. He nodded his acknowledgement and assent, emasculated and powerless in the face of such autocratic authority.

"Pull that chair over here will you," the Headmaster said, pointing to the one-armed chair in the corner of the room that Ben had noticed earlier.

Ben got down off the seat, the skin on the back of his legs sticking to the wood as though reluctant to let go of its safe haven. He walked over to the chair and moved the two cricket bats against the wall, placing the bowl of cricket balls on the floor next to them. He then pulled the chair over to the middle of the room, and as he did the headmaster walked to his desk and opened the top draw, from which he pulled out a broad, flat, leather strap. It looked like a short belt. He turned and walked around behind Ben.

"Now, pop those pants down and bend over this side," the headmaster said, pointing to the solitary arm of the chair. "Hold the seat on the other side."

Ben pulled down his shorts and moved to the chair.

"And the underpants," the headmaster said tetchily.

Ben blushed and pulled his underpants down so they joined his short around his ankles. Gripping Ben's shoulder hard the headmaster moved him over to the chair and positioned him so he had to bend over the arm and reach down to the edge of the seat on the opposite side. Bent almost double, Ben could no longer see what the man was doing behind him. He could hear his movements, his shoes scuffing the carpet. A breeze from the open window chilled his naked, taught bottom. He felt completely exposed, humiliated. The headmaster moved the tail of Ben's shirt up his back.

The exquisite sting of the leather strap across his naked buttocks shocked him to the core. Ben started to rise but the headmaster pushed his head down. Five more strokes fell in quick succession, marked by the complete absence of sound from the headmaster, apart from his quickening, excited breathing. Strangely elated, when the strokes stopped he patted and caressed Ben's naked flesh, gently and almost lovingly stroking it as he ran his hand over his bare skin. He momentarily pushed his hand between Ben's legs.

"Right ho," the headmaster said suddenly, jovially satiated. "Stand up and pull up those togs and then pop the chair back in the corner will you."

Ben stood up and pulled up his underpants and shorts self consciously, acutely aware of the act of once more having to bend over before the ogre to reach for them from their resting place on the floor. He returned the chair to its corner and rearranged the cricket balls and bats when the headmaster told him to leave everything exactly as he had found it. His backside was stinging, his senses affronted by the humiliating assault on his naked person. The headmaster seemed oblivious to his feelings and stood before him, his face and eyes animated.

"Now, remember what I said, we'll just keep that between ourselves. There will be more of the same if I find you have told anyone, and I will find out, believe me. And let's make sure there is no reason for us to have to repeat it when you return to St Nicholas' next term."

It was many years before Ben learned that St Nicholas was the Patron Saint of prostitutes, which was a shame as the eight year old boy would have loved to have told the headmaster, although perhaps not at that precise moment.

As the headmaster finished speaking, Ben's parents returned from their impromptu tour of the school. He listened to the exchange of pleasantries and banalities between the adults, whilst feeling a curious, light headed detachment. They say those at the point of death who are revived tell of having had an out of body experience, of being part of their surroundings but floating above them as a disconnected, dispassionate observer. That is how Ben felt as he watched the ritual shaking of hands.

Suddenly aware that he was expected to participate in the ceremonials of departure, he held out his hand to the headmaster.

"I look forward to seeing you next term, young man, and I enjoyed our little chat," the headmaster said.

"Oh, thank you!" Ben's mother exclaimed. "That is such a relief and I just know Ben will be very happy here.

"Of course he will," the headmaster said. He turned to Ben and held out his hand.

"Thank you, sir," Ben replied, taking the proffered hand. The headmaster held it longer than he felt comfortable with. The man's large, sylvan hand was damp with sweat. It was hot and unexpectedly soft. He held Ben's eyes knowingly, his unbroken gaze an unspoken threat. Ben retrieved his hand and turned to follow his parents from the study and out of the building to the sanctuary of the car. As they left, his mother suddenly stopped and turned to ask a question at the door of the office. Ben cannoned into her in his hurry to leave the room. He never wanted to see the man again, and yet knew he would have him as an omnipotent presence and threat in his life for the next five years.

The family reached the car and Ben quickly opened the back door and jumped in, slipping down in the seat so he could not be seen from the outside. Ben remembered that car so well. An old, grey Standard Vanguard with its sloping back, round and bulbous, always reminding him of a bumble bee's bottom. Now it was his haven, his sanctuary. His father swung it around on the wide gravel forecourt in front of the school, and set its nose down the tree lined drive, past the now empty playing field on their left. Only the cows grazing in the fields on the right saw them leave, their distended udders brushing the long grass and yellow buttercups.

As the car cleared the school gates and turned onto the road, Ben's mother swivelled around in her seat, looking at him over her shoulder, her brow furrowed.

"I really do think you could show a little more gratitude and good grace," she said. "The headmaster has very kindly agreed to take you and all you can do is look sour-faced. You will need to pull your socks up, young man, or you won't last there. And if you don't, I really don't know what we can do with you. I can't think of any other school that would take you."

Satisfied she had made herself clear, and evidently irritated at Ben's lack of response, she turned back in her seat. Ben stared out of the window as the unseen countryside passed them by. Somehow, life had become just a bit more complicated.

CHAPTER 2

September 1957

The opaque moonlight from the blue moon filtered through the tall window above Ben's bed. Its ghostly light revealed the contents of the curtained cubicle in which he lay, chasing elusive sleep and its soothing balm. A slight breeze from the open window moved the curtain at the foot of the bed. As he rolled over on the unforgiving thin mattress, he wondered why his mother had said it would be a blue moon that night. The moon always seemed to be pretty much white to him.

Ben had arrived at St Nicholas' earlier in the afternoon. The school's drive was filled with cars disgorging boys, parents and large, blue school trunks, each with the owner's name painted on them. Tuck boxes clattered onto the gravel. The trunks were harvested by two men who carried them into the school, like worker ants disappearing into an anthill with the trophies of a foraging expedition. Ben's bare kneecaps, which protruded from beneath his grey shorts, seemed to have started an involuntary shaking. A fierce grip of dread knotted his stomach. He shivered in the cool September air and wished with every sense of his being to be somewhere else. No one had asked him if he wanted to leave home, but then looking back in later years he came to realise a post war eight year old had no say in the big decisions affecting his life. It never occurred to him then that his opinion was sought or desired. As he walked behind his parents towards the steps leading up to the large wooden doors of the school he was reminded of images of a prison entrance he had seen in a photograph in the newspaper at home. Forbidding and isolating, the intimidating doors represented a hermetic seal, keeping the inmates isolated from the outside world.

One of the men collecting trunks looked at the name on Ben's and consulted a list he took out of his pocket. He picked up the trunk and hefted it up onto his shoulder. He turned and smiled kindly at Ben and then beckoned to the three of them to follow him. Going through the open front doors they crossed a large mosaic floored hall and then into a wide corridor running behind it. A large staircase was in front of them and they followed the trunk and its carrier up it, turning left at the top into a wide corridor. At the end of the corridor was another large door that opened into a long dormitory. Cubicles ran down either side of the large room, each with a curtain that could be pulled across the front to offer the occupant a semblance of visual, if not auditory privacy. Ben's cubicle was at the far end, the last one in the corner, up against the end wall and with a large, ceiling-high sash window above it. His name was written on a small label that slotted into a holder on the wooden cross frame from which the curtain hung. He felt he was being ushered into a stable, like a horse being brought in from the field.

On one side of the cubicle a simple metal framed bed was pushed up against the wall. On the other side stood a small chest of drawers with a large ceramic bowl on it. In the bowl stood an enamel jug filled with cold water. Ben had not expected ensuite facilities. A plain wooden chair sat between the chest of drawers and the bed. Spartan and minimalistic, for better or worse this was his new home, somewhat devoid of the 'better' in an adage that had never made much sense to him. He wondered how many marriages, created on the mistakenly solid foundations of the phrase, foundered on the sharp rocks of the reality of life, when the better stopped and worse knocked on the front door, as welcome as the knock of a travelling troupe of evangelising Jehovah's Witnesses are to a housewife at the critical point of making a soufflé.

The moment of his parents' departure had come too quickly, leaving him uncertain of what to do and where to go. He had mingled with a group of similarly disorientated boys who were eventually shepherded into a large refectory for a supper of fried egg and chips. Now, lying on his side in the body shaped hollow generations of boys had created in the middle of the prickly mattress, Ben felt he could smell those preceding generations of young heads of hair in the musty scent of the emaciated pillow. How many young boys had lain there before him, staring at the chipped white wood panels of the cubicle, tears trickling down their cheeks and falling onto the wafer thin pillow?

Further down the dark dormitory a boy coughed. Nearer, Ben could hear one or two others moving in their beds. Someone was sobbing quietly. Were they too struggling to sleep, fellow eight year olds unhappily torn from home and imprisoned for the seemingly interminable weeks ahead? A bed creaked and a loud rattle disturbed the still of the night. The tinkling sound of running water was a broadcast to all in the large room who were awake that one of the boys was kneeling by his bed, relieving himself into the porcelain chamber pot he had noisily dragged across the bare wooden floor. One of these handy receptacles huddled underneath every bed, gape-mouthed like a grouper under a rock, tremulous at the prospect of liberal sprinklings in the nights ahead. As all the boys had been getting ready to go to bed, just before lights out, Matron came into the dormitory and announced that she expected all the new boys to fill the chamber pot in their cubicle. Looking at the size of it, and being a somewhat literal child in those days, Ben felt daunted at the task of the 'filling' part of her diktat. He trembled at the consequences of not producing a receptacle with a meniscus standing proud of its rim. His list of fears grew exponentially. At home he always slept with a glass of water by his bed but here such a luxury was clearly deemed superfluous. If one had been available in his cubicle he could have used it to produce a reservoir and headwater sufficiently large to rise to the challenge of a brimful chamber pot.

Unaware he had fallen asleep, Ben was startled awake by someone clapping their hands loudly at the far end of the dormitory. Since watches were not allowed he had no idea what the time was but assumed from the sound of creaking beds and general movement that it was time to get up. The early morning light through the window above him washed through the cubicle, casting dancing shadows of the autumnal leaves of a large oak tree outside the window on the bare cubicle wall. Swinging his legs out of the bed he sat on the edge, his feet on the cold, bare floorboards. He shivered in the cool morning air of the unheated dormitory and wondered what it was going to be like getting up in the depth of the winter. Stepping over to the basin he poured some water into the bowl and splashed some on his face. It was freezing and he tried to work some heat into his hands by rubbing them hard to make a lather with the new bar of Pears soap his mother had put in his washbag. The translucent soap's unique and distinctive scent filled his nostrils as he breathed it in, bringing instant memories and thoughts of home.

Rinsing the soap off his face, Ben reached for the towel that hung on a peg on the side of the small chest of drawers. He could see his name tape on the top edge where his mother had sewn it. Everything he possessed that was with him at the school had been named, even the brushes to polish his shoes. He had watched his mother sewing name tapes into his clothes as she sat in her armchair in the darkening autumn evenings. The light from the standard lamp behind her put her face in shadow. He could see in his mind's eye her head bent down in concentration as she pushed the needle and thread through the material in her hands, light glinting off the metal thimble she wore on her finger whenever she sewed or darned his socks. The sight of the label, and the realisation of the love that had gone into that simple act made Ben's eyes well up as homesickness took its hold. Her sudden absence in his daily life opened an unbridgeable chasm of longing, of unrequiteable need.

Determined not to let this weakness show, Ben buried his face in the towel to soak up the tears and dry his eyes so he could face the world beyond the curtain with his true feelings hidden and suppressed. The scents of home in the towel only served to heighten the sense of loss and separation. It brought memories of Henry, the family dog. A hound of dubious genetic quality and sub-normal intellect, he was nevertheless affectionate and a constant companion to Ben. Other memories flooded his mind. Of his mother's perfume. Of his father as he greeted him off the train from London, exuding the aroma of commuter trains and City smog. Ben took one last deep breath with his face in the towel in the hope of absorbing the memories that might sustain him through the day ahead, and then put the towel back on its hook, sitting back on the edge of the bed to take a few moments to compose himself.

Down the length of the dormitory curtains were being drawn back on the cubicles and Ben could hear Matron talking to some of the half asleep boys. He quickly changed, doing up his tie and tucking his grey flannel shirt into the top of his shorts as he pulled them up. He pushed his feet deep into the long grey socks that were part of the school uniform and turned down their tops over grey garters, each with their ubiquitous name tag. Last came the black shoes as he slipped his feet into them and did up the laces. He dared not think about the high polish on them, and the maternal love burnished into their sheen, so keen was his mother that her son should fit in amongst his contemporaries and not feel ashamed. Fully clothed Ben pulled back the curtain and stood at the end of his bed, uncertain what to do, of what the morning routine required of him.

Matron was moving down the dormitory from cubicle to cubicle. She was a woman of stately proportions, built on the grand scale of an ocean liner, cutting a swathe through all before her in the majesty of her progress. As this leviathan walked, the metronomic lurching of her substantial, meaty buttocks under her crisp white uniform reminded Ben of the movement of the carriage of his father's secretary's typewriter. He had visited his father in his office in London once, his hair carefully combed and evidence of the morning's breakfast wiped off his face and the front of his clothes by his ever vigilant mother. She despaired at Ben's ability to look like a creature from the swamp and on occasion would refuse to have him sit with the family in public.

The secretary, a kind faced lady with grey hair swept back in a bun on the back of her head, was busy typing as Ben and his mother sat on chairs waiting for his father to finish a meeting. He remembered being mesmerised by the to and fro shuttling of the typewriter's carriage. Matron's gargantuan backside held the same fascination in its rhythmic, hypnotic lurches with each step, left and right, left and right as she juggled what looked like two bowling balls beneath her reinforced underwear. Her shapeless breasts, evocative of the bags of coal delivered by sweating coal-men to fuel the fires at home, created a mantlepiece on her chest on which it seemed an upright piano could be balanced. She was the sort of woman who, if she were ever fortunate enough to have sex with a man of sufficient stamina, endurance and resolve to make her experience the ecstasies of an orgasm, would not so much come as arrive. The adult Ben could only look back over time and imagine sex with her would have been like making love to a burst sofa on the pitching deck of an ocean liner in a storm.

Matron was carrying a large tray on which stood a range of bottles of assorted shapes and sizes. Ben watched in horrified fascination as she placed the tray on the end of each bed she came to. The boys stood holding the chamber pots they had retrieved from under their beds. Most were still in their pyjamas. As she arrived at each cubicle she placed her tray on the bed and reached out for the chamber pot with an expectant air, and would then proceed to pour some of the contents into one of the narrow-necked bottles she picked off the tray, seemingly oblivious of the inevitable spillage running over her fingers and hand. Each filled bottle was carefully labelled with the boy's name. Ben could see where the ink had run on the damp labels and wondered how she was going to be able to attribute the contents of each bottle to its original owner. Panic overtook him. Having fallen fast asleep and not woken until the hand-clapping alarm, he had not produced the demanded specimen. His chamber pot was as full of liquid as the arid wastes of the Atacama Desert. As Matron was preoccupied further down the dormitory he ducked back into his cubicle, picked up the water jug in the wash bowl and poured some of its contents into the pot that was under his bed. Replacing the jug as quietly as possible he quickly returned to the foot of his bed to await Matron's arrival, the now refreshed and satiated chamber pot in his hand.

Matron was now about half way down the line of cubicles. She had reached a boy who had introduced himself to Ben in the refectory the night before. They had settled down on the bench on one side of one of the long tables designated for the new boys to the school. The boy was sitting next to Ben on the backless bench.

"I'm Kennedy" he said through a mouthful of the greasy chips.

"I'm Grayson" Ben replied, following his lead in not including his Christian name. His response required no reply, and indeed got none as both turned back to their plates. Ben assumed Kennedy's mind was in an equal whirl, assaulted by the unfamiliar and fearful of the unknown.

Matron held her hand out to Kennedy and he handed her his chipped chamber pot. Ben was comforted to see even this Regency terrace of flesh visibly blanch when she peered into the malodorous pot. Kennedy had obviously copiously and enthusiastically emptied his bowels into it in a scatological haemorrhage. Hosing his offering with a couple of litres he had stored up in his bladder, he had obviously produced a toxic soup slopping around in the pot's depths. He had evidently misinterpreted her instructions the night before and seemed pleased, indeed proudly delighted, with his efforts. The breeze from an open window at the far end of the dormitory wafted the scent of the contents of the offending receptacle before it. Matron recoiled from the pot's entrails as the first hint of what she was staring at hit Ben's senses. He wondered if perhaps she was possessed of an Achilles heel after all. She grabbed Kennedy by his ear, twisting it and forcing him to turn his head sideways, his face grimacing in pain.

"What is this Fellow?" she demanded.

"A poo Matron" Kennedy replied, perhaps just a little too proudly for his own safety and well being. It was a little surprising to everyone Matron needed help in identifying the obvious and brought into question her ability to recognise the slightly more serious medical conditions the boys in her charge might present to her, such as flu or perhaps leprosy, which Ben had recently read about in a magazine at home. He could not see inside the pot but from where he was standing, and from what he could smell, it seemed pretty certain it wasn't a pot full of jasmine petals. Not for the first time, Matron's response tested the boys' confidence in the extent of her medical knowledge. From Kennedy's expression, he clearly felt this was a bit of a prize winner, and perhaps pretty obvious as to what it was.

"I know what it is!" Matron spluttered. "What's it doing in here?"

"I didn't know where else to put it Matron," Kennedy replied.

"Well, not in here" she shouted. "Just….. oh just take it away" she added in dumbfounded exasperation, pushing the offending pot into his chest. "Try again tomorrow, and I only want you to pee in it."

Kennedy stood by his bed, clutching the pot in his arms, looking bemused as to what to do next and where to put its noxious contents. Matron turned her back on him impatiently and moved on to the next cubicle where an ashen faced boy called Johnson stood with his pot in his hand. She took it from him, this time peering cautiously over the edge, fearful of what she might find lurking in its depths. Her brow furrowed in irritation.

"You didn't do anything Fellow," she shouted at the blushing boy, her exasperation growing, perhaps in reaction to the catatonic shock of Kennedy's efforts and its assault on her senses.

"I didn't want to go Matron" he replied.

"Why not?" she demanded.

"I don't know Matron" said Johnson tremulously, revealing to all the others that he lisped, a fatal weakness in an environment where any aberration from the mean is an opportunity for public ridicule.

Matron glared at him and then moved into his cubicle where she pulled back his sheets.

"You wet the bed," she shouted at him. "Why?"

"I don't know Matron," Johnson stammered, "I had a dream…"

"A Dream, you say! Well dream again and do it now," she said, holding the pot to his pyjama bottoms. Johnson stared at her, blushing with embarrassment, disbelieving of what she was asking of him.

"Come on, come on, I haven't got all day," she shouted, jabbing the rim of the pot against him.

With cheeks turning crimson, Johnson thrust his hand through the gap at the front of his pyjamas and extracted his cowering penis, as one might pull a tortoise's reluctant head from inside the shelter of its shell. Matron pushed the chamber pot up against the top of his legs so his genitals followed their companion and hung forlornly over its edge, like a sparrow's giblets on a line. Inevitably, in the full glare of publicity and Matron's frustrated sighs, Johnson's bladder refused to cooperate and give up its precious cargo. The well was dry and his little penis retreated from the limelight, ducking back into the warmth and dark of his pyjamas.

"This is not good enough" Matron said impatiently, adding helpfully "Do a hundred lines."

With the memory of his interview with the headmaster still vivid in his mind, the sheer unreasonableness of this was not lost on Ben. He began to wonder if punishment and humiliation was going to be the staple ingredients of the school's penal code. The tension within him grew and he prayed that since Matron had clearly skipped the class on 'Empathetic Nursing,' she had also absented herself from the class on how to tell the difference between tap water and urine.

Matron continued her harvest down the line of cubicles in the long dormitory, finally reaching Ben's cubicle in the corner at the far end. He held his breath as she slowly poured some of the surprisingly clear contents of his chamber pot into one of the bottles. With the bottle filled, Matron handed the pot back and moved over to the other side of the dormitory to repeat the process, moving up the opposite line of waiting boys whilst scattering mortification and derision like a farmer sowing seed into the wind. Reaching the far end of the dormitory, she turned around and called out to the boys who continued to stand at the end of their beds.

"Right boys, finish washing and changing and get down to Chapel for morning prayers. You have five minutes."

She turned and left the dormitory with her tray of filled bottles clinking merrily against each other in synchronised rhythm with her heavy, clumping footsteps. The bowling balls took on a life of their own and began to fight each other.

Ben soon came to learn how absolute dominance, married to ruthless and unemotional physical or mental brutality, can subjugate the masses or an individual. It enforces abject compliance in those with no power, no authority. For the oppressed, survival is the only ambition, at any price. Any mechanism that secures that becomes acceptable. The boys were powerless in this Hades in which they found themselves. Winnowed chaff, they were blown about by forces infinitely more powerful than them, by people with absolute authority over their every moment, every act. But not over their thoughts.

    The school's Chapel was built in an imposing style, with a high, arched roof and dark wood-panelled walls. The boys filed in and started filling the pews, the senior boys sitting at the back whilst the new boys who had arrived at the school the evening before were directed to the front. Catholicism and Christian values were advertised to prospective parents as part of the school's attractions, an integral part of the establishment's DNA. The school boasted an ethos of caring paternalism that purportedly guided and governed the pupils' daily lives. The day would come when Ben would read an old copy of that prospectus and, with a sense of outrage, liken it to a political manifesto. Meaningless cynical promises, not worth the paper it was written on. He would wonder at the fantasist who had written it, with its breathtaking detachment from the dystopian reality Ben and his contemporaries had experienced in their relationship with the school. Perhaps that long ago Walter Mitty had believed in the words that dribbled onto the page from his pen, the wet ink washing the lies clean. Perhaps he too had been duped, in concert with the trusting parents who would accept the document's promise of five years of care-free and cared for fulfilment. For Ben that morning, that far off moment of enlightenment did not exist. There was only the now and he wished with every fibre of his being that his 'now' could be someone else's. Never before had he felt such a sense of utter abandonment, such a passion to be with his family. Never before had he had such a burning desire for the nightmare of newness and strangeness to stop, for the warmth and comfort of the well worn jacket of familiarity. For home.

Morning prayers turned out to be the full package. England and the English have a well deserved reputation for putting on a show, a talent for ceremony. The Catholic Mass, with servers on the altar ringing bells, thurifers swinging the hot thurible spreading its incense, is the apogee of the Catholic liturgy. Others servers poured water and wine for the priest, and Ben had been brought up to believe this somehow turned into blood, an act of voodoo he struggled to believe. The choir in the choir loft trilled hymns like birds singing in the dawn. Accompanying the treble voices was a hand pumped and emphysemic organ, vigorously played by an octogenarian organist. Taking Communion seemed to be de rigeur. Everybody in the Chapel was going up for it at the appointed moment so Ben joined the others as, row by row, they all filed up to the altar for their pre-prandial gossamer wafer of salvation. For the more devout perhaps this represented another credit for entry to Heaven, like collecting Air Miles. For Ben it was more in the vain hope of assuaging his early morning hunger. Breakfast was a far more appealing repast than someone's body disguised as an early forerunner of the nacho.

Ben had always thought it strange that, at the most sacred part of the Church's liturgy, that divine moment when the transubstantiated form is reverently offered to devotees, they stick their tongue out at it before committing what seemed to him to be an act of liturgical cannibalism. With the insulted host melting on his tongue he returned to his place and knelt with his head hanging down over the pew in simulated devotion, leaning far over in solidarity with every other boy who seemed to be doing the same, all praying to the same God. Except there was no prayer for Ben, and none likely to come to him other than a plea for deliverance. There were only thoughts that randomly meandered over his predicament, as he now viewed his new life to be. His mind pecked through the entrails of its horrors, like a vulture looking for something delectable in the rotten carcass at its feet. He had heard his father talking to a friend as they debated the Prime Minister's recent comment that the country had never had it so good. In relative terms Ben found it hard to agree with this sentiment. Life had definitely got worse.

With Mass completed and blessings administered,

everyone filed out and walked in silence to the refectory for breakfast. Two rows of rectangular solid wooden tables lined the long room, each with benches standing parenthetically under the long sides as they awaited the arrival of the diners. Ben took his place at the table by the doors into the kitchen, where he had sat for supper the night before. A large green enamel bowl of fresh milk stood on a long serving table in the kitchen and the boys formed a queue to file past it, picking up a mug from the table and dipping it into the thick, creamy milk before returning to their table. In the weeks to come Ben learned the milk came from the school's own herd of cows, the same cows he and his parents had passed on their way home from his somewhat memorable interview. In his naive innocence he assumed this to be perfectly normal and that all schools had their own herd of cows. Of course the news of the dangers of tuberculosis and Listeria being transmitted through unpasteurised milk was either unknown to the school, or discounted as being preposterous and of little concern when served to grubby boys already infused with every pathogen known to man.

    Breakfast was a helping of industrial strength porridge that had the consistency of a brick. Ben followed the example of others and poured some of the milk in his mug on it, watching it splash off the glazed surface like raindrops bouncing off a tarmac road. A slice of cold, soggy toast followed, supposedly made palatable by the accompanying albino margarine, and glutinous red jam of unidentifiable provenance. One of the boys on the table helped himself to the food with a self assured air and with knowing looks at the others. Large and confident, it transpired he had already been at the school the year before, having arrived from overseas a year earlier than was necessary.

"I was here last term," he said. "My name's Mason."

His disorientated companions were all impressed with the self-assuredness his experience gave him over them. He was immediately the old lag of the penitentiary, the hardened old timer who had seen it all. The death row veteran who had done his time and survived the system. Being boarding school virgins, they looked to him with a sense of awe, grasping at the thin thread of hope that it was possible to get out alive. Stunned by the apparent callousness of the world in which their parents had abandoned them, they sat silently around the table and ate the tasteless and alien breakfast, each fearful of the prospect of the day and term ahead. The hum of conversation ceased when the headmaster entered the refectory to announce that all the new boys were to have a medical examination.

"After breakfast" he called out, "go to your dormitories and take all your clothes off except your underpants, and then make your way to the First Year classroom and wait outside. We shall call you in one by one to see the doctor." His peremptory instructions completed, he turned on his heel and walked out of the refectory without a backward glance.

When breakfast was finished and all the dirty plates removed, the boys all stood and filed out. Ben fell in with the clatter of boys up the narrow spiral staircase to his dormitory. As he had no idea where the First Year classroom was he decided following the herd seemed the most sensible solution. On reaching his cubicle he quickly stripped off and stood at the end of his bed again, waiting to see where everyone went. To his relief the enlightened Mason led the way to the long gallery that opened off the dormitory which Ben had walked along with his parents the afternoon before as they followed the man carrying his trunk. Doors to classrooms lined the left hand side of the gallery. The bright autumnal morning sunshine filtered through the large lead framed windows opposite the classrooms, from which the sounds of teachers' voices could be heard as the first lessons of the day got under way. The boys lined up outside the first door, shivering slightly in the cool air, each self-conscious about their nakedness. The headmaster strode down the gallery and as he turned into the classroom gestured to the first boy in the queue.

"You, Fellow, come in," he said, pointing at the boy called Kennedy before disappearing into the classroom.

As the others waited with their backs to a large window overlooking a small quadrangle below, Ben could hear a large fly buzzing and bumping against the glass in its quest for freedom. A more mature mind might have found the trapped insect's bid to escape a symbolic metaphor for how he felt but his thoughts were more focussed on the mystery of what was happening behind the closed door. In the quadrangle stood a statue of a saint, hand raised in supplication and face lifted to heaven. As Ben watched a pigeon landed on the statue's nose and immediately defecated on the saint's upper lip before flying off again, its rest break completed. and leaving the saint with fetching moustache.

One by one each boy was summoned and when it was his turn, Ben walked into the room, closing the door behind him. The headmaster and Matron sat next to each other in front of an elderly gentleman who had a stethoscope hanging around his neck. The headmaster was reading the morning newspaper and did not look up when Ben walked in, while Matron was writing some notes on a pad.

"Stand here young man," the doctor said not unkindly, gesturing to a spot in front of his chair.

The doctor was tall and slightly stooped. He had a trimmed white moustache that was more luxuriant than his thinning white hair, which was neatly parted down one side. Ben could see age spots on his pink scalp and on the back of his long, slender hands. His glasses were perched on the end of his nose and he peered at Ben over the top of them. As he lifted his head so he could see through the spectacles, Ben could see up his nostrils, marvelling at the amount of hair one nose could contain. The doctor felt under Ben's chin and around his neck, his long thin fingers probing and pushing, feeling cool on his skin. He tapped on Ben's chest and listened to its machinations through the stethoscope before peering into the darker recesses of his throat, pushing his tongue down with a wooden spatula that Ben noticed was already damp from the tongues of the boys who had gone before. He choked and gagged slightly as it was pushed far into the back of his throat.

Putting the spatula down the doctor suddenly leaned forward, hooked a long index finger over the front of Ben's underpants and pulled the elasticated top forwards and down. As he did so Ben noticed the headmaster lower his paper to his lap. Both he and Matron leaned forward in a synchronised movement to peer at his exposed genitals. Without warning, invitation or preamble, the doctor thrust his other hand into the lowered underpants and started feeling Ben's testicles, hitherto a hobby he had felt was his sole prerogative. He rolled them around between his fingers and then lifted them as though weighing them. Seemingly satisfied, the doctor let go of the pants which snapped back against his skin. The headmaster returned to his newspaper, his face disappearing behind it, and Matron sat back in her chair.

"Thank you, you can go now," he said. "Please ask the next boy to come in" he added as Ben turned to leave.

Ben noticed the doctor's testicle fondling hand reach out and select a biscuit from a plate on the table by his elbow, delicately offering it to his mouth to be nibbled at. He opened the door and left the room before he could be called back for another assault on his privacy.

CHAPTER 3

1957 - 1962

The early weeks and terms passed quickly in a mélange of new experiences and rules. The establishment traditions that had taken decades to evolve had to be absorbed instantly, no allowance given for transgressions born out of innocent ignorance. It seemed there was only guilt, with punishments to fit pointless rules. Obscure and meaningless customs appeared to have been devised solely to fit punishments. Penitential credits with no natural crimes as corresponding debits. Clearly much time had been expended on dreaming up methods of retribution, some seemingly borrowed from blueprints left by the Spanish Inquisition. Having created the punishments, many corporal, suitable reasons for administering or distributing them had to be devised in an illogical form of 'cart before horse' penal logic.

Needless to say, not all were able to survive this Siberian gulag. The lack of sympathy the students were shown by their contemporaries and elders amongst the pupils was in direct proportion to the level of any displays of weakness on their part. Johnson, the newcomer whose inability to produce a specimen for Matron on the first morning increasingly failed to cope with the alien milieu. The state of his bed that morning only added to his sense of public humiliation. He was not alone in his trepidation at returning for the second term of the first year, but failed to master his fears and absconded, to be returned from the neighbouring village to face the kiss of the cane in the headmaster's study. His response of disappearing once more, and leaving a suicide note on his bed, fuelled the gossip machine that lies at the heart of any institution. The fact it was a false alarm, a cry for help, was evident from his reappearance for breakfast in the refectory the following morning. The cry had been heard and was ignored, with only a beating as an acknowledgment. His suicide note quickly becoming public knowledge throughout the school, the news carried swiftly on the jungle network. As Johnson sat at his allotted place at his table the next day, staring forlornly at the bowl of congealed porridge before him, senior boys filed past on their way in and as they did, one stopped by him and looked down at him.

"What are you doing here Fellow? I thought you were dead."

Johnson looked up with tear filled eyes.

"I don't know," he said.

"Well, you need to try harder next time," the senior boy said, moving on before Johnson could reply. The laughter of the older boy's colleagues could be heard for some time after they took their places at their own table. Johnson's companions squirmed in their places, trying and failing not to laugh too. A solitary fat tear trickled down Johnson's crimson cheek.

That first holiday from school had been something of a curate's egg for Ben. Term ended four days before Christmas and, although he no longer believed that Santa would somehow be extruded down and out of the chimney, in many ways the fat man's spirit lived on in all the boys as the excitement grew in the combined joys of going home and the advent of Christmas Day, with all the familiar and comfortable rituals it would bring each family. Ben's parents collected him from school and, as they drove down the drive, he had an intense sense of escape, of liberation. He buried the thought that this would be short lived and that in no time he would be returning when the holiday was over. Perhaps escaping prisoners enjoy the same sensation, no matter how fleeting they know their freedom will be. For Ben, in that moment, there was only the now, and school played no part in that. The only fly in the ointment was when his mother turned in the car and told him about the dancing. And that there would be girls.

"I've put your name down for dancing lessons," she said, smiling at the gift of all the social skills and pleasure he would get from them.

"Why?" he asked. "I don't want to do that."

"Don't be silly dear," she replied. "Of course you do. Everybody does. It will be fun."

Now fun is a subjective issue. To a masochist, thrashing their naked body with a mixed bunch of nettles and brambles whilst scraping their naked buttocks across a flinty driveway like a dog with blocked anal glands is fun. For a surprising number of people though, it isn't, although Ben would have taken the brambly hedge thrashing and anal scarification any time rather than go to dancing lessons. His shyness in the presence of girls was all encompassing and for a fleeting moment he was tempted to ask his father to turn the car round and take him back to school. Suffering is relative.

Like everything else, his opinion in the matter had no value and so the die was cast and dancing was on the holiday agenda. The first lesson was the day after Boxing Day. Classes were to be held in the local village hall where his mother deposited him before driving off into the gloom of a low mist that hung over the village green in the cold, damp air. Ben could hear music in the long, low wooden hall. He was tempted to hide outside behind some dustbins but, afraid of his mother's wrath if she found out, he plucked up courage and pushed open the door.

Warmth and noise hit him as he stepped in. A number of girls were milling around, chatting to the boys, all press ganged to be there to balance out the gender divide. There was a record player on a low table against the far wall and Matron's larger twin sister was changing a record on it. Ben assumed it was Matron's sister as she seemed to be a carbon copy, built by hairy stomached Glaswegian riveters on the Clyde, only on a grander scale. She was wearing a paisley patterned blue dress of some textured material that he assumed must have been an off-cut of industrial strength carpet. For a brief moment a horrifying vision came into his mind of her sunbathing on a beach in a bikini, which were just beginning to be accepted as beachwear, despite the Vatican's declaration that they were sinful. In his mind's eye and imagination she looked like an obese butterball turkey with a couple of rubber bands around it.

Ben stood around awkwardly, not speaking to anyone, and in turn ignored. After suffering his isolation for a few minutes, Ben was relieved when the dance teacher asked everyone to take up positions alone and in rows facing the far end of the hall. She put on a record and then, standing in front of them, took them through the basic paces of the Cha Cha. For about ten minutes, her students repeated the steps as she called "One two cha-cha-cha, one two cha-cha-cha." At first Ben did a remarkable imitation of someone dancing the steps with his shoelaces tied together. The class glisséd left as he shuffled right. He corrected by stumbling to the left in a tangle of feet, bumping into the girl next to him as she went right in unison with all the others. The teacher called out to stop and walked over to the record player to reposition the arm on the record.

"Right, choose a partner please and we shall now try the steps in pairs together."

Her words had the affect of throwing a rock into a pile of feathers as everyone lurched away from Ben, each finding a partner of the opposite sex and all avoiding the boy with a deep sea diver's leaden boots on his feet. It was at this moment it dawned on him there was an uneven number of boys, with the inevitable outcome there was always going to be one left out. The paired couples spread themselves around the room, leaving him standing alone and exposed in the middle. The teacher started the music and waddled over to stand in front of him. Ben could hear her thighs rubbing against each other as she bore down on him, her stockings rasping against each other and making a scratching noise, as hessian does when rubbed together. She held out her right hand and placed her left hand on his shoulder.

"Take my hand" she said, waving her right hand.

Seeing the position the other boys took, Ben grasped her meaty hand in his left hand and stepped forward to put his right hand around her back. This placed his nose directly into her exposed cleavage where it neatly nestled between her two large, soft breasts. They closed over his nostrils, as the sea overwhelms a drowning swimmer. Ben had some sympathy for the Egyptians swallowed by the the Red Sea as they pursued Moses. His right hand behind her back closed on a roll of fat that had been pushed up and out of her corset. It formed a shelf of protruding flesh, like a complete fillet of beef ringing her back. He froze in horror, breathing heavily through his open mouth, his nose now redundant. The teacher stood motionless and he slowly slid his nose up her breasts as he lifted his head and looked up at her. No words were necessary, but she said them anyway.

"Move it," she said.

Ben pulled his head back and smiled weakly.

"And your hand" she said.

He moved his hand further down her back until it rested on the top of her vast left buttock, which felt like a burlap sack full of rocks.

"Up" she said.

Ben's hand moved up off the buttock and settled on the plains between the two continental shelves of meat north and south of it. Satisfied they were appropriately positioned, she set off in time to the music, dragging and throwing him around like a matador's cape. Ben managed to spend much of the dance with one or other of his feet on hers, and sometimes both at the same time.

At every corner his face collided with the woman's breasts like a train running into buffers at the end of a station platform. Not surprisingly, when the music stopped she told everyone to take up solitary positions again and no more was mentioned that afternoon of partnered dancing. When his mother returned to collect him Ben noticed she and the heavily carpeted teacher speaking quietly in a huddle, with occasional glances and frowns in his direction. He didn't go dancing again after that and strangely, the subject never came up again.

Returning to school after that first Christmas holiday was difficult for all of the new boys. Arriving for the previous term, they had been innocents with no idea of what lay ahead. This time, the reality stood out in stark relief in their imaginations. As they settled in on the first evening back, they swapped stories of their Christmas holidays. Ben deemed it sensible to keep his dancing exploits to himself as he listened to others speak of parties and fun.

The daily rhythm of life at the school carried on, picking up seamlessly from where it had ended brief weeks before. Ben was already much troubled by a hairstyle that resembled a dysfunctional rook's nest. Having hair sticking out of the crown of his head did little for his self esteem, at an age when blending with the crowd and not being an object of curiosity or derision were career ambitions.

A new low moment that plumbed the depths of Ben's embarrassment occurred in that second term when he was struck by a stomach ailment, born out of some salmonella ragù the cook had bubbled and brewed on her stove for a couple of months. It had been served with her speciality of spongy, bright yellow Brussel sprouts which weeped water if squeezed under a spoon. For a couple of days after the meal Ben spent much of his spare time hobbling to the lavatories where his ecstatic relief at making it in time left him slumped on the chipped wooden seats. Classes were spent squirming in his seat, oblivious of anything that was being taught while he listened in horror to his intestines gurgling and effervescing loudly as the irresistible magma within them boiled angrily. He felt great empathy with any early vulcanologist perched on the lip of Krakatoa's caldera at the moment the volcano blew up. Whilst they might have had the option of leaving the danger zone, Ben's danger zone went everywhere with him. Krakatoa's explosion was heard a mere 1,900 miles away. He was convinced that if what he was brewing saw the light of day in a cataclysmic eruption, it would be heard in Sydney and take out most of London on the way.

Inevitably, given the distance down the long school corridors to the lavatories, there came the time when their safe harbour was a frustrating pace too far. Sitting on one of the now too familiar seats, Ben stared down into the depths of his destroyed underpants as they encircled his ankles. An unfeasible quantity of his inner self nestled in them and he began to regret the second helping of cabbage the evening before. He had no idea what to do with the defiled pants, or where to put them, so took them off and cleaned himself up with paper dipped into the water in the cistern. He rolled the toxic underpants into a ball and stuffed them into one of the pockets of his grey corduroy shorts. Miraculously his shorts had escaped any damage, largely thanks to his mother's insistence that he needed large sized woollen underpants as they could last the full five years he would be at the school. She was unconcerned by the fact they showed below the bottom of Ben's shorts and when he protested, she told him to roll up the bottoms so they were raised into his shorts. She also had some little knowledge of the destructive force of a small boy's alimentary system, the earliest form of a weapon of mass destruction, and serendipitously had provided underpants that were up to the task. There was still some break time left so Ben made his way to the sanatorium where Matron lurked at her desk. She looked up as he entered her office.

"Shouldn't you be going to class?" she said. "Is there something wrong with you?" This came out as an accusation, as though illness was a mortal sin.

"I have something for you Matron" Ben said.

She beamed with delight, expectant of a box of chocolates or a scented handkerchief as a gift from a grateful mother. She held out her hand. Reaching into his pocket Ben pulled out the soggy underpants and plopped them into her open palm.

Revulsion takes many forms. There is sexual revulsion, where the lack of chemistry is so great that someone can actually repel us. Ben's formative years ahead were blighted with revulsion pheromones that clearly flowed from him like a babbling brook spreading out onto oestrogen soaked floodplains that were soon deserted. There is revulsion at a food or taste that we dislike intensely, like tripe and onions. There is revulsion at an act of violence. Clearly in Matron's opinion these would all have paled into insignificance in comparison with the revulsion she felt for the still warm pants in her hand, gently giving off a thin vapour of scented steam in the cool air. For once she was speechless, frozen in her catatonia as she stared in horror at the sewage farm nestling on her palm.

Ben stood before her, not sure what to say or do. He assumed showing pride in his efforts was not an option. Matron placed the underpants in a tray on her desk, picked it up and told him to follow her. Without a word to him, she led him to some large cupboards in a dark corridor behind the infirmary and opened one of the doors to reveal shelves of the boys' folded clothes. The shelves were divided into small cubbyholes, each labeled with a boy's name. She pointed silently at the cubbyhole with Ben's name on it. From her sign language he inferred he should delve in and extract some clean underpants. Armed with them, he turned and left by the door at the end of the corridor. He glanced back as he went through the door to see her standing staring at the contents of the tray, like Hercules contemplating the enormity of the task ahead of him as he stood at the doors of the Augean stables. He wondered if he had just witnessed the beginning of the end of her Matroning days, the step too far, the straw that broke her nursing back.

Of course, Ben was in luck that the exchange of gifts with Matron had taken place in the privacy of her office, away from the prying eyes of his peers and contemporaries who would never cease from reminding him of his shame. This was not luck that stayed with him in an institution where acts, words, failures and successes were all played on an open stage for all to see. In Chapel one day a boy called Ford who sat behind Ben started flicking small bits of paper at him. It was a day on which missing home featured quite large in his thinking and, eventually losing patience with the aerial bombardment, he turned round and punched Ford in the face. Whilst this had the desired affect of stopping the fusillade of pellets, the unintended consequence was to find one of the masters waiting for them outside the Chapel door after the Service.

Mr Scully was tall, fair-haired and powerfully built. One of his duties was to be the Sports Master. In retrospect he was probably in his mid-thirties but to Ben he was bordering on decrepitude. The school rumour mill had started muttering that he had 'intentions' for one of the female teachers. Miss Hyde was an attractive woman who taught the second year class and had become the object of every boy in the school's darkest fantasy. Despite his rudimentary knowledge of the facts of life, as told to him by his mother just before arriving at St Nicholas's, Ben had absolutely no idea what 'intentions' were. He had found it quite difficult to relate his mother's well meant description of how humanity keeps the production line and the human race going with the reality of life as he saw it. He didn't care what she said, he had absolutely no intention of sticking any part of himself in another human being. Whispered descriptions of female anatomy by other boys at the school brought to his mind the dauntingly cavernous entrance to the Christmas turkey's carcass, which didn't appeal to him much. Not having a sister, the female form was a complete mystery to him and what little he knew was gleaned from conversations and overheard comments at school, as recently when he had eavesdropped in the library on two of the senior boys discussing the finer points of female anatomy.

"I saw my sister's tits in the holidays. She left her bedroom door open a bit and was standing in front of the mirror with no shirt or bra on, looking at herself and playing with them."

"Was she excited?"

"I think so, except I heard you have to play with their clematis to get them excited. Where do you think they keep it?"

"That's a plant isn't it?"

"No, that's a chlamydia. I heard my mother on the phone and she said Mrs Wilson has one. She got it from the gardener."

"You two, come here. " Mr Scully beckoned with a crooked finger. Ben and Ford stood in front of him looking up at his enraged face as other boys flowed past and around them.

"I saw that," he said. "What was going on?"

Ford started to answer, justifiably and understandably framing the blame to fit neatly on his assailant, but Mr Scully was not interested, waving his hand to silence him, which made Ben wonder why he had bothered to ask the question.

"Get three strokes each of you" he said, turning and walking away.

Ben's first official corporal sanction, openly announced unlike the clandestine session with the headmaster at his interview, was heard being imposed by passing boys who later at breakfast whispered to him of the terrors of the punishment that awaited him. The psychology of punishment is arguably a more important and effective part of retribution than the act itself. The anticipation of inevitable pain induces stress and a corrosive sense of dread that is all pervading through the waking hours. Ben was quickly informed by those who had gone before that he was to choose his own moment of execution. The headmaster's office was open for business at a number of times through the day. He issued pocket money, sick notes and beatings with equal gay abandon and apparent pleasure. In the case of corporal punishment it was up to each of the condemned to choose which of the opening times he would opt for to get his sentence served. There was always a Damoclesian threat that if he had not received them within twenty four hours, they would be doubled. Sometimes boys would arrive at the office to find the headmaster was not there. They would have to go away with a bitter sweet sense of relief that the pain was deferred, but with the dread of having to go through the whole process once more, again summoning the courage to do the unwanted. Death Row inmates strapped to the instrument of death must endure the same sensations if a temporary last minute reprieve is phoned through and they are taken back to their cell.

Plucking up his nerve later that morning, Ben made his way up to the headmaster's office and joined a queue of boys outside. He was the only one in the line who was going to be beaten that morning. His fate created a frisson of excitement amongst the others who continued to hang around in the gallery outside the office to listen to the beating when it happened. Reaching the head of the line he entered the office. The headmaster was seated at his desk, head bent over it as he wrote a note on a slip of paper. Ben stood silently, waiting for him to finish. Putting his pen down he looked up at him.

"What can I do for you?" he asked

"Mr Scully said I had to get three Sir," he replied.

The headmaster smiled slightly. "Close the door," he said.

Ben walked slowly to the door and saw a group of grinning faces outside as he closed it. As he got back to his position by the desk, the headmaster opened the top drawer, reached into it and took out something wrapped in tissue paper. He gently unwrapped the paper, careful not to tear it, and almost lovingly lay a long, flat, black, spatula-like object on his desk. This was clearly what he was going to use, the instrument of execution. Ben felt like a criminal at Tyburn looking down from the scaffold on the array of instruments at the executioner's disposal. The headmaster reached into the drawer again and pulled out a hard-backed notebook which he opened on the desk. Picking up his pen he wrote the date and Ben's name in two of the columns that had been drawn on the page.

"How many did you say?" he said.

"Three sir," Ben replied. Time seemed to have come to a standstill and the process seemed to be eternal, the final moment delayed interminably.

"And who ordered them?" he asked.

"Mr Scully sir," he replied. He felt like screaming "Just do it. Get it over with," but the man was in no hurry as he savoured the coming moment, carefully writing the number in the next column.

"And what are they for?" he said.

"Fighting sir," Ben said.

"And where was that?" he said, turning his head to look at Ben over the top of his glasses.

"In Chapel sir," he replied.

He gave a little intake of breath as he turned back to write down the details of the crime, obviously now significantly more heinous with the admitted choice of venue for it. Closing the book and returning it to the open drawer, he stood up, picked up the spatula like cane and came around the desk to stand by Ben's side.

"Hold out your hand," he said.

Ben extended his right arm with his hand open and facing upwards. Grasping his wrist in his left hand the headmaster lifted the cane to the ceiling. As he did so the telephone rang. He dropped Ben's wrist and went to answer the phone, leaving him waiting, the tension building within him. When the telephone conversation ended, the headmaster came back and took Ben's extended wrist again. The cane fell at speed from far above his head onto his open palm, the splayed end neatly fitting its shape. The shock of the pain was excruciating, and there were two more to go.

"Other hand," the headmaster said as he let go of the wrist he had been holding. The process was repeated with his left hand and then he beckoned for the right for it to receive it's second dose.

When it was over the headmaster returned the cane to the tissue paper and carefully wrapped it up before replacing it in the drawer. Ben stood transfixed, his hands stinging.

"You can go now," he said. As Ben turned to leave the headmaster said "What do you say?"

"I'm sorry," he replied.

"No, not sorry. Thank you," he said.

"Thank you sir," Ben said.

With some difficulty because his hands were now completely numb, he turned the large, round brass handle on the door and left the room, walking into the small group of boys still congregated outside. Tears were not an option, no matter the urge, and so he smiled as some patted him on the back. Others asked to see his hands which had sprouted large and raised welts around their edges, now to be borne with pride like duelling scars.

The terms passed in a succession of bullet dodging days. The boys felt they were being burnished in a particularly fierce cauldron. Beatings for misdemeanours were sprinkled liberally, like icing sugar on a lemon drizzle cake. They were also used as an aid to the learning process. Regular tests of hard won knowledge were rewarded by privileges for the enlightened who passed. For those who failed, a selection was made from the offerings of a smorgasbord of detention, lines or beatings. Ben assumed the educational theory behind this illogical practice was that since beating a nail with a hammer drove it into wood, knowledge could be beaten into a boy's brain in the same way. An accumulation of careless mistakes in work or loss of memory in tests or exams all had the same outcome. Cheating became normal behaviour as an avoidance tactic.

Sport played a large and life-saving part in school life for the more physical amongst the students, and Ben grasped every opportunity to take part. The activities were a time where he could temporarily escape the reality of his life, where he could lose himself in the cathartic therapy of physical exertion. A time in which he could forget his surroundings and mentally abscond to a happier place. He enjoyed the physical impact and release of the contact sports. Whilst smaller than many of his year, he made up for his lack of stature with enthusiasm, and a competitive spirit that lurked beneath a carefree mien. Excelling on the sport's field became a school career objective for him, and for a number of others. The desire to be selected for the teams that represented the school became an all-pervasive emotion, not least because matches away against other schools gave the opportunity to get in a coach and escape the confines of the school grounds. Glimpses of the outside world were a greatly valued privilege, much as they must be for prisoners being moved between prisons who can see day to day life passing them by on the other side of the transport vehicle's windows.

One day a strained muscle at the top of Ben's leg left him limping and forbidden to play sport by an uncompromising Matron. He had tried to reason with her, asking for some form of treatment to speed his recovery, but lost his resolve as her capacious chest began to quiver and undulate above his head at his temerity in questioning her authority. He limped slowly and dejectedly from the sanatorium. On his way back to the main school buildings he met one of the schoolmasters in the corridor. The humourless Mr Sinkfield, a bachelor who lived in a room high in the old part of the school, was evidently something of a fixture at the school. It transpired he had himself been a pupil there and had returned, perhaps to spend the rest of his life within the comfortable security of its institutional confines. Seemingly possessed of a pathological hate of boys, generations of students at the school had secretly questioned why someone who appeared to detest the youth of the country should choose a career that brought him into daily contact and conflict with them. It quickly became evident that his autocratic air was companion to a singularly sadistic streak.

    Mr Sinkfield was the school's Maths master and Ben's inability to grasp any part of mathematics more complicated than addition and subtraction infuriated the man. On discovering Ben's lack of skill or talent, he proceeded to select him for special attention and public humiliation in classes. He repeatedly presented him with questions and then shouted frenziedly at Ben's inevitable and quite foreseeable inability to answer them. Where he deemed any answers to be particularly careless or stupid he would send him to the headmaster to be beaten. Monthly maths tests were marked and judged against the benchmark of a minimum passmark. Those who just failed to pass were given detention or lines to do, whilst those who fell far short of passing were sent for another beating. Yet again Ben repeatedly questioned how being beaten could possibly help to drive in the finer points of Maths, Latin or French. Years later, reflecting on the day he finally 'got' long division, he wished he had been able to find the courage to have asked to be beaten for his Latin as it had clearly been so helpful with his Maths. There would of course have been only one outcome from such a show of insolent sarcasm.

On one memorable morning Mr Sinkfield spent the entire forty-five minutes of a class working himself up through ever more stratospheric layers of hysteria, shouting at Ben while he stood by his desk for the entire period. Flecks of froth lined the corners of the master's thin-lipped mouth, like salt drying in the harsh sun on the shores of a soda lake.

The cause of Mr Sinkfield's apoplectic fit was Ben's perceived stupidity at not being able to calculate a simple logarithm. He stared at the log tables in the book, feeling punch drunk in the gale of shouted invective. The more the teacher screamed at him, the further from the answer he felt he was and the more humiliated before his classmates. It was not until the bell for the end of class was about to ring that Mr Sinkfield stormed up to Ben, his face inches away as he covered him in a fine mist of saliva, and snatched the book from his sweating hands. It was only then that he realised Ben had the book open at a page of cosines. Suddenly becoming icily calm, he ordered Ben to report to the headmaster to be beaten for deliberate insolence and wasting time. He turned and walked out of the room with a thin smile, oblivious of the fact he had conducted an entire class during which he had taught absolutely nothing.

That evening Ben settled at his desk to write his weekly letter to his parents. He filled the page with news of sport and the school's food, a perennial subject for discussion between the boys. He enquired after the health of his dog and his younger brother, closing with a short sentence of his eager anticipation of seeing them all on the following Sunday for one of the rare outings from school. As was common practice, he showed the letter to one of the masters before sealing it and putting it in the post box. Because of this compulsory and habitual censorship he had become circumspect about what he wrote in his letters to his parents, fearing recrimination for any complaints about his life away from home, or even anything resembling the truth. He never mentioned beatings or any other form of punishment he or others had received.

Now, limping back from his failed visit to matron, he was presented with his bête noire.

"Fellow, what's wrong with you?" Mr Sinkfield said as they passed each other. "Why are you limping?"

"I've hurt my leg sir," Ben replied.

"Meet me up in my room in ten minutes," Mr Sinkfield said peremptorily, turning and walking in the direction of the stairs that led to the higher floors.

Ben's heart sank at the prospect of having to face this apparently psychopathic man, no doubt to be upbraided for malingering or for the transgression of some irrational dogma of his devising. Arriving at his door ten minutes later, he knocked on it hesitantly.

"Come," Mr Sinkfield's voice called from within the room.

Ben opened the door and entered a small bedroom. An iron bed stood against one end. A crucifix hung on the wall at the head of the bed. An old desk piled high with a shamble of papers and exercise books seemed to lean for support against the opposite wall, exhausted and bent under its burden. Mr Sinkfield occupied the middle of the room in a chair that was pushed back from the desk.

"So, what have you done?" he asked.

"I don't know, sir," Ben replied. "I've done something to the top of my leg."

"Well, we'd better take a look at it," he said. "Drop your shorts and pants." As he said this he leaned forward and reached into a drawer of his desk from which he pulled out a bottle of white fluid. Ben undid his trousers self-consciously and let them fall to the floor.

"And the pants, Fellow, and the pants. Come on, come on," said Mr Sinkfield impatiently. Ben had become reluctantly used to being seen naked by Mr Sinkfield as he was in the habit of watching all the boys when they were in the communal showers after games, but there he had the protection of the herd about him. All were uneasy at the man's unblinking and silent gaze but somehow felt united in their common discomfort. Here, in the isolation of his room, he felt exposed in every sense of the word, vulnerable and helpless like a leaf tossed in the wind at the mercy of a greater force and authority.

Ben blushed, feeling his face become suffused with hot blood, and slowly did as he was told. His underpants joined his trousers about his ankles and he noticed the master's fixed gaze on his groin. Mr Sinkfield knelt down in front of him, poured some of the contents of the bottle into his hand and started rubbing it into the top of the injured leg, running his hand between Ben's legs. He stood transfixed, staring out of the window, conscious of the man's hand rhythmically brushing over his flaccid penis. The smell of the embrocation rose to his nostrils, masking the strong bachelor smell of the room, with its overtones of tobacco, sweat and unwashed hair. He glanced down at the top of the kneeling man's head. He could see Mr Sinkfield's scalp through his greasy, thinning hair. Clumps of dandruff littered his head, like crumbled rancid feta cheese. Some had cascaded down onto the shoulders of his jacket. Ben could smell the man's dirty hair. The scent of the gamey grease of it mingled with his panting, fetid breath and combined in an anabatic flow up to Ben's face.

Ben could hear Mr Sinkfield's breathing becoming louder and more rapid as he silently attended to the task in hand, rubbing his exposed genitals enthusiastically as they flopped backwards and forwards under his hand, inches from his face. In time he seemed to tire of his ministrations, perhaps frustrated by the lack of a desired response as Ben's outraged penis obstinately stared at his feet, refusing to get on its back legs and wave a flag in jubilant celebration. Mr Sinkfield leaned back on his heels, beads of sweat on his forehead and temples catching the light from the window. He stared at the recalcitrant groin and its attachments, which now felt hot from the friction of the adult hand over it and from whatever astringent Mr Sinkfield had used as a lubricant.

"Pull your togs up Fellow," he said curtly, standing up and facing the window. Ben noticed Mr Sinkfield rearranging the front of his own trousers as he stared out at the fields beyond. Presented with the man's silent back, he pulled up his pants and shorts over his stinging genitals and let himself out of the room, assuming he could leave as there was now no acknowledgement of his presence. He hurried down the stairs as fast as possible before he could be called back. He felt a deep sense of shame and embarrassment, already wondering if he had been complicit in the act, whether somehow he had unwittingly encouraged it.

The encounter in Mr Sinkfield's room came to represent a watershed in the relationship between them. He never again called on Ben to answer a question in class, and indeed seemed to become largely oblivious of his existence, only engaging him in conversation when it was essential and unavoidable, and even then avoiding his eyes, seeming to address someone standing behind Ben. Ben was aware of the sexual dimension to Mr Sinkfield's ministrations, and for a long time during his schooling days worried that this seemed to be the only form of sexual approach he would ever attract. He wondered if he should worry about his inability to rise to the occasion, perhaps an early sign of lifelong impotence.

Worse was the spectre of whether he was homosexual. Was that what had attracted the predatory Mr Sinkfield to him? Had he seen in the young boy what he could not divine himself, pheromones of latent desire for his own sex that just needed awakening? Ben found a sliver of comfort in the thought that if he really was a homosexual he would surely have been excited by the man's ministrations, and he hadn't been so maybe he wasn't. He didn't want to be one, given the stigma it carried with it in the testosterone infused community he lived in, and took succour from the fact he thought penises rather revolting little things. When partnered with a full scrotum, Ben felt they looked like poultry offal that would be better placed on a butcher's slab than bouncing and swinging around in men's crutches. Whilst he conceded he was no Adonis, and for his formative years wished he could have the easy manner his friends displayed when in the company of girls, something within him resisted the thought he might somehow be different to his hormonally charged contemporaries. For him, being in the presence of the opposite sex was terrifying and accentuated his shyness, making him feel every comment he made was gauche and risible. But like a moth to a flame, he was attracted and he clung onto the small glimmer of hope that gave him.

Confidence in our own sexuality in our youth is easily shaken. Mr Sinkfield's attentions had troubled Ben but he metabolised and rationalised what had happened with a nascent understanding of the power of logic. He emerged from the process convinced he was going to be alright and not be the felonious one in the community, ultimately to end up on the road to Reading gaol in a time when homosexuality was illegal. All of that was thrown into disarray in the middle of the night a couple of years later. He was fast asleep in his bed in his cubicle, untroubled by the noises of other sleeping boys around him. He awoke, conscious of feeling cold as he lay quite still on his back. He stared up into the darkness, still in the fog of deep sleep but with a sense that all was not well. He felt a strange, almost tickling sensation at his waist as he rose through the different levels of unconsciousness to becoming fully awake.

Lifting his head and staring down the bed, he could see in the pale moonlight that the sheet and blanket covering him had been pulled down to the bottom of the bed. One of the senior boys was kneeling by the side of the bed, unaware he was now being watched. He was pulling the drawstring of Ben's pyjama bottoms, slowly undoing them. If he was looking for additions to his marble collection, Ben didn't feel inclined to be the one who provided them. He sat bolt upright, startling the boy. Wordlessly the boy stood up and slipped silently out of the cubicle, either to go and rummage in others' pyjamas, or to return to his own bed to play with his own little collection. Ben leaned forward and pulled the bedclothes back over himself before lying down, bemusedly wondering if he was in a dream.

He woke in the morning knowing that what had happened had not been a dream, nor in his imagination. The boy who had been kneeling by his bed and starting to undress him was called Russman. He was in the senior year and on a couple of occasions had pinched one of Ben's buttocks as he walked past. Undoing his pyjamas to delve into the sweetie cupboard of his inguinal region implied Russman wanted to take their relationship to a new level, from flirting to fondling, not that Ben was particularly aware they had a relationship. He hadn't inferred from a couple of unwelcome nips on the bottom that he was betrothed and thus contractually committed to some pre-nuptial foreplay as a precursor to Russman's presumed desire for full blown consummation, which Ben gathered was a pretty messy business. He had heard through the school grapevine that the top class were studying Biology and had been dissecting rabbits.

For a few brief seconds he wondered if Russman's nocturnal attentions were nothing more than the inquisitiveness of an enquiring scientific mind doing some research into the comparative texture and dimensions of rabbit and human genitalia. Being rational about it, he realised he was being generous and that Russman's intentions were somewhat short of platonic. At best he hoped he had washed his hands as

Ben had recently read about a myxomatosis outbreak in the area. He wasn't particularly enthralled at the prospect of suppurating lumps and puffiness around his eyes and genitals.

The shorter term impact of Russman's first-footing in his cubicle was for him once again to have to face the unpalatable notion of the reality of his sexuality, leaving him once again confused and scared of what might be the truth. The doubts created by the encounter with Mr Sinkfield in his bedroom resurfaced from the stone under which Ben had hidden them. If heterosexuality was his longed-for career choice, was he mistaken? Could the empirical evidence of his patent attraction to Russman, Mr Sinkfield and the headmaster mean they could see something in him that he could not? Was there some subliminal enticement he exuded? Once again he clung onto the logic of his own instincts, which were repelled by the interest being shown in him.

Just as he began to lay the festering worries to rest, they were yet again resurrected in the following term. Ben had showered when he came in from afternoon games and went up to his cubicle in the long dormitory to change. He peremptorily brushed his wayward hair, still trying to flatten the untidy nest it created at the back of his head. As he walked towards the stairs he passed a cubicle where the curtain was drawn. Coming level with it he heard a noise from behind the curtain.

"Psst!"

Turning to look, Ben could see the amorous and this time naked Russman. He had pulled the curtain back a few inches and shoved his erect penis through the gap. From the look on his face it was evident he was quite proud of it, although the effect might have had a bit more impact if he hadn't felt it necessary to drape his towel over the end of his penis so the cloth hung to the floor like a despondent flag, or a serving cloth hanging over a waiter's arm. At first sight Ben thought the towel was levitating in front of his aroused suitor. This seemed a clever party trick, albeit one that might be better received at genteel soirées for dowagers and maiden aunts if he put some clothes on and not put his engorged penis under it. Some birds build bowers to attract mates, and humans put on nice clothes and wear perfumes and aftershaves. Not many think the height of sexual allure is to wave a towel off the end of your penis at your intended paramour. Perhaps it was a show of strength. Ben wondered if Russman could have managed it if the towel had been wet, or indeed how many towels he could support before the whole edifice collapsed in exhaustion. Could this become an Olympic sport, an extra category in which the weightlifters could compete? If Russman's idea of sexual attraction was articles hanging off pegs, Ben could not begin to imagine his reaction if he were to see a rack full of coats in a restaurant. Fitting under the dining table would be difficult for him without some clever tailoring. Whatever his intentions, his idiosyncratic choice of boudoir wear would make a condom somewhat surplus to requirements. Not much that is likely to impregnate anyone was going to get through heavy towelling made with fine Egyptian cotton. Only the best for Russman, whose mother was known to dote on him and spoil him.

Russman grinned and looked down at the towel before looking up again and winking at Ben. He turned and hurried on to the end of the dormitory and down the staircase, once more taking the steps two at a time, a new level of uncertainty rolling over him, tumbling in his confused mind as an unseated surfer is tumbled by the crashing waves. Yet again he was the object of unwanted male desire. To add to that were the embryonic horrors of penis envy. We live in an obsessively comparative world where quantity, quality and frequency are the essential ingredients of the recipe of life that culminate in our often half-baked sense of self worth.

It was difficult for Ben to judge the quality of Russman's penis, partially hidden as it was behind its penile burka, and indeed he had no benchmark with which to compare it as he had no criteria on which to base a comparative assessment. Additionally, since this private viewing of Russman's intimate parts was Ben's first exposure to a penis with attitude, he could not comment on frequency. On the issue of quantity however he had his own version of a penis with which to compare Russman's prizewinner and he had to admit, if they each were to enter them into the village Harvest Festival, Russman would win by a country mile. What the older boy possessed had all the dimensions needed to become a weapon of mass production one day. It looked dangerously close to the point of of eruption, like a hand grenade with the pin out. Ben had recently read about how the Japanese liked to practice the art of cultivating Bonsai trees and was now convinced there was such thing as a Bonsai penis. Inadequacy is a corrosive force and in the face of what to him looked like the bowsprit off an aroused Nelson's Victory, thoughts of his own diminutive button mushroom version became battery acid dripping into his subconscious, burning cavernous, festering abscesses in his self-esteem.

Ben's final term at the end of five years at St Nicholas' could not end fast enough. Desperate to escape its suffocating rigours he looked forward to the next five years of secondary education with eager anticipation of release into a greater freedom. Leaving through the front doors for the last time he felt a life sentence had ended, his longed for parole granted.

CHAPTER 4

1962 - 1967

"You're a yob. Do you know what a yob is, Fellow?"

"No sir," Ben said. The lesson was not going particularly well for him.

" A backward boy. And that's what you are. What are you Fellow?"

"A backward boy, sir," he replied.

"Excellent. Glad you agree with me. Just remember that. It'll stop you getting above yourself in life. Help you understand why you have amounted to nothing. You're either a one hundred and ten percenter in life Fellow, or a ninety percenter, and you're a ninety percenter. What are you?"

"A ninety percenter, sir," he replied.

Mr Budwell turned to the blackboard to start the

lesson. He picked up a piece of chalk from the desk on the raised dais in front of the class and walked to the blackboard, peering myopically at it through filthy spectacles that seemed to be made of armoured glass over which a pan of soup had ejaculated. Expecting a clean board, he was surprised to see that someone had already written on it. The class sat quietly as he slowly read the words, his nose inches from them to overcome his appalling vision. He was disadvantaged by the fact his eyes looked outwards, left and right with their backs to each other rather than straight ahead, and so it was impossible to tell who he was looking at whenever he spoke to the class.

Shitui, Shituis, Shituit, Shituimus, Shituitus, Shitunt

Quad Erat Demonstrandum – Quite Enough Done

The master's hair was shaved short, his sideboards ending an inch above his ears in a military short back and sides, enabling the boys to see the colour surge up his shaved neck. His ears reddened and he swung round and glowered at the class.

"Who's responsible for this filth?" he shouted, marching forward between a line of desks to stand in the midst of the sniggering boys. His head swung back and forth, sweeping the class with his divorced eyes. Foam flecked the corners of his mouth, and one of the boys sitting beneath where he stood flinched as spittle landed on his face.

Ben let out an involuntary laugh which he tried to disguise as a cough.

"You like it do you, Fellow?" raged Mr Budwell walking to where he sat at his desk and then seemingly staring at the boys either side of Ben.

"No sir," he said.

"Well, perhaps funny then. Is that it? Well, let's see how funny you find nine strokes when you get them."

Ben remained silent, his sentence delivered and to be carried out later that day.

"Who wrote that?" Mr Budwell shouted.

The principle of 'Omertà' is not the sole prerogative of the Sicilian mafiosi. The unwritten rule amongst the boys was that irrespective of the deed, they were united in never revealing the perpetrator of any crime or rule breach, no matter how heinous it might be and no matter the consequences for the group. Perhaps sated by the punishment served on Ben, Mr Budwell turned and walked back towards the front of the class, walking straight into a desk as he did so, spearing his crutch on its corner as he did so. The entire class bit their lower lip in unison, an unspoken understanding that to laugh would invite disaster. The strabismic man picked up the wooden backed duster used to clean the board, peered closely at its black surface again to see where the writing was and started to clean off the offending words. As he did so, a pale light appeared next to the words, reflected from a mirror held by Mason, who sat at the back of the class and who had been responsible for the offending Latin declension. He was using the mirror to catch the pallid sunlight coming through the window he sat next to, reflecting it onto the blackboard. Clearly thinking it was a chalk mark, the poor sighted Mr Budwell rubbed at the light patch on the board until it disappeared, only for it to reappear on the other side. Again he rubbed it out, and followed its repeated reappearances around the surface of the board. It finally dawned on him that the growing tittering he could hear behind him had something to do with the seemingly eternal regeneration of the ineradicable spot before him. Whirling round, he hurled the duster blindly at the class, following it with pieces of chalk, most of which were deflected as the faster reacting raised their desk lids. The duster ricocheted off the head of one of the boys not quick enough to get his lid up in time. It landed at the back of the classroom, and as it came clattering to rest, loud bells rang to signify the morning break.

"You will all stay here for the duration of break," Mr Budwell said as he walked towards the door. "It will give you time to thank whoever wrote that," he added, waving his hand at the blackboard. He opened the door and out of habit flicked on the light switch for the classroom lights. The old brass switch exploded at his touch as the piece of tinfoil Ben had put in the switch after breakfast shorted the unit. Sparks flew out of it and he jumped back in fright.

"And for that, you can all cancel any weekend arrangements you may have made," he shouted before stomping off, muttering under his breath and slamming the door behind him.

The class erupted in laughter, and in the general hubbub Ben hid his disappointment at the loss of a rare few hours away from the school, a punishment worse than the beating he was now to receive. He had arranged to go out for lunch with his mother, but would now have to write to her to tell her not to come to see him. Stoicism was an essential asset in the survival armoury with which the boys encased themselves.

The honeymoon at Senior school had been brief. Ben's parents had kept chickens once, and when he was quite small he used to enjoy going down to their run at the bottom of the garden to look for eggs and to watch them. He remembered one of the hens particularly because of its entirely naked bottom. His father said fleas or mites had infested its backside and caused the feathers to fall out. The bare skin was red, raw and clearly painful. Out of sympathy for its suffering, Ben had gone into the run and tried to catch it so he could smear the tender looking skin with some moisturising cream he had taken from his mother's dressing table, but the chicken's determination not to be caught had finally defeated him. Breathless from the stooped chase, he went back outside the run and settled down to watch again. The flustered hens calmed down after a few minutes and returned to their ceaseless scratching of the ground, stepping back and looking expectantly at the result of their raking. The infected bird was at the small hatch leading into the little henhouse, it's head inside as it stood on the step peering into the gloom of the interior. It's lurid bottom filled the small opening, throbbing and pulsating like a Belisha Beacon. One of the other hens was slowly strutting past when it noticed what was clearly too tempting a target. It walked to the hut and pecked the sunset hued throbbing flesh in the doorway. The affronted bird squawked and shot inside.

In a peculiar way, the school environment reminded Ben of that moment, where an insensitive disregard for your companions was the staple ingredient of survival. Sympathy was an indulgent weakness and therefore exorcised from daily life. Any weakness of spirit was to be buried deep, and physical or emotional flaws in others were a matter for exploitation, unearthed through native acuity and then to be publicly ridiculed and highlighted. It was as though the social structure was based on a pecking order of physical and emotional strength, and seeking out and working on the vulnerability in others was a necessary occupation to maintain status within the community. Perhaps the callousness shown towards each other was born out of an instinct for survival and a constant search for a weak point in each other's armour. An objective observer might call that indifference sadism, but to the boys it was normal behaviour, the manifestation of Darwinian natural selection where the strong survive. Scores were settled swiftly and often physically, and the more annoying were picked out for particular attention.

A boy called Chapman somehow excelled in irritating everyone. One hot summer's afternoon, as the industrious bees weaved their complicated flight paths amongst the daisies and dandelions in the fields, a number of the boys held him face down in the long grass, pulled his trousers and pants down and proceeded to brand his bare buttocks with concentrated sunlight shone through a magnifying glass, sprinkling a new crop of freckles across them. A trapped bee under a glass mug was then held against his bare flesh and it too must also have found him tiresome since it vented its spleen, and venom sack, into his flesh. A somewhat Pyrrhic final act by the bee but presumably it felt it had made its point. The minor injuries didn't entirely cure Chapman of his irritating habits but did make sitting down a little uncomfortable for him for a few days to remind him of his shortcomings.

Ben's thinking at that time had not matured to the point where he could rationalise his thoughts and experiences of those days. One day he would come to the conclusion that the all male world of his schooldays represented a microcosm of what would be found in a prison. To crowd males into a restricted environment, to remove freedom and the ability to escape and then to apply emotional and physical pressure has the inevitable affect of turning the occupants of the institution against each other. They become callous, gratuitously and casually violent towards each other, creating a milieu where only the emotionally and physically strong survive, and do so as sociopaths. Sympathy is neither sought nor offered. Ultimately he would conclude that there was a direct correlation between the level of stress and pressure being applied or experienced and the degree of violence the inmates or pupils exhibit against each other, and in extreme cases against their own person. Violence begets violence

For now, he knew no more than that he must hide his disappointment at the cancelled weekend. To reveal it would imply homesickness, a heinous crime with Mummy's boy connotations in the eyes of his peers. The tedium of a break spent in the classroom passed with the ringing of bells once more for the second morning session of teaching. Turning to his desk, Ben opened it to take out the books he would need for the next class. Surreptitiously he slid from the bottom of the pile a black and white photograph of his father, whose smile reassuringly gazed up at him from the depths of the desk.

A cold November wind chilled the school the day his father died. Ben was angry with him for leaving him. How could he, and without so much as a good-bye? As if we have a choice in these matters. He had seen his father the weekend before when he had gone home for Sunday lunch. His mother had picked him up after Chapel and driven him home. Many of the autumnal leaves on the trees had already fallen but the mighty oaks clung onto some of theirs, in futile obstinance as they defied Winter's tightening grip as she slowly plucked them off the branches to scatter them across the road, where they flitted on the wind like blown butterflies. Ben's father now remained in his bedroom permanently, too ill and weak to come down the stairs. Oxygen bottles lay on the bed beside him and he gasped hungrily at their thin life giving vapour. It was all that sustained his frail grip on life. After lunch Ben walked around the garden with the dog and then came in. His mother was asleep on the sofa in the drawing room, an exhausted carer enveloped in fear of the inevitability of the widowhood that pushed at her door. A few weeks before, in the holidays, a friend had visited the house and as he arrived he asked her how Ben's father was.

"The knowledge of death is in his eyes" was all she could say.

Ben left his mother sleeping and went upstairs to see if his father was awake. He found him sitting in an armchair, still and silent, staring out of the window at the garden he loved. It had been many months since he had last walked around it. Ben sat down in a chair next to the exhausted man who had given him life, and so loved the life he had created. He turned his head to Ben and smiled, too short of breath to speak. The two of them sat silently side by side, the man's bright eyes looking out of the husk of a body that contained still so active a mind. Somehow Ben was searingly conscious of his father's natural frustration with his failed mortal frame, and of his fear of what he must leave behind. Did his fear of leaving match Ben's fear of his going? No words seemed to be needed between them, and his father appeared to enjoy his company and the closeness of the quiet moment together. But so much was unsaid, so many feelings unspoken. So often we only think of the things we want to say after someone has gone, leaving us alone to deal with our regrets.

When it was time to go back to school, Ben went upstairs to say goodbye but his father was asleep in the chair. He stood silently at the bedroom door for a while and watched the sleeping man, embedding the memory as a squirrel stores acorns for when they are no longer there on the trees. He seemed at peace, despite the heaves of his chest as it searched for that next breath. His hands lay quietly together in his lap, his folded glasses protruding from one of them. Ben turned slowly, reluctant to leave the moment and the man, and went down the stairs and out of the front door to his mother who was waiting in the car, its engine idling as it sat in the drive.

Now, a week later, a master came up to Ben as the boys filed out of the refectory after breakfast.

"The headmaster wants to see you in his study. He's waiting for you." He did not meet Ben's eyes and turned away quickly, as though intent on the next task.

Ben walked through the bustling school corridors and came to the headmaster's study. He knocked and entered at the summons. The headmaster, a kindly man, was standing by his desk speaking on the telephone. He glanced up as Ben came into the room, and murmured into the phone before putting it back on its cradle.

"Sit down, sit down," he said, moving some papers about on his desk. Ben sat in the chair, his elbows on the arms and hands clasped before him as he leaned slightly forwards. He watched as the man seemed to tidy his desk. He suddenly looked up and cleared his throat.

"You know your father has not been very well recently, don't you?" he asked.

Ben wondered if his father had ever been well, but simply replied "Yes".

"Well, I'm afraid he died this morning," said the Headmaster.

Ben sat silent and motionless, absorbing the news he seemed to have been expecting all his life. He turned his head and looked out of the window, aware only that he had not said good-bye, and felt cheated for that. His mind filled with the image of his father in the chair in his bedroom just a week before. And he hadn't said farewell, even thought he had gone upstairs to do so, and the searing pain from that was exquisite. Thoughts ran pell-mell through Ben's mind, a continuous repetitive loop that impaled his heart and mind. 'Did he know I loved him? When did I last tell him? Did I ever tell him? Why didn't I wake him up? I could have hugged him.' Ben became aware that the headmaster was talking to him.

"I will arrange for you to be taken home this morning. There will be a car at the front of the school in half an hour. I should pack a bag for the night, but you will be coming back tomorrow." He stood up, relieved the conversation was over, and held out his hand.

"I'm sorry," he said.

Ben shook his hand and walked out of the room, making his way down to the library where he had left some books. As he went in he bumped into Mason.

"Everything OK?" said Mason. "What did the Head want?"

"Oh, nothing much," Ben replied. He did not feel much inclined to start a conversation or to give an explanation. He had a burning need to be alone with his thoughts.

"Could you just tell Budwell I won't be in class this morning. I'll be back later. I've just got to go and do something."

Gathering up his books off the table he turned and left the library and made his way up to the empty and silent dormitory. He dragged a bag out from under his bed and threw in a few things for a night at home. The school corridors were quiet as he went down to the front door and stood on the steps, welcoming the cold air that helped to numb his feelings as he waited for the car to draw up. As long as he could remember, he had been waiting for this moment, the news of his father's death, and yet he found as he stood alone on the school steps that he was completely unprepared for the reality of the moment. The evidence of his father's failing health over many years had made the knowledge of paternal mortality an ever present but invisible companion. Ben had never shared his anticipation of the event with anyone. Instead he had unknowingly built a protective carapace of self-sufficiency about himself in the instinctive awareness that the calm and gently guiding hand in his life would soon be gone.

Whilst Ben's father's health had failed for years, recent declines in his condition had increased the frequency of visits from doctors and friends. In the last school holidays, Ben had walked into the kitchen at home one morning to find his father quietly weeping as his mother held him to her. Ben's eyes met his mother's, and over her husband's shoulder she frowned and mouthed to him to leave the room. He turned and left silently, going out into the garden with Henry, the family's dog. He retreated to a favourite and secluded far corner of the large garden that surrounded the house, and sat against an aged oak tree, his arms around Henry's neck, struggling to comprehend the image in his mind of a strong-willed man reduced to such grief.

Try as he might, he couldn't think of anything he might have done that could have disturbed his father so deeply, but nevertheless he carefully went over his recent actions and behaviour, a mental audit in which the debits and credits of unregenerate and degenerate behaviour were examined for culpability on his part. Ben included his brother in the process, but he too seemed innocent of any crime heinous enough to reduce a grown man to tears. Only slightly reassured that he was not at the heart of the problem, whatever it was, Ben picked up an old tennis ball lying in the grass at the base of the tree and threw it for Henry, who bounded after it, his tail rotating like a propeller behind him in his excitement. He picked it up and returned to within three feet of Ben and, in the way of all dogs, refused to come any nearer despite being desperate for it to be thrown again. He sat chewing and salivating on it, dropping it on the grass and nudging it forwards with his nose and then grabbing it again when Ben reached for it. Ben suddenly lunged and grabbed the dog's collar, wrestling the ball from his mouth before throwing it again. Wiping his wet hand on his trouser leg, Ben stood up to walk up the garden back to the house. His mother was walking across the lawn, quietly calling for him.

"Oh, there you are," she said as he came around a bush into her view. Henry bounded up and pranced about her, still with the ball in his mouth, wary of being caught again.

'I was just playing with Henry," Ben said. "He still won't drop the ball when I tell him, stupid dog."

"He's just playing, that's all. It's a game. Are you alright?"

"Yes, why?"

"I know you saw your father crying, and you must have wondered...."

"Was it me? Something I did?"

"No, of course not. You know he's very ill, don't you?"

"Yes," Ben said hesitantly.

"Well, it's just, you know, very sad. He's sad. He's upset because he knows he'll never see the two of you grow up, never see you marry or know his grandchildren."

"Oh," Ben said. The enormity of the moment overwhelmed him with the revelation of a man's pain in the self awareness of his impending death and utter sense of loss.

"Yes, so it's nothing you've done and there's nothing any of us can do. Now do you want some lunch?"

"Yes please," Ben said, somewhat relieved his mother seemed eager to end the conversation, whilst leaving hanging in the air so many questions unasked, so many painful answers avoided as she too shared the dread of her own imminent loss.

And now that time had arrived, and despite the fact he had been waiting for it for so long, he was shocked by the actuality of it. The absence of someone we have loved, the aching vacuum they leave behind, is as unfathomable as the concept of infinity. So many details of a person's life die with them and when later we think of something we want to ask them, the shock of realising we can't reopens the wound of their loss. Memories and treasured moments passed through Ben's mind in legions during the journey home. Mr Scully was driving and he somehow sensed that faux joviality would be quickly revealed for the fakery it was and so little was said in the car. Ben welcomed the silence as he contemplated the void he was going home to. The red poppies worn by pedestrians they passed heralded the approach of Remembrance Day and added a poignancy to the journey.

Ben's mother was sitting at the kitchen table when he got home. A mug of tea sat on the table in front of her and she had her hands around it, warming them as she leaned forward on her elbows, her shoulders hunched. A tall, elderly and balding man stood next to her in a long, dark winter coat that covered a black suit that matched the black tie lying stark against the white of his crisply ironed shirt. The man was slightly stooped and was slowly rubbing his hands together in a perpetual hand-washing movement. A dewlap of loose flesh anchored to his throat hung down from his chin, wobbling and flapping as he moved his head. He reminded Ben of a

Marabou Stork.

As Ben walked through the door his mother turned her head to him and looked straight through him, as one might when seeing a complete stranger. She seemed unaware who he was, and was clearly gripped by an unfathomable grief. Ben found her vacuous stare slightly unnerving. The woman before him was as much a stranger to him as he seemed to be to her.

"Hi Mum," he said.

She didn't answer and turned her head to stare out at the autumnal scene. Dark clouds scudded across the sky in the stiff wind that was blowing, whipping up fallen leaves that flitted against the window like brown butterflies. Spots of rain dotted the glass, some then racing each other in a downward plunge. He went up to her and put his arms around her, hugging her as she leant her head against his.

"Where's Dad? Can I see him?" he asked her.

"He's upstairs in his bedroom" the Stork said, giving his hands an extra wash. "I'm Mr Jarvis. I'm the

Funeral Director. My staff are attending to your dear father at the moment and so I'm afraid it wouldn't be convenient for you to be there. We can make arrangements for you to come to the funeral parlour later if you wish. And if your mother agrees," he added as an afterthought.

Ben knew instinctively this would never happen and resigned himself to the memory of the last time he had seen his father, sitting asleep in the bedroom where his body now lay suffering the indignity of being manhandled by the undertakers into a bag, like so much detritus on its way to the municipal disposal facility. 'Is this all it adds up to?' he asked himself. A lifetime of achievements, loves, experiences, all bundled up into a bag to be thrown away, no longer of any use to anyone. Ben lent down and hugged his mother again, holding her longer than he normally would, tightening his grip as once more she leaned into him. She lay her head on his shoulder and whispered a whimper in his ear before sitting back in her chair to resume looking out of the window. Ben turned and left the room to go out of the house and walk around the garden with Henry the dog following uncharacteristically quietly at his heel. The strong breeze in his face was refreshing, somehow blowing away the gloom of the house's sepulchral atmosphere which was not lifted by the melancholic expression on the undertaker's face. From the far side of the expansive lawn he glanced back at the house in time to see the undertakers loading a large black bag into the back of their van, which already seemed to contain two other similar bags, implying business was brisk in the mortician's world.

Returning to school the next day, life quickly settled back into its habitual rhythm. Contemporaries soon stopped avoiding Ben's eyes or being alone with him. He noticed that for some time, many rarely spoke of their fathers in his presence. He tried to remember the sound of his father's voice, troubled that he seemed unable to recall it. For a while he lay in bed at night concentrating on conjuring it back into his mind, desperate to keep that little bit of him alive in his memory, the thinning thread that held him close, but slowly the sound eroded. Like someone walking away into the mist, it inexorably faded from his mind and no matter how hard he tried to recall and hold it, it slowly slipped though his fingers until he eventually resigned to letting go of it, freeing him from the tethers of his memory. Behind the smiles, Ben came to terms as best he could with the fact that the one person who was going to help him choose a path for his life was gone. He must now decide on, choose and then walk that path alone, without his assumed guide.

Of course, death is a natural companion in our lives and when it happens to those we know or love, it leaves an indelible imprint in our memories. It is the one inescapable reality of our lives and we each have to face it for ourselves, and for the loss of those we treasure and think we can't live without. Some deaths are sudden, with no warning, and they bring with them the shock of the suddenness of the loss. Others are expected, and we think we are prepared for them, but nothing prepares us for that emptiness, that moment we look up, for the briefest moment confidently expecting the departed loved one to walk through the door, or to be sitting in that familiar chair. And they do not walk through that do and are not sitting in that chair, and that remains a shock for some time.

Slowly, as the reality of their absence strikes home again, we realise they never will. All we ever wanted to say to them will remain unsaid, unheard. All the questions we had yet to ask them will remain unasked. The sense of loss is complete, overwhelming and always life changing, even if in only the smallest and most subtle of ways. Death leaves its indelible mark on us, through its brutal finality and its reminder of the mystery of a purported after-death timeless existence that so many cling onto to give their earthly being some purpose. Perhaps an after-life, in what some call heaven, is a human invention. Perhaps it's a fiction of the imagination created to alleviate the fear of a vacuum and the terrors of the utter silence of eternity. We are dominated and governed by time, by the change of seasons and by our very existence, so cannot contemplate or understand the infinity of emptiness, of non-existence. And so perhaps our ancestors created a celestial world, with its Managing Director God, for the masses to grasp onto like a drowning swimmer might grasp a lifebelt or piece of flotsam, in a leap of faith that transcends logic. Perhaps, Ben thought, Father Christmas does exist after all.

The arrival of someone at the Styx leaves an ineradicable imprint of the moment on the mind of those left behind, and a reminder it is their lot to continue the same inexorable journey to the same crossing point. They say those alive at the time all remember the day President Kennedy died by the assassin's bullet. Ben was sitting at his desk in his classroom catching up on some work. Mason stuck his head around the corner of the door and said,

"Have you heard Kennedy has been shot?"

"What do you mean?" Ben said, shocked. "I saw

him at breakfast in the refectory this morning. Why would anyone want to shoot him?"

Kennedy was one of the large group of boys who had migrated up to the senior school, and the image of him standing with his heavily filled chamber pot on their first morning together all those years ago flashed through Ben's mind. Perhaps Matron from their previous school had finally cracked and tracked him down to exact her moment of revenge. Ben was glad she seemed to have chosen Kennedy and forgotten his own filled underpants moment.

"No, not him. President Kennedy in America!" Mason said.

And so too, the long expected announcement of Ben's father's death became etched into his memory. An enduring fresco guaranteed to retain its clarity, sheltered from the fading influence of the harsh light of open discussion and the passage of time. He buried it alive, the invisible but omnipresent Minotaur lurking in the darkest labyrinthine recesses of his mind. No one mentioned it to him, the subject somehow avoided. He was taken home again a week later for the funeral by the headmaster and met his mother outside the church, but could not spend any time with her as family friends milled about her, all wearing solemn expressions and whispering condolences in her ear. Ben walked into the small church with the coffin lying before the altar and was ushered to the front pew. The headmaster walked up to him and handed him a prayer book.

"You will be doing a reading," he said. "Psalm 23. I have marked the page for you." He turned and walked back down the aisle to take a seat further back, leaving Ben to assimilate the prospect of having to stand up in front of the large congregation to do the reading. He had no time to prepare for the task as his mother and brother joined him in the pew and the service began.

As the funeral ceremony droned on, Ben's mind wandered, the words and hymns a dulled hum in his ears. His mother quietly wept next to him as a family friend went up to the altar and gave a eulogy, but Ben heard none of it. In his mind's eye he was standing in the doorway of his father's bedroom watching him sleeping in his chair. Now the body that held that mind lay silent in the box within reach of his hand. He suddenly became aware that the church had gone quiet and the priest was looking at him, nodding and signalling. He stood up and, having no idea what was expected of him, turned to face the congregation, standing next to the coffin. It seemed the natural place to be and he took comfort from the proximity of his father's memory lying close by his side. The words he read were cold comfort and meant very little to him. Loafing around in green pastures in the valley of death, wherever that was, with cups that runneth over seemed a pretty messy sort of picnic with which to celebrate a life. He felt a bit of *'My God, my God, why hast thou forsaken me,'* might have been a more apt reference to how he was feeling.

After the ceremony the funeral party made its way to the cemetery behind the church and gathered around the gaping maw of the freshly dug grave. The coffin led the crocodile of mourners and family on the shoulders of the pall bearers, who lowered it slowly onto two wooden poles positioned across the open grave. The priest read words that were meaningless to Ben and at some pre-agreed point, the coffin was lowered slowly into the ground on canvas straps. A few people picked up small handfuls of earth which they threw down onto the coffin lid whilst others threw in flowers before everyone turned and headed back to their cars for the drive to the family's house house where drinks and canapés awaited them. Solicitous adults came up to him offering sympathy and words they felt would be a comfort to him which he politely acknowledged, shaking some by the hand and kissing the cheeks of others when they were proffered.

Back at the house, with plates of food and trays of drinks being passed around, he wished he could be somewhere else, anywhere that would mean he could be alone. Left by himself for a moment he slipped out of the room and quietly went up to his bedroom where he sat on his bed, his head resting back against the wall. He closed his tired eyes but he knew escape was impossible and that he should be downstairs supporting his mother so he returned to the chattering throng in the drawing room. People were beginning to say their farewells and to leave, and soon the house was empty except for the headmaster and the immediate family and hired waiting staff, who cleared the debris before they too left. After a cup of tea, Ben hugged his mother, wishing he could wash away her grief, and drove back to school with the headmaster with a sense that his life was somehow restarting with a new plan. He needed a new blueprint.

CHAPTER 5

As each individual is born with talents, so they usually have a compensating lack of flair or skills in certain subjects or fields of knowledge. Some seem to have no gaps in their arsenal of gifts, the all-rounders who sweep the board of plaudits and awards, destined to run away with the Victor Ludorum of life. Ben seemed to have an Achilles heel in almost every subject, with Latin and Maths vying for position as his most feared. Every piece of Latin homework handed in carried with it the threat of a beating for careless work. Each punishment created within him and his contemporaries a new layer of indifference to authority and the system it perpetuated, and through which it enforced control. But somehow, through it all, Ben and the majority of his companions never allowed the authoritarian state to control their minds. Their thoughts remained their own and they survived within them.

And so, as the terms and years passed, the boys became inured to the harsher aspects of their lives. The underlying unimportance in which they felt they were held meant each of them formed a protective emotional carapace and an instinct for survival. In later years Ben asked himself if this might have been a conscious educational philosophy of the institutions through whose hands he had passed, a way of preparing a generation for the rigours of adult life. This seemed a somewhat far-fetched idea because, if it was intentional, it was a high risk strategy that failed those who collapsed under the system. Some succumbed to the pressure and left for softer pastures, each perhaps irrevocably damaged for their life ahead rather than prepared for it. Since much of our behaviour is learned, what sort of companions, husbands and fathers were they all going to make? And yet, generations before had passed through an education little different to the one Ben experienced, and went out and built an Empire on the back of it. Perhaps they did so because of rather than in spite of their formative years.

Part of those development years were shaped by the school's delegation of responsibility for day to day control of the school to the senior boys who had been elected Captains and Prefects. The range of sanctions available to the putative trustees for liberal distribution amongst young offenders was diverse and arrayed in ascending order to match the quality or quantity of transgression. Lines, morning runs and ultimately caning by the School Captain were all available without reference to the adults in the school administration, and thus lay completely unsupervised in the hands of what became the omnipotent master class. Younger boys consoled themselves with the thought that their time would come. But in the meantime, where authority lies, there also lurks rebellion, the irrepressible need to extract even the smallest taste of victory. Ben was sent to the Captain's room after throwing a clod of earth at a Prefect on the rugby pitch. It took a beautifully balanced arcing trajectory and caught the senior boy in the face. As Ben admired the accuracy of his missile and its parabola of perfection, he became aware the Prefect was a little unhappy with him as he picked earth off his teeth and tongue.

Presenting himself at the Captain's room, he knocked on the door and opened on the shout "Come" from inside. Entering he noticed the Captain and his five deputies seated around the room in shabby armchairs. A log fire crackled in the fireplace and a tea tray lay on a low coffee table. The turf-coated and patently still affronted Prefect sat slightly apart from the Captains, not yet senior enough to be elevated to Government so something of a Junior Minister.

"Stand there Fellow," the School Captain said, pointing at a spot on the worn carpet in front of the fire. Ben could feel the heat of the flames on his legs through his trousers as he faced the kangaroo court. He was fully aware they represented the prosecutor, jury, judge and executioner in one body, an economy of justice that would be the envy of any despot.

"Can you explain what happened please?" the Captain said, turning to the Prefect. The outrage to which he had been subjected still clearly rankled as he explained to the assembled court his innocent enjoyment of the afternoon and the pause in the game when he had been hit by a large lump of turf and soil that had been thrown at him by "this complete anus here in front of us."

The case for the prosecution succinctly put to him, the Captain turned to Ben.

"Have you anything to say?" he asked.

"Well, it was only a joke," Ben said. "I didn't actually mean to hit him, just get close, so I think he should have just taken it on the chin."

As the final words left his mouth, he realised his defence was slightly deficient in its delivery and unlikely to be helpful to his cause. It was framed more in the way of having signed his own death warrant. His case was not helped by one or two of the others sniggering at the joke, which drove the Prefect nearer a state of complete apoplexy.

"Guilty," I think, the Captain said. "Six strokes for thuggish behaviour. Bend over that chair." He pointed at a wooden chair as he reached behind his own for a long thin cane. Taking a piece of chalk, he ran it over the last few inches of the cane, covering it in a white dust. As Ben turned to the chair, the other Captains in the room each picked up a newspaper, each of which had had a large hole cut in the middle allowing them to go through the charade of reading whilst watching the delivery of the sentence. Ben bent over the chair, grasping the legs on the other side, and the Captain moved behind him.

"Hang on a minute, what the hell's this?" the Captain said tapping Ben on the seat of his trousers with the cane. "Take it out."

Ben stood up and pulled two copies of Reader's Digest out of the back of his trousers.

"Two extra for that," the Captain said.

Bent over the chair once more, Ben awaited the moment of retribution to start, happy for once still to be wearing his trousers in front of authority. He could hear the swish of the cane as the Captain whipped it back and forth in the air behind him. Suddenly the first stroke was delivered, its force and impact enhanced by the Captain standing back and taking a long step forward as he struck. The affect was like an electric shock that increased exponentially as each of the next seven strokes fell on the chalked line across his backside, the target the Captain had laid with the marked cane on his first stroke. The end of the cane whipped around Ben's side onto the top of his thigh.

"Right, you can go Fellow, and I don't want to see you here again," he said when the final stroke had been delivered. Ben stood up slowly. He could feel a slight sticky dampness under his trousers and assumed blood had been drawn. Without looking round he walked to the door, opened it and stepped out into the corridor.

"What do you say?" the Prefect shouted after him.

"You can fuck off," Ben muttered under his breath.

The Prefect leapt up and crossed to the door.

"What did you say?" he shouted at Ben's receding back.

Ben turned and faced him.

"I said thank you, it was worth it," he said and carried on walking whilst holding up two fingers over his shoulder.

One of the tasks of the more junior boys was to take their turn in a rota that delivered the Captains' tea to their lounge each afternoon. The boy assigned to the task prepared a tray in the school kitchens, loading it with cups and saucers, teaspoons, knives, small plates, butter, jam and a sizeable quantity of slices of toast which he would have to make. A large teapot filled with freshly made tea and a jug of milk completed the repast which was then carried through the school on the large tray and delivered to the lounge.

The day after his caning, Ben found out who was to be the fag for the afternoon and persuaded him without much difficulty to swap and let him do it. He dutifully laid out the cutlery and china on the tray as the toaster worked overtime to produce the toast. As he placed it in the toast racks on the tray, he licked both sides of each slice. Alone in the kitchen, he undid his trousers and put a couple of the slices between his shredded buttocks as he carried on licking others coming off the production line.

With the defiled toast neatly arranged on the tray, Ben poured boiling water into the teapot in which he had spooned tea leaves. Taking the steaming tea pot over to the kitchen sink he urinated in it, sufficiently he hoped so the Captains would not taste it, and then finished emptying his bladder in the sink. He vigorously stirred the pot and then, his tea making preparations complete, he picked up the laden tray and took it up to the Captains' lounge where he knocked on the door once more. Taking the tray in when summoned, he placed it wordlessly on a table by the window. Ben noticed the victimised Prefect was once more in the room. He looked at Ben.

"Limping a bit today Fellow," he said. "Nothing trivial I trust?" He looked around at the others with a grin, clearly delighted at his wit.

Ben looked at him and smiled before retreating and closing the door on the cholera time bomb he had served up. Sometimes anonymous victory is more sweet, a delicious memory that never loses its flavour.

In those later years of their education, conversations amongst the boys matured in tandem with their physical development, and ever greater energy and attention was devoted to discussing girls. It sometimes seemed to Ben that this was not just the favourite subject for examination and dissection but the only one. Every anatomical, emotional and behavioural aspect was scrutinised and debated. Perhaps sensing their burgeoning interest in the fairer sex, the school administration decided some educational intervention was necessary, albeit probably a few years too late. When the boys reached the senior year they were all summoned to the Physics Laboratory one evening. No reason was given for the gathering and everyone assumed it was probably to do with the choice of Universities and careers they were going to have to make. Ben had already had a career talk with Mr Johnson, one of the masters, so was not sure there was any point in turning up to this latest group meeting. Mr Johnson had called him into his study and told him to sit down, telling him he wished to discuss Ben's future.

"Do you know what I think your problem is Grayson?" he said.

"Er, no sir," Ben replied, not aware he had a problem beyond penis envy, an unfounded sense of body dysmorphia, a growing attachment to anarchy, concern about his sexuality, a distaste for being beaten, a sense of academic inadequacy, self-confidence issues and a complete dislike and disregard of any form of authority.

"I think you have a massive inferiority complex about the capacity of your brain," Mr Johnson said.

"Why, thank you sir," Ben replied. "I can't think where I might have got that idea from. That's very helpful, sir. I shall see if I can build on it."

Mr Johnson sat back in his chair, clasped his hands in front of his bulging stomach and stared silently at Ben, a small smile of satisfaction at the profundity of his thumbnail character assessment creasing his lower face. Ben didn't know what else to say and couldn't see how this far from elevated opinion of him got him any further down the road to deciding on his future, which yawned before him like an abyss of directionless confusion. As the silence in the room began to cross the boundary of awkwardness into embarrassing discomfort, Mr Johnson suddenly sat forward, as though breaking out of a trance. He picked up a book on the table by his elbow and held it out to Ben.

"As you won't be applying for a University you can choose a career from this," he said, again sitting back, once more smiling as though satisfied at being seen to be helpful. Ben was not aware he would not be applying for University as there had been no discussion about the matter with him, but he did not see much profit in challenging the presumption.

The title of the book was *"Careers for Sixth Formers."* Ben quickly leafed the pages, creating a small and welcome breeze on his face in the stuffy room. He could see it was an alphabetic list of careers, jobs and vocations. He wondered if the first job listed would be Aardvark Keeper and the last Zebra Keeper. The conversation appeared to be over so he stood up and left the room.

"Thank you for your help and advice sir," Ben said. "It was very inspiring. I'll be sure to come back if I need any more guidance." The years had instilled an understanding of good manners in him, but sarcasm was becoming an irresistible force. He opened the door to leave.

"Not at all Grayson, any time," Mr Johnson replied. "Don't hesitate to ask. There's a good fellow," he added as he reached for his pipe and started stuffing tobacco into its bowl.

Ben had taken the book back to his room and thumbed through it. Its contents only served to increase his confusion and to highlight the stark paucity of any direction for his life in the months and years ahead. Now on the evening of the grand summons he joined his friends and peer group as they filed noisily into the Laboratory and took up places in the back row of the tiered seats that rose high up to the back of the room. They had been sitting talking for about five minutes when Mr Johnson came in and went behind the lecturer's bench that formed a barrier between the audience and the large blackboard behind his back. He waited a few moments for the hum of conversation to die away. Clearing his throat hesitantly whilst fiddling with the end of his tie and fiddling with his gown, he looked flustered and flushed.

"Right, erm, you will all soon be leaving here and entering a new and, …er…., somewhat grown up world. You will be tempted by temptations boys."

Mr Johnson paused and glared around the room, scanning all the faces before him as though looking for symptoms of temptations.

"Temptations!" he almost shouted. "Yes, indeed. Here, under our care, you have been free of …er, outside temptations." He paused as if to let this thought gather gravitas in his audience's minds. "Some of you may have been personally tempted whilst here and let me tell you gentlemen, that path leads to poor eyesight and blindness so must at all costs be avoided."

As he said this he stared directly and meaningfully at a thickly spectacled and rather femininely effete boy called Willshaw who was sitting in the front row.

"I'm talking about masturbation." he said, nodding at Willshaw. "A meaningless exercise in my opinion, with no beneficial outcome except money in the coffers of the opticians."

For reasons Ben failed to understand for years to come, he lifted his hand to ask a question.

"Yes?" asked Mr Johnson, irritated at being interrupted.

"If I masturbate Willshaw, will we both go blind or just him sir?" Ben asked.

The astounded Mr Johnson stared at Ben open mouthed and momentarily speechless. He suddenly shuddered, like someone breaking a fever.

"Get twelve strokes Fellow," he shouted, froth spitting out of his mouth.

"Thank you sir," Ben replied as Mason and all the boys around him guffawed and laughed. Willshaw squirmed in his seat.

"Quiet, you lot!" Mr Johnson shouted, seemingly aware he was losing control of the boys and the direction of his homily. The boys settled down and quiet settled back in the room.

"As I was saying, you have not been tempted by external influences and so you probably don't know how to deal with them, these temptations. Temptations come in many forms boys. Yes, they do. Long, short, thin and fat, but they all have one thing in common. They are tempting, very tempting. And because of that they can be dangerous to you. Dangerous temptations can lead you astray if you know what I mean. Astray, into unchartered waters where ships shouldn't go, where those on board have no navigational skills. Crumbling cliff edges it's dangerous to walk near."

Mr Johnson paused again, this time to let his dire allegorical warnings sink in. His minestrone of mixed metaphors were impenetrable. He slowly looked around the room, swinging his head back and forth as he moved his gaze up the tiered benches, trying to catch and hold each of the boys' eyes to emphasise his prophesy of impending doom. Not one of his audience had the faintest idea what he was talking about, nor where his ramblings were leading.

"It is my unpleasant duty to instruct you about these unsavoury temptations, how to recognise them and how best to avoid them. As I have said, temptations come in many shapes and sizes. You will notice differences from yourselves. Bodily differences if you get my meaning?" He looked at the bemused boys with a satisfied expression on his face, as though they were at one with him and his theme.

Having seemingly run out of what to say next, the stumbling man turned to the blackboard, picked up a piece of chalk and drew a large outline of a cow, much as one might see on a poster behind a butcher's counter where all the cuts of meat are delineated on the side view of the animal. The udders of Mr Johnson's cow were particularly pendulous, probably resting on the ground underneath any poor beast unfortunate enough to be in possession of anything so outsized. It reminded Ben of the dance teacher's cleavage he had buried his nose in all those years ago, as indeed did the whole cow.

"You will recognise the female form here boys. Quite unlike the male. The bull would not possess these,

…..er…. these……hmmm… appendages." He pointed at the udders, stumbling over his words, clearly ill at ease with his subject, whatever that was.

"These, er…..appendages are the first signs of temptation boys and you may find they are thrust at you at times, and you might be tempted to………" He paused for effect, allowing the horrors of thrust udders to sink in……. "Hold them, or even feel them!" He shuddered, aghast at the very thought.

SEX!!

He was talking about sex. The penny dropped and there was a collective snigger throughout the room.

"Yes, indeed boys, the first temptation and you are right to be shocked," he shouted, misinterpreting the suppressed laughter as agreement with his thesis and as a communal understanding of his message. He was on a roll now, happy that the room was with him at every step of the meandering, obfuscated journey he was taking the boys on. Picking up the chalk again, he drew a large arrow pointed at the cow's arse.

"The point of entry boys," he shouted, "Oh yes, indeed. But where there's an entry, there's an exit and this is where babies come from! Yes, if you hold these," he pointed at the udders, "a baby will end up coming out of here. And you don't want one of those, let me tell you. Do I make myself clear? Babies are the work of the devil."

There was utter silence in the room as the boys contemplated a life of unfondled breasts, when this was all they had ever dreamed of for the last few years, dreams that entailed rolling naked in a sea of breasts. Mr Johnson obviously took the silence to be a united understanding and acceptance of the principle of human reproduction. In the form in which he had explained it, a less intuitive audience might leave the room convinced that feeling a cow's udders resulted in babies. Did that mean dairy farmers had large families, given they milked twice a day? Ben began to wonder if Joseph in the Bible had really been a dairy farmer rather than a carpenter, one who'd played fast and furious in the milking parlour. Perhaps in one eureka moment and leap of imagination he had solved the parthenogenetic conundrum of the virgin birth, one of the central mysteries of Christianity. No wonder that miraculously implausible birth had been in a stable.

There was an obvious flaw in asking an asexual, aged and clearly virginal, misogynistic bachelor, who had not the slightest knowledge of the female emotional or physical form, to give a sex talk to a group of matured adolescents. It was quite clear Mr Johnson had not one shred of empirical evidence of his own to support his dire warnings of the hazards of women. Testosterone oozed from the boys' every pore and orifice as they knocked loudly at the doors of manhood and full sexual enlightenment. Their sole ambition and focus on leaving the confines and strictures of their education and incarceration was total immersion in the most fascinating aspect of their physical development. Each one had been brought into the world through an orifice, and every one of them had every intention of putting as many parts of themselves as possible into as many female orifices as they could find. Causing post pubescent but unfulfilled and unrequited teenagers to become bonded with a cow's udders as the portal to sexual nirvana was perhaps, on reflection, foolish.

"Excellent. Capital." Mr Johnson said. He turned and left the room, clearly delighted with his erudition in the facts of life, and in the clarity of his delivery of them. More likely he was delighted and relieved his ordeal was over. His relief was matched by the boys' surprise, not only at the discovery their future sex lives were going to be conducted in cow barns and milking sheds, but also by the mere fact the little homily had been given. They left the room not entirely convinced. Temptation was exactly what they wanted. Whilst as yet not many had first-hand evidence of the ecstasies to be derived from the charm's of a woman's body, they were tantalisingly aware they existed from their study of the well thumbed and illicit copy of the banned book *Fanny Hill* that had passed through all their hands, and from their hidden collections of magazines such as *Health and Efficiency* and *Parade*. Mr Johnson was perhaps a little late in the day with their education. In addition, the subject was never discussed or brought up by any of the masters, and indeed was hidden in a form of unspoken censorship.

When Christine Keeler and her dalliance with Profumo and others was in the news, the newspaper the boys were provided with by the school looked like a Gruyère cheese, full of large holes. All articles relating to the infamous affair were cut out of it in an act of social vandalism by extreme redaction. The inevitable result was to lift the boys' inquisitiveness to new heights. When they finally saw the legendary photograph of Keeler astride the hourglass chair, she became the subject of every fantasy in the school for months. Kennedy vowed to take up furniture upholstery as a career. To this day there may be many who unwittingly sit nonchalantly on sofas and armchairs stuffed with female pubic hair.

It was shortly after Mr Johnson's helpful discourse that the school unaccountably organised a dance, to which girls from a neighbouring school were invited. Perhaps the school authorities felt this would be a way of testing the boys' resolve to resist Mr Johnson's temptations, unaware most of them would want to use the occasion to put into practice as many of the illicit acts they had heard their elders discuss as could be fitted into the course of the coming evening. The sheer novelty of the event generated a frisson of excitement amongst the majority of the boys, but put the fear of God in Ben. He still lived in a private mortal dread of the opposite sex. When first arriving at the school, where the hormone infused pubescent boys were waking to the dawn of sexual attraction, he had been shown naturist magazines. The pre-sexual liberation era censor's airbrush had removed any external evidence of reproductive equipment. Breasts were allowed but any mid-body genitalia were blurred out. Couples were photographed cavorting on windswept beaches, usually with a large, inflated and colourful beach ball and each with their crutch area hidden behind an opaque mist. This only served to deepen in Ben the mysteries of the female form.

The evening of the dance arrived, and the senior dormitories reeked of cheap aftershave, hosed into armpits and underwear by the already tumescent boys as they boasted of the conquests that awaited them.

Ben dressed with the enthusiasm of a condemned man preparing for the short walk to his fate.

    Two coaches arrived at the front of the school where the girls selected for slaughter disembarked onto the gravel drive under the gaze of the throbbing throng pressed to the windows above them. To Ben they seemed like lambs being delivered to the doors of the local abattoir, nervously giggling at the fate that awaited them inside. He could hear their shoes scrunching the gravel as they milled about before walking as a close-knit group through the front doors, huddled together as a flock for protection. As they filed into the school hall where the dance was to be held, the boys rushed down the stairs to greet them. The girls were gathered at one end of it, ready to face the bachelor herd huddled at the other end of the room, two opposing armies in their respective trenches waiting for the first shot to be fired. The two boys who had volunteered to provide the music for the evening quickly put a record on as some of the bolder and more confident boys crossed the no man's land dividing the two groups and started talking to the girls, some of whom stood arm in arm in mutual support.

    Slowly, the two groups mingled and partnerships began to form. Ben was aware that the group of unattached about him was dwindling as connections were made and couples went off to dance, or to sit and chat on sofas and chairs scattered about the room. The embryonic relationships and connections being made were kept under the watchful gaze of a couple of chaperoning teachers, tasked with the unenviable responsibility of ensuring the girls all returned unimpregnated, each with their little store of eggs yet to be introduced to an amorous and stampeding herd of sperm already muscling their way up dark corridors, elbowing each other out of the way in the race of life.

Ben realised with horror that he could not walk up to any of them and start talking, the fear of rejection or derision was so great. Apart from abject shyness, fashion played a large part in his reticence. Over recent years men's trousers had become narrower, to the point where in some cases it seemed a physical impossibility for anyone to get a leg down a trouser leg that was no more than a narrow pipe. His friends and companions all showed off their chiseled and honed calves and knotted thighs through the tight fitting material around their legs. Ben's clothes were somewhat different. After his father died, his mother donated his suits to Ben. She told him the dark one with thin red stripes that closely resembled the material used for the uniforms worn by the staff of British Rail would be perfect for his school suit.

Being from a different, wartime generation, Ben's father's trousers were more of the Oxford Bags design. The legs were made from sufficient material for him to feel able to walk about in them without it being apparent that his legs were moving. Basset Hounds have similar freedom of movement within their skin. The toxic fashion disaster of the suit was completed by it having a double breasted jacket and turn ups on the trousers, defying the modern trend of pop groups and fashion icons like The Beatles for thin single lapels and straight bottomed narrow trousers. Being so far removed from the zeitgeist of current fashion, when all you want to do is blend and conform, is like being the only zebra in the herd with no stripes. You tend to stick out for all the wrong reasons and just know you are the laughing stock of the crowd, a natural and obvious target for derision.

Ben quietly slipped out of the room to seek refuge in the lavatories where he found safety, seated behind a closed and locked door. He knew he could not stay there all evening, but the brief respite was delicious and he leaned back against the wall and savoured it. By the time he came back into the hall, the evening's food was being served. Large trestle tables had been laid out with a buffet style meal. Ham, chicken, salad and cheeses lay on plates that had clearly been vigorously attacked and pillaged. Couples were moving along the tables, spooning food onto their plates, chatting animatedly to each other. Ben joined the end of the queue, acutely conscious of his isolation. As he picked through the debris of food on the tables, the girl ahead of him in the line turned around to face him.

"Hello," she said, holding out a beefy, shot-putter's hand, "I'm Veronica".

"Oh, hello," Ben replied, glancing sideways at her and taking her hand to shake it. Given his less than limited contact with girls, he had no idea what they liked to talk about so the conversation floundered on the rocks of his social incompetence.

Veronica was a big girl, seemingly designed from the blueprint of a butcher's block. Built for comfort rather than speed, more of a Clydesdale than a Newmarket thoroughbred, she was not tall but very substantial. Ben thought she had the makings of a formidable rugby prop-forward. She appeared to have no waist, her body falling vertically from her armpits to her substantial hips, the whole encased in a red dress of a thick textured material that reminded him of the wallpaper usually seen in Chinese and Indian restaurants. Large breasts, like buffers on a steam train, strained at the material. He wondered if she was suckling a couple of baby hippos under it. She reached across Ben and delicately with her forefinger and thumb, picked up the last chicken leg on the table. She chewed on it as she surveyed the remnants of the buffet. She reminded Ben of a cow masticating on regurgitated grass. He noticed the remains of her first helping on the empty plate in her hand. As she leant to the back of the table to reload her plate with fresh supplies, he also noticed how her dress was stretched taught across her back, her flesh bulging conspicuously in spongy lumps around her bra-strap. The sight was reminiscent of the dance teacher he had offended with his foraging hand as it sought a safe haven on her back. Perhaps Veronica was that woolly mammoth's daughter. Unsure whether her greeting was an invitation for more conversation, Ben self-consciously continued to select from what was salvageable to eat on the trays and dishes on the tables.

    Having filled his plate, Ben looked around for somewhere to sit, embarrassed at his solitariness, feeling the stigma of being the social pariah. He was unsure how to break into the conversations of the groups around the room, even though each group contained friends and boys well known to him. They were all so at ease with the girls, and he envied them that casual comfort they had as they chatted to their newfound companions. Walking over to the side of the room, he sat alone on a chair by the wall. As he settled into his seat he was horrified to look up to see Veronica heading his way. The floor seemed to tremble at her every step. Without hesitation or invitation, she sat down on the empty seat next to him, wordlessly continuing the conveyor belt of food into her mouth. Clearing her plate, Veronica leant down and pushed it under her chair. Ben glanced sideways as she bent over. Her torso resembled a stack of used car tyres he had once seen piled outside the local garage at home. Sweat marks had appeared under her armpits, like an encroaching tide. Ben looked around in desperation, praying there was somewhere he could hide, or that some escape route would magically open up for him. The majority of the others in the room had finished eating and were drifting back towards the dance floor in pairs.

"Is this the first dance you've had here?" Veronica asked, turning to him.

"Yes, I think so," he replied.

She pushed a stubby finger into her mouth and worried at something stuck in her teeth.

"Thought so," she continued. "Do you want to dance?"

Before Ben could think of a plausible reason for avoiding the inevitable confrontation of dancing by spiriting himself out of the room to find sanctuary in the lavatories again, she stood up and headed confidently in the direction of the music. The dance floor held all the charm of the front line at Passchendaele. It was impossible for him not to follow, and he did so with leaden legs as he left the safety of the trenches to engage in hand to hand combat with a future ladies' weightlifting champion. The music was slow and the crush of bodies enforced proximity.

Veronica turned and clasped Ben to her, pulling him relentlessly into the middle of the melee, her breasts like a scuba diver's air tanks pressed hard against his chest. He put his arm around her and his hand landed on a large roll of flesh that had somehow escaped and pushed itself upwards and over the confines of a corset she was wearing. It formed a small mantelpiece across her back and as he grasped it, Ben had an intense sense of déjà vu of the nightmares of his encounter with the leviathan dance teacher a few short years ago. Perhaps she was Veronica's mother. Moving his hand down towards her waist, Veronica's constraining undergarments gave him the sense of stroking the sides of an ironclad in a dry dock. He was conscious of the dampness in his left hand and assumed it emanated from Veronica's palm. Beads of sweat had pupated out of her skin and lay quivering on her down covered upper lip. Ben prayed they were not the first signs of arousal in her. She manoeuvred his body around the crush of the dance floor as effortlessly as though he had been attached to the front of a battle tank. He felt like one of the sides of beef that are hefted about Smithfield market by burly porters.

If he was honest with himself, he had initially felt acquiring any partner was preferable to the discomfort of wandering alone about the fringes of the room, which was his usual role at dances and parties when he wasn't inhabiting the lavatories, but that small benefit was beginning to lose its appeal. Ben noticed the tempo of the music was beginning to slow further, and couples were becoming more closely entwined, some stationary as they kissed. With alarm, he felt Veronica's grip on him tighten as she pulled him closer to her. She moved her left hand from his shoulder to the back of his head and started to push her fingers through his hair. The erotic intentions of this foreplay were somewhat diminished as his hair became caught in rings on her fingers, pulling strands from his head with sharp, eye watering stings. Veronica seemed oblivious of these minor obstructions to the free passage of her fingers, and pressed a brawny leg like a haunch of ham between his thighs, lifting her knee and crushing his testicles up into his pelvis. He could feel her chest beginning to heave like the bellows of a blast furnace, and suddenly became aware that the hand on the back of his head was pulling it inexorably down to meet hers.

Looking down on her upturned face, Ben could see her eyes were closed. Her voluminous and somewhat hirsute lips were puckered like a large anemone fringed clam. The charms of a clam were marginally more appealing than Veronica's mouth, with crumbs of supper framing it and its row of beads of sweat balanced precariously on top of her upper lip. Their mouths met in the kiss she presumably deemed her reward for her labours on the dance floor, and a tongue like a Toulouse sausage was thrust into Ben's mouth. Arriving uninvited, it thrashed about like an epileptic python in the darker recesses in its quest for treasure, ricocheting off his teeth and drumming off his epiglottis like a boxer on a speed-ball.

Unsure what to do next in this, his first real sexual encounter, and aware his tongue had involuntarily retreated like an eel seeking refuge in a cave, Ben stood transfixed, waiting for her next move. Veronica continued to search the extremities of his mouth, her tongue lashing around in a desperate search for his, at times seeming to forage inches past his epiglottis. His own was now cowering behind his molars, terrified out of its wits, but hers found it and somehow seemed to drag it out and slam-dunk it to the floor of his mouth, encircling it like an anaconda squeezing the life out of its prey. It dawned on Ben he should show some enthusiasm and respond to what was becoming an increasingly inelegant and violently rugged sexual encounter. He began to fill his lungs, sucking the breath out of hers. He noticed her eyes suddenly open wide in some form of exophthalmic hernia as her oxygen debt accelerated and her cheeks imploded. Mistaking her look for passion he sucked harder, convinced her gargantuan breasts were beginning to deflate. Veronica suddenly broke away and inhaled deeply.

"God, what are you trying to do?" she gasped, stepping back and removing her knee from Ben's crutch. His testicles dropped back into place and blood began to flow freely through them once more. Until that moment he was not aware you could get scrotal pins and needles.

And in truth, that was the end of the evening as far as he was concerned. His inauguration to the temptations the boys had been warned about by Mr Johnson left him feeling the cow might have been a more alluring proposition. Perhaps Mr Johnson was right and temptations were not what they were all cracked up to be. His first sexual encounter with a human Land Rover had not quite lived up to expectation, and the fantasy was considerably more alluring than the reality. Veronica left the dance floor and joined a group of girls who had broken off from dancing to have a drink. They huddled their heads together as she spoke to them, and Ben heard them all laugh and then glance in his direction. He slipped out of the room, his trousers flapping around his legs like out of control spinnakers, and went back to the security of the lavatories where once more he went into a cubicle, locked the door and sat down. Leaning back again, he closed his eyes, relieved to escape the mating game but at the same time at a loss as to how he would ever be able to become engaged in it. So far its charms eluded him, leaving him frustrated and somewhat lonely in the age of youthful revolution where the mass introduction of contraception opened up a cornucopia of opportunity for a newly liberated and guilt free generation which was eager to experiment.

    Ben woke up a couple of hours later, still lying back on the lavatory with his legs stretched out before him, his head thrown back against the wall. Glancing at his watch, he stood up quickly and immediately collapsed on the floor as the blood surged back into his lifelessly cold and numbed legs. For the second time that night, pins and needles pricked like hot coals, this time under the soles of his feet. He sat leaning against the side of the cubicle, waiting for feeling to return to his limbs. When it did, he slipped out and made his way through the sleeping building to his bed, where he lay worried and confused at his inability to mine even the minimum of excitement from his encounter at the dance. Women remained a mystery to him and as a sexual dyslexic, all he could say about them was they were like men but tragically deformed.

On top of that, what was he going to do with his new life? His contemporaries all knew what they wanted to do in theirs, and all he could come up with was aardvarks to look after. He felt he faced a chasm of emptiness, a parachutist at the door of the plane without a parachute and someone's hand pressing firmly into his back. He was supposed to be choosing a career, eager to plough his furrow in the fields of capitalism and he had neither a field nor a plough.

Quietly Ben slipped back into his room and into bed where he quickly fell into a deep sleep. He dreamt a rampant octopus with Veronica's face attached itself to his face and thrust the majority of its tentacles down his throat in an attempt to rip his testicles out by their roots, a vengeful act of emasculation by an Amazonian feminist.

    A whole new world awaited Ben in a few weeks and he asked himself if he felt prepared for it. The inevitable conclusion was, not in the slightest. However, ready or not, the caged bird was about to be freed, or in his case, evicted. By the end of it all he felt overdosed on academia and the constraints of the educational world, on petty rules and above all, on authority in any of its many forms. Despite the abyss it presented, the prospect of his unknown future was both exciting and exhilarating and when at the end of term he walked out of the school buildings for the last time, it was with a light step and a sense of euphoric liberation.

CHAPTER 6

1967

Ben's sense of euphoria at his new found freedom was short lived as reality in the guise of an empty bank account arrived at the front door. The newspapers were spread out on the floor in front of him like prayer mats as he knelt before them in supplication for inspiration. They all lay opened at the Job Vacancies pages and were as enlightening and inspirational as the book of careers he had been given a few months before. He had no idea that such an eclectic range of jobs and occupations existed in the wider world. The variety before him just made the task of choice harder as he realised he was not qualified for anything that resembled a career. Whilst probably perfectly capable of the task, he definitely knew he didn't want to be the Quality Control Officer for a company that manufactured mobile toilets. He assumed generations before him had refined the design of the condom to the point of perfection so didn't feel a long career opportunity existed in the sales department of a new manufacturer breaking into the market, no doubt eager to capitalise on a sexually liberated generation fixated on free love. He had penned circles around a number of offerings and started making phone calls which led him to the first of a number of meetings with prospective employers, none of whom had any idea just how much they really wanted to employ him, nor more importantly quite how much he and his bank manager needed the job.

Lombard Street in the City of London seemed to be the banking capital of the world and the prancing horse hanging from one of the fine buildings guided Ben to the doors of Lloyds Bank. Gliding through them in his voluminous suit like a small hovercraft, he announced himself to the concierge and was directed to the fourth floor. Stepping out of the lift he saw a small reception area in front of him. A few leather armchairs were arranged around a low coffee table. Assorted banking magazines and other offerings from the financial press were arranged neatly over the table and an empty ashtray sat in the middle next to a half drunk coffee cup. There was no one there so he sat down in one of the armchairs to wait for something to happen, or someone to appear. Looking around he noticed the corridor stretched both ways from the lift. The walls were lined with perfectly polished dark wood and there was not a sound, any footsteps muffled by the thick, soft carpet. The place was sepulchral, each door leading off the corridor an entrance to a dynastic mausoleum. The ambience exuded power, stability and authority and Ben could sense the power the bank exercised over the lives of its customers. There was something intensely solid and reassuring about the place, an ocean liner sailing serenely through the troubled seas that most people were tossed about in, even if this one appeared to be the Marie Celeste.

He heard a door open out of sight somewhere down the corridor and shortly a well fed man appeared and stood in his sight.

"Mr Grayson?" he said. Ben stood up.

"Yes sir," he replied.

"Barker" he said, holding out his hand. "I apologise for keeping you. My secretary is not well today and I was on the telephone. Please follow me."

Mr Barker turned and started to walk back down the corridor as Ben followed him. The man's hair was cropped quite severely, above his ears. It was black and shone from whatever unguent he had smeared all over it and which plastered it to his head. His parting was completely straight and revealed a thin pale line of scalp with a light sowing of greasy dandruff flakes. A thin moustache, a dark pencil line across his upper lip, overshadowed a thin humourless mouth. Arriving at an open door along the corridor Mr Barker walked through and Ben followed into what was obviously his office. There were two desks in it, a large wooden one by the tall windows that looked down onto the busy street, and a smaller one in the corner with a covered typewriter on it. Ben assumed this must be the ailing secretary's desk. He could see the carpet was slightly worn underneath her chair where its wheels had ploughed furrows. Perhaps she had been overcome by the fumes off Mr Barker's oil slick hair and was at home on oxygen. Every inch the sober banker, Mr Barker walked around behind the desk and gestured to one of the chairs in front of it.

"Sit down, sit down" he said sweeping his arm across the front of his desk.

Ben sat in one of the upright chairs, at first with his arms on the armrests but then, wondering if this was too informal, brought his hands together in his lap as he waited for the man to open the batting with a question. Ben's voluminous trousers spread over his legs like a warming blanket, hiding any evidence of human body parts beneath. Mr Barker held Ben's completed application form in his hand, the one he had carefully filled in a couple of weeks before. He had become quite adept at completing the myriad of forms he had received as a result of responding to the various advertisements he had unearthed in the back pages of a number of newspapers. Name, address, exams passed, interests, hobbies and sports all increasingly easily written by rote in the relevant boxes on the forms before they were posted off with his low expectations of a reply. Lloyds Bank were the first to respond, asking him to attend a meeting at their Lombard Street head office which was what had brought him to the chair he was sitting in before a man who looked like a rather well fed Fred Astaire.

"So, you studied Zoology did you?" he said, looking up as he laid the form back on the large, white and unblemished blotting pad on his otherwise empty desk.

"Yes sir," Ben replied, glad to be on familiar territory although uncertain what the twelve cranial nerves of a dogfish or reproductive systems of frogs and rabbits had to do with banking.

"Of course, you know it's pronounced incorrectly by everyone?" Mr Barker said.

Ben didn't know, but realised he had nothing to fear from this gap in his education as Mr Barker was clearly eager to enlighten him.

"The way it's pronounced is illogical because it should have three 'o's'. Zoo'ology. D'you see what I mean? With only two 'o's' it should be pronounced Zo'ology. As in Zoe without the 'e'. Now why do you think it is everyone gets it wrong?"

It was quite hard to know what to say that would match the man's pedantry. Ben had prepared for the interview by reading up a bit about the finer points of banking, about managing risk and customer relationships, about overdrafts and interest rates, but the financial reference books had been a bit light on the subject of how many 'o's Zoology should be spelt with. Ben decided banking was not for him if this was the sort of person he would have to work with, or even worse, might become. Given the brevity of the rest of the interview, Mr Barker rather felt the same, perhaps influenced by Ben's lack of enthusiasm for his view of erudition. They parted company and he found himself back on Lombard Street with the Bank tube station to his right.

Having finished somewhat earlier than he had

anticipated, Ben decided to walk through the City to the offices of P&O, the cruise liner company. He remembered they had advertised for ship's Pursers. Whilst not entirely sure why their passengers could not carry their own purses, he felt the qualifications for the job wouldn't be overly onerous. The prospect of seeing the world whilst overseeing the welfare of people's wallets was attractive and he thought he would pop in and accept the job they would undoubtedly offer him.

Turning left outside the building and following a map, he made his way through the streets of the financial powerhouse that is the City of London, absorbing the sense of its global power and influence. He pictured his highly salaried self one day hurrying through the streets between important meetings, assistants and advisors trailing in his wake. On arriving at P&O's Head Offices, he stood on the pavement opposite the building, looked up at the imposing edifice and lost his nerve. The reality of the ridiculousness of his intention to walk in and ask for a job overwhelmed him and so he turned and made his way back to the station, confident the company's passengers could carry their own purses without his skills.

A few days later Ben found himself at the Head

Office of a large paper manufacturer and supplier. It's job description in the newspaper had the added lure of overseas travel and postings, which Ben felt brought an exotic element to the job, and was the main attraction for him. He arrived slightly early for his appointment with Mr Charlton whose secretary had confirmed would see him in the first instance. The interview seemed to go reasonably well and he was excited at the end of it when Mr Charlton conducting it said he would be very interested in Ben working for the company. He said he wanted him to go to their offices in the East End of the City where he would initially be based to learn about the company's business. Picking up the large black phone on his desk, he made a call and arranged for Ben to see a Mr Albright later in the afternoon. Mr Charlton gave him a slip of paper with the address written on it and bade him farewell, stressing he was looking forward to him joining the company.

Ben walked out onto Cannon Street feeling elated. He had no money and no income but could now get the strong scent of a salary cheque, with the delicious prospect of all the bacchanalian delights it would afford him. He would be able to afford alcohol and turn his back on conjugal relationships with cattle, buying a real girl a drink instead, if he could find one who'd stay with him long enough to drink it. But first, he'd buy a suit whose trouser legs moved in unison with his legs inside them.

When Ben arrived at the address in Aldgate later that afternoon, he found it was a tall and very old red brick warehouse, built on the subtle and welcoming lines of a Victorian workhouse. This was a long way from the opulence of the imposing grandeur of the marble halls of the Head Office. The whole area was run down and the narrow streets were lined with other equally ancient and tall warehouses, the two sides forming steep sided canyons. The depressed air was emphasised by the buildings cutting out any sunlight at street level.

The large, aged front door of the building he had been directed to opened into a bare stone flagged hallway with a wide wooden staircase rising steeply into the gloom above. It resembled the vestibule of a tenement building in the Gorbals, but without the elegance or charm. Each step on the staircase had a deeply worn dip in it where countless feet over the decades had trudged upwards into the musty building. A notice on the wall informed visitors that they were to report to the offices on the fifth floor. As Ben climbed he noticed a mist of dust in the pale afternoon light behind him that had been disturbed by his shoes.

Reaching the fifth floor he stepped onto a large landing. Wide double doors blocked his path. The top half of the doors was filled with opaque yellowed glass. He knocked quietly on it. An indistinct and shadowy figure appeared on the other side of the glass and the door slowly opened. An elderly, stooped and grey-haired man stood before him, rheumy eyed and with a care-worn expression on his lined face. The frayed and grubby collar of his shirt was too big for the scrawny neck that sprouted out of it, and the weight of his stained tie seemed to drag his head down.

"Can I help you?" he said.

"Yes, I'm here to see Mr Albright," Ben replied. "I think he's expecting me."

"Follow me," the man said, turning and walking out of sight behind the door. Ben went in and quickly caught up with him as he shuffled forwards, scuffing his feet on the worn, bare wooden floorboards. His dirty and worn shoes were clearly too big for him and the heels clunked loudly on the bare floor with every forward step. He wore an old grey cardigan over his shirt and Ben could see the elbows had been repeatedly darned by a blind tailor. Looking around as he walked Ben could see they were in a large, high ceilinged room that was filled with old desks set out in rows. Each desk was occupied by clones of the man he was following. Not one head lifted to watch them, each bent over papers, dog-eared files, half-filled ashtrays and the detritus of an office. Ben noticed not one of the desks had a telephone on it. The atmosphere was thick with cigarette smoke and foetid armpits, with some top notes of feet in crusty socks, a sort of pied-en-croute aroma. Apart from the sound the man's shoes made with each step, there was complete silence in the room.

At the far end of the long room a glass sided cubbyhole that passed for a small office sat like a goldfish bowl in the corner. The door was closed and inside the small room a large, fat, bald-headed man sat behind a desk that was piled high with more of the dusty files the business clearly bred. The man had his jacket off, exposing braces that were stretched to their breaking point over his stomach as they strained to reach his trousers. A cigarette hung out of the corner of his mouth, a thin smoke signal drifting up the side of his face and into his eyes, making him squint lopsidedly. The elderly man leading Ben reached the door and knocked on it, stepping back to wait. The fat man inside looked up and beckoned them in.

"Someone to see you Mr Albright," the old man said, opening the door and stepping to one side to let Ben pass. He squeezed into the small cubicle between the old man and the door, and then up against the desk so the door could be pulled shut behind him. Leaning back as the elderly man went past, Ben knocked over a pile of files on the corner of the desk, toppling them across it. They swept a half-eaten cheese and tomato sandwich across the desk from where it had been lying, cowering in front of Mr Albright's stomach.

"Careful, be careful!" he cried out in an irritated tone. "Just sit down before you do any more damage," he said, gesturing to an old chair in front of his desk. Ben sat on the hard chair, which leaned precariously to one side as it took his weight. Mr Albright made a great show of rearranging the collapsed tower of files, tutting and fussing as he did with no attempt to disguise his displeasure. The desk rearranged to his satisfaction, he sat back in his seat to stare across at Ben, his fingers entwined as his hands lay in the wilderness of his expansive stomach. His cigarette remained in his mouth where it bounced up and down as he spoke, like a wagging finger, while the long drooping piece of ash at the end of it hung on like a man to the edge of a cliff. Presumably exhausted, it finally let go and showered down Mr Albright's grubby shirt, adding potash to the compost of the meals he had recently eaten. Ben wondered if any of the tomato seeds from the mangled sandwich that had also fallen on the fertile expanses of his shirt would start sprouting.

"Paper," he suddenly said. "That's what we do. It's what we are. We make it and distribute it. We live it. We breathe it. Do you know how many uses there are for paper? No, I didn't think you would. Not many people do."

The wagging cigarette admonished Ben for his ignorance. Since he had said absolutely nothing, he had no idea how the man knew whether he was up to date with paper's full panoply of talents, but he didn't seem to be the sort of person who was interested in anyone's opinion.

"The Egyptians were the first people to make paper. They used papyrus, which is where the word paper comes from, but it was the Chinese who were the first to use trees and to develop paper as we know it now. Clever little people those Chinese. Mind you, they have a lot of arses to wipe over there so not surprising they found a way of dealing with that, is it?"

He chuckled to himself at his little joke before

going on to spend the next twenty minutes giving Ben the history of the love and passion of his life. Paper was clearly an aphrodisiac to him. Ben wondered whether the bedding on the Albright marital bed was made with old newspapers. Probably a bit alarming for the redoubtable Mrs Albright if her paper fetishist husband approached their marital bed in a perpetual state of nocturnal arousal. He learned from the impromptu lecture that the Americans were a bit late in the day in getting into paper, beaten to the post by centuries by most European countries. In Mr Albright's expressed opinion, this showed the Americans weren't as smart as they thought they were and still had some catching up to do.

Having finished the history lesson, Mr Albright moved on to Lesson two on Ben's road to enlightenment. He launched into another twenty minutes of a run-through on the many types of paper that existed. Ben was beginning to realise Mr Albright lived in twenty minute sound-bites, during which an opinion or interruption was not invited nor welcome. A bramble and nettle scrub in the genital area would have been preferable to the agonies of listening to his monotonous, monotone voice as he eulogised about the most commonplace of materials. He picked up a piece of A4 white paper, holding it lovingly in front of his shirt on which Ben was sure he could see signs of radicles appearing from the tomato seeds. On the other hand, perhaps the little shoots he thought he could see were slumbering maggots, exhausted from feeding on shrapnel from past meals.

"Paper breathes you know," Mr Albright said, holding the sheet of paper towards Ben. He reached forward to take it so he too could feel and examine it, assuming he was expected to do so, but Mr Albright pulled it back sharply with a horrified intake of breath, caressing it as one would a frightened child or pet.

"No, don't touch it," he said sharply. "Paper is delicate. It responds to humidity and can easily be damaged."

Mr Albright glared aggressively at him with a protective hand over the sheet of paper. From the man's demeanour, this obviously needed no explanation but Ben assumed it might reveal a jealous streak in his interviewer who was clearly fearful the philandering sheet might transfer its affections from him to Ben and worm its way into his pocket in a state of folded bliss, reducing the spurned Mr Albright to the role of a cuckold.

Looking to his right and through the glass wall of the little office Ben could see the afternoon sunshine slanting through the air in the long office where the clerks laboured. Its rays cut through the fug of exhaled cigarette smoke coming from the worker bees at their desks. It created shafts of light and shadow that shimmered and stirred as the air moved lethargically around. Fine dust floated in the yellowed sunlight, particles dancing like Mayflies over a Hampshire river on a summer's evening. Ben's back was beginning to ache from sitting upright in the straight-backed wooden chair and he leant forward to ease the discomfort, resting his arms on the thin armrests and with his face lowered closer to the desktop.

"Paper's a living thing. It responds to the atmosphere, the humidity" Mr Albright droned on. "Opening or closing the window can change its nature. Subtly, but if you know your paper you will notice and know its moods, likes and dislikes. You will learn to care for it, how to keep it. After nine years here with me, I can assure you there is nothing you won't know about paper. Not many people can say that. You are very lucky."

Ben had gone to sleep with his eyes open. In his daydream he could see the obsessive Mr Albright at home, kneeling before a little altar on which rested a couple of reams of the stuff. Candles flickered in homage before the neatly arranged pile. Little circular clippings from the reservoir of his hole punch had been scattered about the place as an offering to St John the Evangelist, the Patron Saint of papermakers. In the background, his gargantuan wife, swaddled in lavatory paper, lay on their bed, crinkling the paper sheets and winking salaciously at him.

The words *'nine years here with me'* wormed their way through Ben's narcoleptic trance and he coughed and laughed at the same time, straight into the overflowing ashtray that sat close under his nose on the front of the desk. A huge cloud of ash blew up and across the desk where it came to rest on Mr Albright. In an instant, he was turned into a facsimile of an exhibit at Pompeii, petrified for eternity in carbonised tobacco.

Ben could not think of a more effective way to bring an interview to a close, not that he had been interviewed, more lectured at. It dawned on him he had not uttered a word throughout the meeting. The only thing that now stirred in the silent office was the piece of desecrated paper in Mr Albright's hand where it trembled. Red, watery eyes peered out of the man's pudgy ash covered face as he stared at the defiled paper in his hand. Ben took this as his hint to leave and stood up to go. Mr Albright appeared to be in some form of catatonic state so Ben said goodbye and slipped out of his little cubbyhole of an office into the silence of the larger room, closing the door quietly behind him. The gathering of scribes continued their work, again not one of them lifting an inquisitive head. Perhaps they were too worn down by their dire working environment, any spark of ambition, hope or pleasure in their work leached out of them.

Glancing at them as he walked between the desks, Ben could not think of a better incentive to 'get on' in life. All he had to do was to find something to 'get on' with. When he reached the door he opened it and glanced back to see the traumatised Mr Albright was still sitting in the same position, a man now in desperate need of bereavement counselling as he stared at the violated paper in his hand. The relative fresh air of the vehicle fume filled street was pure nectar and Ben walked down the road with the sense of an escapee, a man wandering in a forest who realises he has narrowly avoided putting his foot in a bear trap.

CHAPTER 7

1968

Ben could not recall the exact moment he decided on a life in advertising. Perhaps it found him. He could never remember. Desperation is a powerful motivator, and between writing letters of application he had been keeping himself in some limited hard-earned funds by doing manual labour on building sites. This exposed him to a cast of characters he couldn't have made up, aliens in his more sophisticated aspirational life. Spending the rest of his working life with itinerant Irish navvies, whose greatest joy in life was to shift a couple of tons of soil a day with their trusty shovels, selling the sweat on their brows to the highest bidder, was not one of the options that had jumped off the pages of the careers book he had perused. Once he had learned to cut through the accents of the hardened labourers he toiled with, he learned a version of the English language he had no idea existed, a pithiness of communication that left no uncertainty in the message being delivered.

For some of those he worked with comprehension

was a bit more complicated. An elderly Polish man was employed as the tea boy on one large building project where Ben was earning blistered hands. The wizened little man ran the tea hut with military precision, sweeping the floor of food scraps and the mud from the labourers' boots. At regular intervals he brewed tea that had the consistency of engine oil. When the tea was made he would stand at the door of the hut and announce it to the workforce at the top of his voice. Given the company he had kept for many years, he knew that every sentence in the English language had the words '*Fuck*' or '*Fucking*' in it, but he had no idea where they went in the sentence, so the end of it clearly seemed to be as good a place as any to him. Perhaps this allowed him to feel he was one of the boys, armed with the password to full inclusion in the band, blending into the herd despite his ability to torture and mangle the language with every utterance.

"Tea's ready, fucking!" was his regular clarion call to everyone to come and sample the muscular tea he had made. "Wipe your boots, fucking!" was his greeting to each man entering the hut to sit at the two long tables running the length of the bare room. "Put rubbish in bin, fucking!" was his farewell as the men went back to work at the end of their break.

In between digging or filling holes, or carting huge bags of cement off lorries and moving the mobile toilet around sites, Ben continued to go to interviews and scan the papers. In researching jobs and careers it occurred to him that advertising seemed a fun thing to do. From what he read about it, it seemed to be a young person's world, and he couldn't imagine finding the likes of Messrs Barker and Albright employed in it. They had become the benchmark of the sort of people he never wanted to spend time with. Ten minutes with one of them would be like a life sentence.

Advertising on the other hand must surely be populated by the young and vibrant, at a time when the young and vibrant were rebelling against the old order, taking possession of their own destiny. British and Merseyside music was ruling the world and London had been declared its fashion capital. The air was full of revolution, of a generation that no longer wished to conform to the establishment's expectations of them. The Vietnam war had come home to America where the National Guard were soon to fire on their own, on students who only wanted to express an understandable horror at a conflict that had nothing to do with them but which was stealing so many young American lives. The students quickly learned that flowers of peace pushed down National Guard gun barrels didn't stop bullets. The Second World War had not long finished and it seemed to the youth of the world that those who had been involved in that horror were determined to sacrifice another generation of young and innocent in yet another abattoir of meddling. The world's youth were outraged that a generation that preceded them seemed to have learned nothing from two global conflicts in one century, and yet demanded and expected respect as an entitlement for their greater experience and seniority.

Violence begets violence and Ben joined the great outraged who turned up on an early Spring day in Trafalgar Square to protest. The assembled throng of young protestors listened to speeches by the leaders and then set off to march to Grosvenor Square to voice their dissent against the war in front of the American Embassy in London. When the crowd reached the Square they found the authorities had already formed a cordon of mounted and riot police in front of the Embassy to protect it. Ben didn't know how it started but he suddenly found himself in the middle of what seemed to be a full blown riot. The air was thick with thrown missiles, placards, and marijuana smoke. Protestors repeatedly charged at the police line, but it held and in brutal retaliation police horses charged back in return, some rearing high as they too were frightened or injured. People were trampled and many heads were bloodied by batons in the battle as the fights spilled over into the gardens in the centre of the square. Spring daffodils were trampled underfoot, as were the poppies of Flanders, once again innocent victims of the inevitable collateral damage that is always the by-product of any conflict.

The Embassy's defences remained un-breached. Veterans of the day gathered in bars later and speculated on how many guns had been trained on them from within the Embassy as the melée played out in front of it. The police won the fight but lost the respect of a psychedelic, free-loving floral generation, whose resolve to change the established order hardened. The Establishment's pyrrhic victory brought a new sense of anarchic liberation that incited those at the threshold of their adult lives to create a new way of living for themselves and for following generations. The benchmark of what was normal changed and respect now had to be earned, not just considered an entitlement, a right based on seniority. Music became a powerful medium for voicing protest, a weapon to irritate and horrify the establishment with the weapon of a shock culture.

Against this backdrop of freedom and flower garlanded hedonism, capitalism continued its relentless march. The corporate monoliths dreamt up new ways to open wallets and plunder their contents, like hungry picnickers opening ripe figs and plunging their teeth into the soft unprotected flesh hidden inside. Credit cards had recently arrived in Britain and for the first time people woke up to the fact they no longer had to wait for their pleasures or desires. The future became the present and the waiting was taken out of the wanting, whether the newly financially liberated had the money or not. Advertising agencies seemed to be riding the wave of retail incontinence as companies sought ever more persuasive ways to sell things to people who had no idea they wanted them, let alone needed them.

When devaluing its currency Harold Wilson had told the Nation that the pound in everyone's pocket would remain the same. That seemed to Ben like telling a slimmer he is the same person, despite having shed twenty percent of his body weight. Nevertheless, advertising was clearly flourishing and was exactly where he felt he needed to be. It had a future and without any concern to how parasitic that might be, he wanted to be part of that. A retail fixated population that wanted it all and wanted it now were ripe for exploitation by cynical capitalism.

With this inspirational thought, and the realisation

that it was one of the careers he could consider that didn't seem to require qualifications, Ben scoured the newspapers and visited a number of recruitment agencies that specialised in placing aspiring marketeers in advertising jobs. For the first time he felt his life had some direction, an objective he could target, and this brought comfort to him. It lit a fire of ambition he had no idea existed within him. One of the agencies seemed particularly adept at obtaining interviews for the unqualified incompetents of the job-seeking population, which was how Ben found himself sitting in front of the Personnel Director of a large advertising agency. He had read some background information on the agency when the recruitment company told him he was going to be interviewed. It seemed the agency had a reputation for innovative creative work, whatever that was, but Ben wasn't sure whether that was the agency's opinion of itself or an independent view. The agency was looking for trainee account executives and Jonathan, as the Personnel Director liked to be addressed, was keen to *'take in raw material that we can mould and fashion in our ways, with our ethos, through our dedicated training programme.'*

Jonathan was from a different planet to the pedant Mr Barker and the paper fundamentalist Mr Albright. Dressed in an expensive and à la mode suit that had obviously been hand crafted, he smelt of exotic fragrances, like a Mediterranean herbaceous border, which amplified his carefully groomed persona. His hair was fashionably long, covering the top of his ears and the collar of his hand made Jermyn Street shirt. A pastel silk tie, unsullied by the shrapnel from cheese and tomato sandwiches that formed such a fertile environment for the bacteria living on Mr Albright's front, was perfectly knotted and lay casually across the crisply ironed shirt front that must surely have covered an exercise honed stomach. His face was tanned from some exotic holiday and the gold cufflinks in his double cuffed shirt glinted in the sunlight. With his silk socks and expensive brogue shoes, he exuded success, clearly the beneficiary of a salary to envy and an expense account to desire. And Ben wanted to be part of that. Ambition beckoned alluringly and he wanted it all. The whole enchilada.

"So Ben, why do you want to join us?" Jonathan asked at the end of the interview, after he had elicited the heavily edited framework of Ben's life and had outlined life in a busy and successful award winning Agency.

"Well, I come from a small family, I live in a small village and I went to a small school. I think it's time I did something big in my life," he replied.

Ben had no idea where his answer came from. Unrehearsed, it was spontaneous and heartfelt. There was nothing to be gained from trying to explain it.

"Well, thank you, and thank you for coming in to see me. As you can imagine, I have quite a number of people to see so I shall be in touch with you when we have made a decision."

Jonathan stood up as he was speaking and held out his hand. Ben took it and shook it firmly.

"Thank you," he said. "I've enjoyed meeting you, and would really love to work here."

He was amazed at the audacity of his comment. Closing the door behind him, he left the office and made his way down through the building and through the revolving front door to the street outside. Now the waiting started, the frustration and strain of not knowing, but wanting so much. It was the intense desire and need that was so hard to deal with and if he was not going to get the job he would much rather have been told at the interview. Instead, the postman's daily steps on the drive would lift the palindromic daily tension, only for it to drop as no letter arrived, leaving the bitter taste of disappointment and the growing sense of impending rejection. Ben felt as though he was peering over the edge of an abyss, an empty future of directionless wandering whilst all about him forged ahead with the joys of success and fulfilment. It was terrifying and he felt isolated and alone as he had never done before. The barren days were long and hard to fill.

In fact, the letter arrived a week later, on the day Russian tanks rolled over the Czechoslovakian border on their way to the capital, their autumnal intervention signalling the swift and brutal end to the Prague Spring that had shown the first buds of a new dawn. It had gathered momentum and a heady sense of freedom for the oppressed population but enjoyed the briefest of summers with the tantalising hope of lives freed from the communist yoke. Ben held the envelope in his hand, readying himself for the inevitable rejection. He was alone in the house and took it through to the drawing room where he sat in an armchair in the bay window looking out across the sun-drenched lawn.

There was no point in delaying the pain so he tore open the envelope and pulled out the letter that offered him his first real job. Trainee account manager, starting in a week's time on the princely salary of ninety pounds a month. He was on the threshold of wealth beyond his dreams and the opportunity of independence. Having been relieved to be alone for the letter opening moment, he now wished there was someone in the house with whom to share the good news, someone with whom to celebrate. Ecstatic at the opportunity to fill his days, with the added bonus of untold riches, he couldn't settle to anything for the rest of the day, apart from quickly writing a letter of acceptance and walking down to the post box to send it on its way before the Agency changed its mind. Walking back to the house in the late summer sunshine, he decided he needed to get a new suit to shed his past. His new self was going to metamorphose and appear in public wearing something that didn't look like a re-tailored parachute. With the prospect of a salary he decided to ask his mother if he could borrow the money for a few new clothes.

CHAPTER 8

The Agency's offices were in the West End of London. Situated near fashionable Carnaby Street, where beautiful people wandered aimlessly, dressed in floral print clothes like flower arrangements, or in flowing kaftans. Pretty girls with flower filled hair flowing freely and dreamcatchers on their wrists wore skirts that made belts look wide. Young people strolled about, nonchalantly disseminating peace and love in a haze of marijuana and more exotic cocktails of mind reshaping stimulants for those for whom a mere spliff was an inadequate escape from reality.

Ben felt he was at the very centre of modern Britain, an irresistible force that was driving and leading music and fashion in the world beyond its shores. The future belonged to the young, determined to overthrow the old order, a rebellious generation that believed things could change, that the old mores and values were outdated. Experience became a devalued currency, to be replaced by meritocracy, a sense of worth that only bore allegiance to demonstrable actions and results. During his first weeks at work Ben came to feel he had entered some form of parallel universe, an alien life where he had left his previous existence at the top of the heap, and started a new one at the bottom. He wondered if his life was going to be like a game of snakes and ladders, a series of episodes of reaching the top of one chapter and then starting again on the first rung of the next.

The Agency had synchronised the start date of four new trainees. Ben arrived for his first day clutching an ostentatious and embarrassing briefcase his excessively proud mother had bought him. He wondered if it was obvious to everyone there that there was absolutely nothing in it apart from a peanut butter and jam sandwich. He had been tempted to leave it in a left luggage locker at the station but was running slightly late and didn't feel he had the time, so he walked into the building with it slightly behind him to hide it. Introducing himself to the receptionist, he was directed to take a seat in comfortable black leather sofas by the front windows, where two other young men were already seated. As he took his place next to them, a pretty, short skirted girl with long blonde hair came in through the front door and walked up to the receptionist where she waited for the girl behind the desk to finish a phone call. Being seated in the low chairs, the three young men's eyes were level with the hem of her skirt, which was short enough to reveal the first hint of her firm and perfectly formed bottom as it curved inwards and down to meld into the top of her leg.

Ben was completely transfixed. He had never seen anything so erotic, so far removed from his entanglement with the voracious buffalo Veronica, and from a brief but failed encounter shortly after her. In his last year at school, a new assistant matron had arrived to a fanfare of priapic posturing from the boys. In her early twenties, she was a wholesome girl with a pneumatic figure and an earthy and pragmatic enjoyment of the carnal needs of youth. Shortly after the fateful school dance, Ben had had need of some minor medical attention one evening, and had gone up to her room. She was watching a film on television, a glass of wine by her hand, and after her ministrations asked Ben if he would like a glass as well.

One glass led to another, and he had found himself in an alcoholic haze naked on the carpet with her, realisation dawning on him that the bottle of wine he had been sharing with her was almost certainly her second of the evening. He was also acutely aware a copious helping of wine was not the aphrodisiac he had hoped it would be and that he was somewhat lacking in the ready for action department. The troops were still in the barracks and being somewhat truculent and uncooperative. She rolled onto her back, pulling him on top of her and wrapping her legs around his waist. As she did so, the school tomcat strolled into the room with a struggling mouse in its mouth. In the way of any arrogant cat, the animal walked over to the entwined couple on the floor and sniffed Ben's face. Startled at the touch of the cat's cold nose on his, he opened his eyes just as the cat turned around, lifted its tail, arched its back and languidly emptied the contents of its anal scent gland in his face and into his open mouth. The affect on his passion was the same as if the girl's mother had walked in and started playing a blowtorch over his naked arse in that it was a bit of a distraction from the task in hand. He had quickly disentangled himself from the writhing but ultimately frustrated body beneath him so that he could retrieve his clothes and return to his room to wash his face and rinse his mouth with sulphuric acid if he could just find some.

Now, in one brief cataclysmic moment, heterosexuality arrived like a juggernaut, sweeping aside his fears about his sexuality. He was overwhelmed with desire as testosterone flooded his system, undiluted by a barrel of wine. Less is so often more, and the tantalisingly teasing hint at the treasures her body promised could not have been more arousing if she had been completely naked. He blushed at the realisation he appeared to have acquired a demented and frenetic squirrel in his underwear.

The girl said something quietly to the receptionist who pointed at the seats where Ben and the other two were seated. She turned and walked confidently over to join the three young men. When she took her seat on the sofa next to Ben, it seemed to him that fifteen yards of soft golden thighs were stretched out by his side. Soft downy hair on her bare legs had been bleached by the sun. Desperate not to be seen looking down at her legs, he smiled at her.

"Hi," she said turning to him and holding out her hand, her returning smile and even white teeth captivating beneath sky blue eyes. "I'm Jo."

"Ben," he replied, taking her hand and shaking it firmly whilst remaining doubled over in his seat to hide the monster that seemed to be trying to thrash its way out of his trousers. It felt as though the rampant squirrel had metamorphosed into a woolly mammoth in musth. He was aware he probably looked like someone with food poisoning on a lavatory, but the alternative of standing up and revealing to the world that he appeared to have a throbbing cantaloupe melon down the front of his pants was less appealing. Jo's handshake was strong and self-assured and she held his gaze with her sky blue eyes. She wore very little make-up and he noticed a few delicate freckles sprinkled across her nose. She turned to the other two young men, leaning forward and across Ben to shake their hands. Each time she did so her crisp white linen shirt, with its top three buttons undone, fell forward. Ben was mesmerised by the sight of her cleavage, his gaze fixated on the soft skin on the swell of her breasts. He fought a desperate urge to push his finger down the gap between them.

"Graham," the dark haired and slightly acned one sitting next to Ben said, dropping his gaze.

"Ed," replied the other, tossing back surfer's blonde hair out of his eyes, even white teeth showing as he smiled at Jo. His suntanned face hinted at summers on a beach, drinking beers around camp fires in the sand and catching big waves in the dawn light. He held her hand longer than Ben thought was polite or necessary, and his own sense of arousal was now diluted with jealousy. He wanted her attention to be back on him but remained tongue tied. She was close enough to him on the sofa for him to pick up the scent of the perfume she was wearing, with its subtle understated blend of petitgrain, jasmine and rose enhancing her allure. Brutalised and hardened by his formative years, steeped as they had been in masculinity undiluted by compensating feminine influences, he was overwhelmed by her soft femininity and realised he had absolutely no idea how to communicate with her on any level that wouldn't repel her. In that moment he knew ten years as a trainee Trappist monk had not been a fully holistic preparation for the real facts of life. They were years that had left him knowing so little about the opposite sex, breathtakingly unprepared to relate with or understand a woman's mind.

"Good morning, I'm Jonathan's secretary. I see you're all here so will you follow me please and I'll take you up."

Ben realised someone had walked up to them, breaking his fantasising if somewhat confused reverie. The four of them stood and started after the girl as she walked ahead of them towards the lifts. Ben hung back slightly so he could walk behind Jo, glad of the shelter of his mother's gift to him which he now held in front of him. At least he would be able to answer his mother honestly when she inevitably asked him if he had found it useful. Now they were on their feet, he realised Jo was a few inches shorter than him. Slim waisted and straight backed, she walked with a lilting sway to her gait, placing one foot directly in front of the other, with the affect of moving her hips seductively from side to side. It brought to his mind the contrast of the disturbing memory of the violent lurching of that first Matron's bovine buttocks as they fought to herniate out of whatever galvanised foundation undergarments she had used to restrain them. The dissimilarity with the vision before him could not have been more extreme and Ben felt he could quite happily walk behind Jo and her bottom all day. The lift door opened as they arrived at it and they stepped in and lined up around the side of it. The secretary pushed the button for the fourth floor and an uncomfortable quiet descended, as so often happens when strangers are confined in a small space, agonising about ways in which to avoid their travelling companions' eyes.

"So, this is where it all begins," Ed said. Ben noticed he had carefully positioned himself next to Jo and was looking at her when he spoke into the empty silence in the lift. "I wonder what the day holds for us all."

Ed was clearly very confident and easy about women, an Alpha male determined to stamp his authority on the group. He smiled at Jo and gave her a wink before turning to the other occupants.

"You're going to meet the Client Services

Director with Jonathan who you've all met," the secretary said with a smile. "They will explain the induction process to you and allocate you to your account management teams."

The lift stopped and the doors slid open quietly. The secretary led the way out onto a long and wide, modern open plan floor that was filled with desks huddled together in small groups. Floor to ceiling windows ran down the far side and the daylight streamed in, brightening the farthest corners of the room. There was a steady hum of conversation, and people walking about with armfuls of papers and note pads. Telephones rang and the clatter of typewriter keys added a background chatter. It seemed to Ben that the average age of everyone in the room was about twenty five.

The secretary turned and started walking down to the end of the room where there was a glassed in meeting room. The newcomers followed her like a line of ducklings, except for Ed who fell in step next to Jo. Walking just behind them, Ben saw the precocious Ed lean into her, their shoulders and upper arms touching, and whisper something in her ear. She laughed and turned to him with a smile. Ben felt a small stab in his heart and distracted himself by looking around the room as they walked. He could not help but think about the cardigan clad worker bees in the yellowed light of the silent warehouse office where he had been interviewed by the slightly less than inspirational deviant obsessive, Mr Albright. The comparison between the vibrancy of the office he was walking through and the sepulchral silence of the paper company was stark. He felt like a soldier in the front line who had dodged a bullet. How could two such opposite worlds exist? What held a man chained to a visionless, hopeless and passionless job, one that emasculated him and cauterised the slightest germinations of individuality? Were their lives at home as monochrome? Ben could not think of a more powerful incentive to fill his life with colour and fun, to achieve and get on. The first seeds of real ambition sown at his interview with Jonathan had fallen on fertile ground.

The four trainees followed the secretary into the meeting room and she told them to sit down the long side of the large table.

"Jonathan will be with you in a minute," the secretary said. "Help yourselves to tea and coffee." She pointed at a sideboard at the end of the meeting room on which mugs and flasks were neatly arranged, and then left the room, closing the door behind her.

"Coffee or tea anyone?" Ed said, walking up to the sideboard.

"I'd love a coffee," Jo said, following him. "Black, no sugar please."

"Coffee for me too," Ben said, "but with milk. No sugar."

Graham followed the others but said nothing as Ed poured the coffees out. He held up the flask to Graham who nodded acceptance. They each returned to the table and sat down.

"So, where are you guys all from?" Ed said, again taking the lead in conversation, turning to Jo who was sitting next to him, telegraphing his complete disinterest in Ben and Graham's origins, his question clearly not intended for them. Before she could answer, the door opened quickly and Jonathan, who had interviewed Ben, strode in, accompanied by a shorter, broad shouldered man who seemed to bristle with energy. His bull neck was accentuated by his unfashionably short hair. A small, trim moustache lay like an anorexic hairy caterpillar over his thin lips.

"Good morning and welcome," he said, taking a seat on the other side of the table to face the four of them. "This is James, our Client Services Director. James has overall responsibility in the Agency for our client relationships and for ensuring we deliver our promises to clients. Everything's going to feel a bit strange to you at first but you'll get the hang of it soon enough. We are going to allocate you to account management teams, each of which looks after designated clients. Advertising is a process and your first priority is to learn that process, from the first briefing by the client through to the finished product, whether that is a television, Press or a poster campaign. It will be some time before you can be let loose on clients by yourselves so you will shadow your team and work under your Account Director who will send me regular reports on how you are getting on. Any problems you take to your Director or the Account Manager. Any questions?"

"Yes," Ed said. "Is it all to be learning as we go or are there any specific training sessions?"

"No," James said, "we will be giving you specific training at various points but the majority of the time you will be picking it up as you work in your teams. They are all experienced and will help you. Anything else?"

The four newcomers each shook their heads and so Jonathan and James turned and walked towards the door.

"Right, follow me and I shall introduce you to your teams," Jonathan said over his shoulder as James opened and held the door for them.

The four pushed their chairs back and followed Jonathan out into the main office. They stopped at the first group of desks they came to and Jonathan beckoned Ben to come forward.

"Ben, this is Celia, your Account Director," Jonathan said. "She will introduce you to the team so I'll leave you in her capable hands." The small group moved on down the office to another group of desks where Ben noticed Graham was handed over to a tall, serious looking man who was wearing a bright bow tie. Celia turned around from some documents she was reading and stood up. Dark curly hair that was fashionably cut off at her jawline framed her face, and her short dress was straight out of Biba, black and white panels competing for attention. Celia obviously believed in being à la mode. Small eyes peered at Ben through glasses and a thin mouth was a red slash beneath her slightly hooked nose. Ben wondered if he could detect the hint of a moustache on her upper lip. Perhaps a little lip hair was a fashion statement in the Agency.

"Good morning," she said without offering a hand to complement the greeting. "We have prepared a desk for you over there next to Jason." She pointed at an empty desk by the window. "Go over and make yourself at home and I'll be with you when I have finished reading this contact report."

Ben walked over to his desk which was directly opposite and facing one occupied by a tall man who was also wearing a colourful bow tie. Ben made a mental note to buy one for himself. As Ben approached, Jason leant back in his chair and reached for a cigarette packet on his desk.

"So, it's Ben is it?" he said with a smile. "I'm Jason. Welcome to the sweat shop." He held out his hand and Ben reached across the desks to shake it. Jason put a cigarette in his mouth and lit it with a silver lighter.

"Yes. First day," Ben said with a slight shrug.

"Don't worry," Jason said. "You'll soon get the hang of it. We are on three main accounts here, with a few smaller ones, and it gets a bit hectic at times. I imagine you'll work with me to begin with. Needless to say, I haven't been told."

And so Ben's introduction to Planet Work was Jason's friendly greeting. It relaxed him a bit, easing the tension of the unknown. Secretly he was terrified. He had not the faintest idea of what was expected of him, of how advertising worked. Everyone in the large office seemed preoccupied by what they were doing and, as yet, he was unnoticed, the wallflower in the room. He welcomed his anonymity whilst at the same time longing for the familiar. He quietly hid the embarrassing briefcase under the desk and set about rearranging the few items on it, marking his territory and putting his stamp on it. The drawers were empty apart from dust and a few mangled paperclips on which the previous occupant seemed to have vented his frustration. The last drawer he opened had an empty pill bottle that, from the prescription note on it, seemed to have contained some form of calming sedative. It was lying on a piece of paper with a gibbet and hangman's noose drawn on it. Under the drawing the amateur artist had written;

'This is all you need to work here.'

Disenchantment with a career choice takes many forms but depression and suicide seemed to be a bit extreme to Ben. He chose to ignore the harbinger of doom that lurked in the desk, throwing both the empty bottle and the paper in the wastepaper basket by his chair.

The rest of that first morning was spent listening to Jason describe the building blocks of an advertising campaign. His discourse was repeatedly interrupted by the shrill ring of the telephone on his desk, and by regular visits by people in need of a decision or advice. The vibrancy and pace of the work excited Ben, and he determined to master the intricacies of the marketing craft so he too could become as confident in the subject as those he observed about him. Jason explained that, whilst those on the Creative floor above assumed the whole Agency had been set up as a life support system for them, the heart of any campaign and management of a client was the Account Director and his or her team of Account Executives and Managers. It seemed to

Ben that every role in the Agency carried a title with it, each designed to elevate the importance of the individual, anointing each with an aura of importance that bore no relevance to their actual function or position in the hierarchy. He wondered at the futility of the need for this orotund self-aggrandisement, when all must be in the know and realise the reality behind the titles. Perhaps they were fig leaves for low self esteem, an aphrodisiac for the ego.

Just before lunch, Jason asked Ben to take a package of artwork down to the post room in the basement. It needed to go immediately and by express post to a client.

"I've got a meeting there the day after tomorrow and they want to have a look at the artwork for the campaign before we get there. They are like that, a bunch of failed creatives who think they can do it better than us. Anyway, whatever, we just have to humour them and pretend their opinion is important. Tell Joe it's urgent and has to go out straight away."

Ben made his way down into the basement, stepping out of the lift and turning down a long corridor. Pipes and tubes lined the ceiling from which hung a couple of bare bulbs, the anatomy of the lifelines of a building. Coming to a door at the end he entered a large, brightly lit room. A large, fat and bald-headed man was sitting in an armchair at the far end, reading a newspaper with his feet up on a waist high shelf that ran around two sides of the room. The shelf was littered with letters, packages and parcels, some that had clearly arrived in the post and others awaiting dispatch. Two young men sat in chairs with a table between them. They were playing cards, mugs of tea sitting by their elbows, a cigarette dangling from each mouth. None of them looked up as Ben let the door close behind him. He stood by it for a moment, expecting an acknowledgement of his entry. When none was forthcoming, he cleared his throat.

"Hi, is Joe here?" he asked.

The large bald man lowered his newspaper with a slight sigh and turned his head.

"Who's asking?" he said, looking at Ben.

"I'm Ben," Ben replied. "Jason asked me to bring this package down. It's urgent and needs to go out early this afternoon. Express delivery I think he said." Ben held up the package in his hand as evidence of the importance of his mission into the uncharted bowels of the building.

"No chance mate," the bald man replied. Ben assumed he must be Joe. "We're a bit busy here." Joe picked up his newspaper again and carried on reading to express his lack of interest in Ben and his parcel.

Some deep instinct warned Ben this was not a good time to debate different people's definition of 'busy,' given that he appeared to have come into a crèche for recalcitrant overgrown children enjoying play and rest time. Intuitively he felt that pleading and begging were also inappropriate and unlikely to produce a satisfactory outcome. Caught between the opposing influences of authority and petulant obduracy, he was at a loss as to what to do next, emasculated as he was by the lack of any form of authority or influence. He continued to stand by the door, trying to conjure a response to the rebuttal of his request when Joe lowered the paper and looked at him again, an irritated expression on his face.

"You go and tell that Jason we're not here to take orders from him, not from anyone up there. You see, this whole place is like a body, a living thing. D'you get my meaning? The Creative department tell me they're its lungs. Without them 'breathing' as they tell me, this place would die. Account Management tell me they're the 'eart of the place, beating away they say to keep everything flowing. Well, you can tell them from me, we're the arsehole here and if we close up, the body stops working, which makes us top dog. At the moment, the arsehole is shut because it's taken enough shit down the line from that lot upstairs. It's always urgent they tell us. Will we drop everything? Will we do this or that favour? All their airs and graces. I'm sick of it and all of them. You can tell Jason the arsehole is taking a bit of a rest 'cos it's got constipation, and that bungs up the works ."

Joe picked up the newspaper once more, and the two younger men carried on with their game of cards. Neither had yet acknowledged his presence.

"I'm sorry, it's my first day here," Ben said, almost plaintively. "I didn't mean to disturb you. It's just that I was asked to bring this down. There's a meeting on Wednesday apparently, and this needs to be there before then. If you're busy, can I do it for you?"

"You touch anything in here, son, and we walk out." Joe said, taking his feet off the shelf and sitting up. "Bring it over here." Joe beckoned Ben forward.

Ben walked over and handed him the package. Joe looked at it and then threw it up on the shelf where it landed on top of a pile of letters awaiting stamping.

"We'll get to it as soon as we can," he said, picking up a mug of half drunk tea and and the newspaper before settling back in the chair again.

"Thank you," Ben said. "I'm very grateful. It would be, you know, a bit awkward….."

Ben left the consequences of failure hanging in the air as he turned and left the room. Clearly, the post room was somewhere that needed handling with care. This was his first exposure to the protectionism of the powerful Unions that were increasing their grip on the country. It revealed the affect of the transfer of corporate power from supine Board Rooms to the shop floor, making so many companies ungovernable under the strictures of the stranglehold of non-cooperative workforces practising the politics of obduracy and belligerence. The consequences of the irrational and unsustainable economics of socialism squaring up to the unacceptable face of capitalism.

The rest of the day followed the same pattern for

Ben, visiting various departments on errands for Jason, studying the impenetrable intricacies of status reports and production schedules and learning about the clients he had been assigned to in the team. It soon became apparent to him that the much vaunted dedicated training programme that Jonathan the Client Services Director had eulogised about at Ben's interview didn't exist. He was going to have to pick up the skills of the job by experience rather than by any formalised in house education programme. It did not take long to realise everyone had time for lunch, but no one had time for him. He was however heartened and excited when Jason announced in the afternoon that he wanted Ben to accompany him to the client meeting to which the important package of art work had been sent that day. A meeting seemed very grown up and mature and Ben immediately prayed that the package would indeed be sent by the post room.

The client was a large manufacturer of toiletries and bathroom accessories. The campaign they were working on related to a new luxury toilet paper the client had created and wished to promote and Ben wondered if Mr Albright had put a hex on him and he would always be stalked by paper in its many forms. The client's importance to the Agency was based on the wider range of products for which they ran campaigns. The toilet paper division was a new venture for the company and the team were working on the product launch. For one awful moment, Ben panicked they may be going to see the traumatised Mr Albright in his garret office, perhaps still in a state of rigor and bereavement over the desecrated paper on his desk, but logic returned as he reminded himself the client was a different company. To prepare for the meeting, Jason arranged for a final briefing from the Creative department late in the afternoon and asked Ben to attend it with him.

As they walked through the building, Ben kept an eye open for Jo and spotted her at a desk next to Ed. It seemed they had been assigned to the same team. They were laughing over something Ed had said. Jo seemed to laugh at whatever comment he had made, her face lighting up as she did. As they walked past she looked up and spotted Ben over Ed's shoulder. She gave him a small smile and a little wave and then turned back to whatever she was doing while Ed continued to talk to her. Ben felt a surge of emotions, a heady cocktail of jealousy, desire and a liberal dash of despondency at the advantage the persistent Ed had gained by working with her. His lascivious intentions were ill-concealed and Ben felt a paternalistic desire to protect Jo from the unwanted rampant advances she was being subjected to. His despondency deepened when it occurred to him the intense attention she was getting might not be so unwelcome. What if she was encouraging it?

Ben's feelings were outside his realm of experience and he had no idea how to deal with them. He only knew he was unexpectedly unsettled by the delicious Jo, and wanted to spend time with her. How could that be when they had exchanged no more than a few polite words? Never having experienced instant attraction before, he was unable to recognise it when it arrived at his door, and equally unable to know whether it was reciprocated.

Arriving at the Creative Department, he pushed the thoughts of Jo to the back of his mind and took a seat at a table in the middle of the room. Looking around he took in a scene of apparent chaos. Large sheets of paper with sketches on them lay scattered on the floor. One desk by a window was completely covered by a two foot deep shambolic pile of papers, books, industry awards, toys and extraneous objects including a plate with a half eaten sandwich on it. A cave had been excavated in the middle of the pile of detritus to allow the desk's occupant a small space at which to work. At the far end of the room a table tennis table was being used by two long haired young men in loud floral shirts. They looked like two flower arrangements dancing around to the syncopated tic-toc of the ball that bounced between them. One of them was not wearing shoes or socks which omission he had compensated for with an impressive collection of beads strung around his neck.

The meeting commenced only when another man, who was languishing prone on a sofa reading a book, got up and walked over to the table to join Ben and Jason. He was introduced to Ben as Steve, the creative assigned to the campaign. It soon became apparent to Ben that his opinion was neither needed, nor going to be sought at the gathering. He listened as the other two talked about the intricacies of competing lavatory paper, and the merits and advantages of the new soft version the client had manufactured over the greaseproof, glissé qualities of Ben's experience. Soft paper was not a new invention, but it had been a luxury he had been denied throughout his formative years. The vaunted soothing qualities of the product, an inspirational example of which sat prominently on the table between them, seemed quite seductive.

Ben listened to Jason's strategic logic as he argued for changes he wanted to make to the direction of the campaign. He explained the changes were based on the empirical evidence of research he had commissioned and on his understanding of the client and its place in the market it intended breaking into. Ben also noticed Steve's defensive aggression whenever Jason appeared to offer a critique of his ideas and work. Jason maintained a placatory mien throughout the meeting, calming the diva in Steve who seemed to take any suggestion or idea that was not his own as an affront to his self confessed prodigious talent and integrity. After an hour of discussion and argument, they eventually reached some form of compromise over how Jason was going to present the creative concept to the client and each returned to their own domain to reflect, Jason and Ben to their desks and Steve to his couch and his book.

"We have to be everyone's friend here," Jason said to Ben as they walked back, "no matter how or what we feel about them."

Apart from the suggestion in his desk drawer of hanging himself after dining on a bottle of tranquillisers, Jason's words were the only piece of advice or education Ben would remember receiving in the years to come. Knowledge was gained osmotically and honed by experience. The weeks and months flowed past like a river in spate and most of the time he felt like a drowning man tossed about in rapids, just managing to keep his nose above the surface. Survival came about by instinct and a desperate will to live, with the knowledge that swimming was the only alternative to sinking, an unpalatable option. Lifelines were in short supply. Without any responsibilities in those early months, he was nevertheless held accountable for things he did not understand and over which he had no control.

Without any true guidance, he found he had to build and develop his own role and his own way. The transfer of guilt was a universal survival mechanism and provided opportunities for enhancement for those cynical enough to use it. Cliques abounded in the Agency, a form of protectionism that did not welcome newcomers. Perhaps clique members were fearful of the change in comfortable dynamics caused by any interloper, a brick hurled into the placid pool of familiarity. Arrogance was a common trait, born of an unshakeable belief in the gift of greatness many felt had been thrust upon them. This bred a sense of entitlement and a blindness to the thought that all they were doing was producing advertisements. Lives did not depend on what the Agency did, but there was an assumption of a First Class, limousine life, where turning left when walking onto a plane was an expectation and a right.

The aspirational needs within Ben were fuelled

one day when he was asked to take a contract to the Managing Director for his signature. Paul Reid was an industry legend, the success story everyone wanted to emulate and the figurehead of hedonistic excess that attracted people to the industry. Ben arrived at the office on the top floor allotted time and was ushered in by a secretary. The company's esteemed leader was seated at an enormous desk at the far end of what seemed to Ben to be an airfield sized office. Peter Reid was seated at the desk and was in the process of finishing a telephone conversation. He gestured towards a separate and smaller table with chairs about it so Ben walked over and sat down to await the end of the call. His gaze wandered around the room from which he could see there seemed to be two of everything. Two large fishtanks filled with extravagantly coloured fish lined one wall. Two paintings by a well known and in vogue artist faced them on the opposite wall. Two large sculptures stood sentry by the door.

Peter Reid put the phone down and walked over to the table as Ben stood up.

"Sit down my boy," he said, taking a seat opposite.

"Thank you Mr Reid," said Ben as he settled back

in the seat and placed the document he was carrying on the table.

"It's Peter, no need for formalities here." He reached across and pulled the document towards him and then placed both forearms on the table, pulling up his shirt sleeves to reveal expensive looking matches on each wrist.

"Patek Philippe or Piaget, which to wear? I couldn't make my mind up this morning so I thought, why not both. Ten thousand, the pair. What do you think?"

"Er, they're very nice," Ben said sliding his Timex up his sleeve, both aghast and fascinated at the sight of such ostentatious opulence.

"Aren't they just," the man replied picking up the papers. He quickly scanned them, signed on the last page with his exquisitely crafted Montblanc pen and handed the document back to Ben.

"Thank you young man," he said and turned to walk back to his desk and his phone as Ben hastily left the room, determined that one day he would no longer feel inadequate, and somewhere on his journey to success he would ditch his Timex and his biro.

In those early months, Ben managed to move into a flat which he shared with five other people. It was a relief to leave home and become more independent. He had found the flat by scouring the pages of London Newspapers. The five flat mates interviewed a number of people and the fact Ben didn't want to bring a piano or trombone into the flat seemed to win the day for him and they offered him the place. Including him there were two girls and four men and he quickly became used to the presence of tights and girl's underwear drying in the bathroom and on radiators about the flat.

The flatmates all led independent lives, the girls in particular as they each had boyfriends, but they all tended to try to have one evening a week together in the nearby pub. This was sometimes used as an informal Board Meeting to discuss issues relating to communal living. At other times, when there was nothing on the agenda or urgent to talk about, the gathering was unashamedly an opportunity to drink too much. At one of the more informal gatherings, mellowed, liberated and emboldened by alcohol, Ben raised the burning issue of Jo at the Agency with Jenny and Rupert, two of his flatmates.

"But why would she be interested in me when she's got someone like Ed, the original Mr Smooth, dancing around her like a Bonobo monkey on speed?" he said.

"What makes you think she wouldn't be?" Jenny replied. "You don't know until you ask her. Why don't you ask her out to a movie or dinner?"

"Where would I take her for dinner?"

"Well, there's a great little bistro called Madame Luba's in Yeoman's Row," said Rupert. "It's just by Beauchamp Place and I took a girl there a couple of months ago. It's mainly Russian food and you have to take your own wine as they don't have a licence but there's great atmosphere and it's not too expensive."

"Just go up and ask her," said Jenny. "The worst that can happen is she says no."

"I know and I'd feel such a fool" said Ben. For some the fear of rejection is an unassailable barrier to a life that exists in their dreams and which will never become a reality.

"I'm sure you'll get over that" said Jenny. "You're not exactly going to die from it, are you?"

"I'm not so sure" Ben laughed. "But you're right, I've just got to ask and hope she doesn't slap me."

"Doubt that will happen," said Rupert "unless of course you put your hand on her arse as you ask."

"OK, so I'll do it tomorrow," Ben said, "but I leave her bum alone. Must remember that. Thanks for the advice. I wouldn't have thought of that myself."

The next morning Ben set off to work steeling himself and bolstering his courage to ask the fateful question of Jo. He needed to get her on her own, away from the omnipresent limpet Ed who always seemed to be within two feet of her, omnipresent and difficult to ignore, like a wasp at a picnic. It was mid-morning before Ben spotted his opportunity. He noticed her get up from her desk and walk over to a kitchen which was in a small vestibule off the main office. She was alone and quite engrossed in the papers in her hands as she waited for the kettle to boil. Picking up some random papers and his empty coffee mug from his own desk, Ben hurried around into the main corridor in the office and immediately tripped over a box of files he had not noticed on the floor, so transfixed was he by the vision that was Jo ahead of him, and by the desperation of his mission. Lying prostrate on the floor under a snowstorm of the papers he had thrown in the air, he watched his now handleless mug rolling towards the kitchen. The phone he had grabbed off the desk as he went down was lying on the floor next to his ear where it had landed after bouncing off his head. Above its irritating buzzing he could hear peals of laughter from everyone around him, Jo included, although she had the grace to hold her hand to her mouth in a futile attempt to hide her giggling.

Dignity is a precious cloak we cover ourselves with. Under it's gossamer protection we germinate and nurture our delicate egos. The fragile tendrils of our self-esteem and confidence feed greedily off it, but wither the moment it is removed, leaving us stranded in the arid desert of shame and embarrassment. Denied the succour of an oasis in his own desert of shame, Ben picked himself up, replaced the phone on its desk, gathered his scattered papers and made his way back to his desk where he busied himself with the finer details of a campaign to promote armpit fresheners to the owners of armpits which emptied whole train compartments with the lift of an arm at the end of busy days. Until that moment he had no idea just how fascinating and attention riveting armpits could be. If he could have found one he would have hidden his puce face in it.

Sadly for Ben, the floor did not open beneath him and swallow him, so he soldiered on through the afternoon, his eyes fixed to the papers on his desk or to the floor, walls and ceiling if he had occasion to move about the office. It was irrelevant that everyone else had already forgotten his dive onto the carpet. He felt the moment would now burn eternally in his memory and probably Jo's. As the working day came to a close and people started to drive off home, Ben continued working, preferring to leave alone and unnoticed. When he felt the office was finally empty, he gathered up his things and caught the lift down to the ground floor. Stepping out into the Reception area, his heart sank as he saw Jo finishing a conversation with Ed, who turned and went out into the street as Jo stood by the doors, doing up her fashionably long dark green maxi-coat which elegantly hugged and flattered her slim waist. She looked up and saw Ben and smiled.

"Hi there," she said cheerfully, "are you off home?"

"Yes" Ben replied. "Home and then to the pub

with some friends."

"I'll walk with you to the Tube," Jo said, falling in next to Ben on the pavement as they set off down the road.

They had gone a few paces when Jo turned to him,

"I'm sorry I laughed when you fell over," she said, "but it was very funny. Quite the slapstick artist."

"It wasn't exactly the highlight of my day" Ben replied. "In fact I was coming to see you," he added, grasping the moment alone with her and his courage at the same time. "I was going to ask if you'd like to have a meal or a drink or something, but of course lying amongst the wastepaper baskets and destroyed telephones I realised that's ridiculous so I summoned up all my cowardice and went back to my desk. Very safe harbour a desk you know. I can recommend it."

"I'd love to do that," Jo said.

"Really?" Ben asked disbelievingly. "Are you sure?"

"No, I just said that to keep you happy," she replied. "Of course I'd like to. It would be fun."

"Will Ed mind?" Ben asked.

"What's Ed got to do with it?" Jo said with a smile and a frown.

"Well, I don't know," Ben replied, "I just thought, you know, you too seemed pretty thick together and I assumed....."

"Good God no!" Jo exclaimed. "Ed's a pain but I just have to humour him. It's just easier because we work together so much and there'd be an atmosphere, but I think the time's coming when I'm going to have to throw some cold water on him." Jo laughed at the thought.

With a date agreed to meet for supper they parted to catch their separate trains at the station. Ben sat in his seat as the train rocked through the tunnels, trying to control the size of the smile on his face and relief in his heart. Ed was a pain and news didn't get better than that. Back at the flat he got the address and telephone number of Madame Luba's restaurant from Rupert and rang them to book a table.

"We don't take bookings sir," the waitress said. "Just turn up and I'm sure we'll fit you in."

And so they did just turn up. Ben arranged to meet Jo at the restaurant. She was on a week's holiday that week so he did not see her at work that day. He turned up early and hung around outside the restaurant waiting for her to arrive. About five minutes after their agreed time, when he was beginning to think she had forgotten, he spotted her walking down the street towards him, moving in and out of the pools of light from the street lamps. Ben noticed how the lights caught her blonde hair as she walked under them.

"Hi, sorry I'm late," she said. "Have you been waiting long? Someone was ill on the Tube, a heart attack or something, so it was held up at Leicester Square. Anyway, I'm here and I'm starving."

Jo put her hand through Ben's arm and they opened the door of the restaurant, which Ben was alarmed to find was completely empty of customers. About five bored looking staff were leaning up against a bar chatting and all moved forward in unison when they came in, obviously relieved to have something to do. A short, square shaped woman with no front teeth stepped around from behind the bar barking orders to the staff in what Ben assumed was Russian. She wore a faded floral dress stained with borsch, beetroot soup, stroganoff and other unidentifiable food and Ben wondered if her dress was the menu from which they could choose their evening's delicacies. Thick flesh coloured support hose stockings bagged around her ankles before disappearing down into the old slippers she wore on her feet. She was every inch and scent the original babushka and looked as though she had just come off the Steppes after milking the yaks, Bactrian camels or whatever other exotic animals Ben imagined they herded there.

The waiting staff took their coats and ushered them to one of the only two tables in the room. Each was about twenty feet long with assorted benches and chairs either side. Both were covered in red gingham tablecloths. Cutlery, napkins and glasses were laid at regular intervals along each side of the tables. Ben and Jo were directed to the far end of the table nearest the restaurant's window that ran down the length of the room and looked out onto the dark street outside. Sitting opposite each other Ben placed the bottle of red wine he had brought on the table. It was immediately grabbed and opened by a waiter who produced a bottle opener from a pocket in front of his apron. He poured them each a glass and stood watching them expectantly. Ben picked up his glass and held it up slightly.

"Cheers," he said, with a sense of foreboding as to where this carefully planned à deux evening was heading.

"Cheers," Jo responded as they touched glasses. The waiter smiled and rubbed his hands in appreciation as two others came up to them, one with a basket of roughly torn, crusty bread and the other with a jug of water. A fourth followed them and thrust two grubby menus into their hands. Looking at them Ben wondered if it might not be easier to use the woman's dress. The menu was in Russian with strange translations beneath each dish. Borscht was fairly easy to detect but fried hamsters hinted at a need for a call to the RSPCA.

"What do you fancy?" Ben asked.

Jo smiled wanly. "I'm not sure," she said. "I think I'll go simple and have the beetroot soup and then the stroganoff. I know what they are."

"Two soup and two stroganoff please," Ben said to the waiter with the pen and the pad. He carefully wrote down their order with the other three waiters peering over his shoulder. The order safely committed to paper and four memories, the quartet disappeared into the kitchen behind the bar. Ben turned to speak but was interrupted by one of the waiters returning and dragging up a chair near to them. In his other hand he clutched a balalaika. He settled down and made himself comfortable on the chair, one foot propped on a bar between its legs. He rested the instrument in the crook of his leg and raised knee and proceeded to strum it whilst occasionally humming and singing in accompaniment.

Two bowls of beetroot soup magically appeared from the kitchen and were plonked down in front of Ben and Jo. The two waiters who had brought them then stood on either side of the polymathic waiter caressing the strings and the three of them smiled and stared at the dining couple. Another couple walked into the restaurant but, on seeing the intimate gathering at the far end of the room, must have assumed a raucous private party was in full swing and quickly turned and fled.

With all the charms and ambiance of a wake in a

mortuary, any conversation Ben started seemed to fall on stony ground. Jo tried valiantly to rise to the occasion but it was pretty obvious it was a disaster that the man about town Rupert was going to hear about later. The stroganoff sauce was delicious and tried its best to complement the old shoe it had been poured onto, a shoe made out of an octogenarian cow that had encountered one too many Russian winters and had stayed frozen in a perpetual state of rigor mortis. When their plates were cleared away, the chewed remnants littered them like the fallen at Stalingrad. The waiters then proudly wheeled out a desert trolly on which there was one item. Clumps of red objects wallowed in thick syrup. It looked as though the fallen and wounded from the main course had been swept onto a new plate and covered in the red mixture.

"Sokva," said one of the waiters, pointing at it with a yellowed, nicotine stained finger. "Fruit Leather," he helpfully translated, as if that would make a difference to their understanding of what it was.

"Not for me," Jo said quickly, recoiling and nearly leaning back into the balalaika player, who had moved his position to sit just behind her.

"Just the bill please," Ben said. "I'm really sorry

about all this," he said to Jo waving his arm around the room but taking in the whole evening in the one simple gesture. "This place was recommended by one of my flatmates. He either thought it a good joke or has different expectations to me."

"It's OK," Jo said graciously.

With the bill ordered, the musician clearly decided his duty was done and for the first time in the evening they were left alone.

"Well, I was really hoping we'd have a good time but perhaps next time?" Ben said. "Only if you want that is," he quickly added.

"Well, that's one of the things I wanted to talk to you about," Jo said. "I'm leaving the Agency in a couple of months. I haven't told anyone yet so keep it to yourself. My boyfriend is going to Australia. He's emigrating there. You can do it for ten pounds and so I'm going with him. Ten Pound Poms we'll be called. We have to stay there for two years but they guarantee us jobs there and we have nothing to hold us here so we have nothing to lose really."

Of course she has a boyfriend, Ben thought, what on earth possessed me to believe someone as pretty as her is not going to have a boyfriend? Suddenly, the condom hidden in his pocket, a gift from Rupert as he left the flat, seemed beyond ridiculous. Ben could only be relieved he had not made even more of a fool of himself with some preposterous proposition to her, someone clearly outside his league.

"Wow," he said, "that's wonderful for you. How exciting and what an adventure. All that sun and kangaroos."

Somehow the pressure was off him and for the first time since he met her he could relax in her company. She was off limits and so he could stop trying to be something he was not. The words came more easily now and he felt less tongue tied. They chatted easily all the way back to the Tube station where they said goodnight. Ben was about to turn to head towards his train west when Jo lent forwards and kissed him on the cheek.

"You're a lovely person," she said. "Don't change, just be you. You'll find someone one day." With that she turned and was gone, leaving only her scent on Ben's face as a memento of their evening.

'She knew all along,' Ben thought as he walked down the tunnel to the platform. Unexpectedly he didn't feel ashamed about that, just glad that she knew he had had feelings for her, even though most of them had been carnal. 'And now for a chat with Rupert' Ben thought as his train emerged from the tunnel at the far end of the platform.

CHAPTER 9

Autumn – 1987

"Where's your father?"

Ben felt his cry of frustration had become a mantra, seemingly repeated hourly as the family's equilibrium was disrupted once again, this time by a frantic search for his father-in-law.

"Where's your sodding father?" was what he wanted to say, but the potential for ensuing grief and angst that would inevitably result outweighed the relief the explosion of his thoughts would give. When Lucy had suggested her father move in with them, it had seemed the right thing to do. A charitable act that pandered to Ben's tendency to play the martyr, an act that would grant him the warm glow of beatification by their friends and his colleagues. A supreme act of selflessness. That was before the old bastard had lost his marbles.

Of course, Lucy couldn't see it. Ostrich-like, he

felt she could see no more in her father's irrational behaviour than a little forgetfulness.

"We're all forgetful," she had said to Ben when he had first raised the issue. "I mean, look at you. If I ask you to collect more than two items, even from the next room let alone anything as remote as the shops, you forget the reason for the entire expedition. I think you're exaggerating about Dad just a little, don't you?"

"I forget things because I am busy," Ben said. "I have so much on my mind, and you have absolutely no understanding of that. The only thing on your father's mind is his hat, and that sits on top of a cranial vacuum. I'm slaving away, trying to keep everyone deliriously happy. You, the children, clients, bank managers, management, the whole bloody world as far as I can see. I really don't need to be having to put up with your father's senility as well."

"Something of an exaggeration again I think," Lucy said. "For one, your devotion to your work borders on the obsessional, so no need to transfer that bit of guilt onto the rest of us. Why do men always do that? Why do they always turn an argument into an exercise in guilt-export? And why do women always take it? Why do we always end up feeling guilty? We're so stupid. Well, not this time Ben. Your work ethos is your choice, not mine or ours. I for one have never asked you to devote ninety percent of your every breathing moment to your bloody clients and their pathetic problems, which are always so much more important than the time you could have with us. So please, get your esteemed creative department to come up with something better than that for you. And in any event, we were actually discussing Dad, who is fine, and who has nothing to do with your chosen career and your infatuation with it."

Lucy definitely could not see it. As far as Ben was concerned, all she could see was his nascent resentment, which she interpreted as jealousy for her emotional attachment to her father. It seemed a subject without resolution, unless he compromised and accepted the status quo. Anything less and he could only ever be accused of turning an old man out. And not just any old man, but his own flesh and blood-in-law.

And yet, to Ben the signs of the old man's incipient dementia were patently obvious. His habitual acts of disappearing. His absurd habits. Forgetting his son-in-law's name, delving instead into a seemingly limitless supply of Lucy's previous boyfriends names.

He had even called Ben by the name of one of the family's long deceased dogs. Bodger might have a certain ring to it if you happen to be a golden Labrador, but it didn't do much for the self-esteem down at the pub where Ben had taken George for a mid-day pint one Sunday to allow Lucy to get lunch ready in peace without her father getting under her feet. Ben had read somewhere that the long-term memory remained intact longest with advancing years, and it was the short-term memory that flew the nest first. Clearly in George's case, fifteen years of a daughter's relationship and marriage constituted short-term memory.

"We've found him," called Sebastian from the front door. For a nine year old, Sebastian seemed to have an unreasonable quotient of inner calm that appeared to enable him to take his grandfather's growing litany of idiosyncrasies in his stride. Perhaps it was his nigh telepathic empathy with Lucy that gave him his mature acceptance of things he could not change. Emma, his six year old sister, had more of Ben's intolerance in her genes. Ben had come to the conclusion that nature had a significantly greater influence than nurture in his children's characters.

"Where the hell was he?" Ben said irritably.

"In a car outside," said Sebastian.

"What do you mean, 'in a car outside'. The car's locked. How did he get in it?" Ben's confusion fuelled his irritation.

"He wasn't in our car," said Sebastian patiently, as though describing a perfectly normal every-day occurrence. "There's another silver car that always parks in the road and he often gets in that if he thinks we are going out."

"You make it sound as though this is some sort of hobby of his. Has he done this before?"

"Lots of times, Daddy," Emma said as she applied one of her mother's curlers to the sleek hair of a new doll. "The man was very cross the first time, but he doesn't mind now. He says Grandpa is sweet and…."

"Which man was cross?" Ben interrupted. His irritation was becoming harder to suppress.

"The man whose car it is," said Sebastian. "He lives

down the road. He thought Grandpa was a tramp the first time, but when Mum explained and said she was sorry, he helped bring him back here. He said he could sit in the car any time he liked. He asked Mum if Grandpa was continental though, and whether he should put plastic on the seats. I don't see why that should make any difference. Why would it matter where he came from? Would that make him a racist if it did make a difference to him, Dad?"

"We haven't got time to chat about all that. We're going to be late for the restaurant. I booked the table for one, and it's nearly that now. Just get in the car and let's get on," said Ben.

Ben's father-in-law, George, was standing outside the house by the front passenger door of Ben's car. Once tall and elegant, he was now stooped and fragile, bent like a poplar giving way to the breeze. His thinned grey hair was neatly brushed, arranged by Lucy to reclaim his dignified past. With his hand on the handle of the front passenger door, his eyes betrayed the confusion that had detached him from the world, guillotining his once nimble and acquisitive mind from its remaining links with reality. They were opaque windows to the fear that lurked behind. Ben opened the door for him and gently helped him into his seat. He smelt George's oldness as he leant across him to fasten his seat-belt, an evocative mustiness that stirred an unease in him that he related to all humanity's apprehension of the ageing process, and its cruel larceny of sentient independence. He shivered involuntarily at the uninvited thought and reminder of his own mortality, and closed the passenger door gently, checking the old man's hand was not in the way.

The meal had been Lucy's idea, a plea to escape the thankless task of producing another meal she felt would elicit no compliment or even comment. Surely some critique would be given as to flavour or texture if anything she cooked came into contact with sensory cells. Perhaps her family had none. Whatever she served up seemed to be met with indifference, and whilst she did not seek adulation for what she agreed were not memorable culinary events, some hint of enjoyment would have signified appreciation. She felt each member of her family was a diminutive galactic black hole. Food and the sustenance of life were sucked in, and no compliment could escape the gravitational pull of indifference.

As Lucy and the children settled into the back of the car, Ben pulled into the light Sunday traffic. He had booked a table in a fashionable restaurant, recently adopted by media luminaries. On the edge of Soho, it was close enough to be accessible for that essential business lunch, without yet charging prices that would exhaust expense accounts that had been pared to the bone in view of the economic crises that bedevilled the country. Its popularity had been enhanced by recent reviews that focussed more on its clientele than its fare. Like the fairy tale of the king's clothes, no one had yet broken ranks and exposed its limitations, or the posturing pretensions of its owner Frank, who professed to be intimate with everyone who mattered. Ben had become a frequent patron, mixing with industry contemporaries, colleagues and clients. Whilst it had been Lucy's idea to go out for the meal, the restaurant had been Ben's choice. His instincts told him that despite it being a week-end, he was sure to meet someone of a career enhancing status there.

The restaurant was in an old converted house, spread through a number of rooms on two floors. The building was set back from the road. A low stone balustrade separated a tiny parterre from the pavement. The family passed through the door, where a waitress stood to take coats and confirm bookings, or to turn away those foolish enough to think a spare table might be available to anyone not already known to the owner.

"'Allo, monsieur Ben," greeted the waitress, her shoulders held back so her pert firm breasts must rise to greet his entry, reaching out for him through a white blouse that was unbuttoned just sufficiently for him to see the valley of her cleavage. "You 'ave brought your family aujourd'hui. Zat is nice."

"Hello, Marie," said Ben, winking at her, comforted by the familiarity of the greeting and its implicit recognition of his status as one of the chosen, welcome in the incestuous comradeship that was "Frank's." It occurred to him the warmth of his smile to her might betray to Lucy his fantasies of afternoons spent with a naked Marie, cavorting in a field of corn that matched her aureate hair. He was relieved to see Lucy was preoccupied with ushering the children and her father through the door into the small hall that served as a reception area.

The warm glow of belonging to a select club appealed to Ben's tribal instincts. He handed his coat to Marie as Frank, the eponymous owner, came forward, hand outstretched.

"Ben, it is good to see you again," he said. He turned to Lucy and took her hand, raising it to his lips as he bowed slightly. "Enchanté, Madame," he said, "why so long Ben has you hidden from us?"

Lucy blushed as the children grouped behind her, terrified this man would want to kiss them too. She was conscious of an almost tangible haze of cologne that swarmed about Frank, an aura of scent that marked his territory wherever he passed. His carefully bouffant hair swept meticulously back over his ears, steely grey and still full on his leonine head. The gold identity bracelet that loosely encircled his wrist slid back under the sleeve of his black silk shirt as he raised Lucy's hand. As his eyes swept over her, Lucy felt she had been completely undressed, her clothes peeled off her with the surgical precision of a serial philanderer used to assuming feminine favours were his as of right.

"Oh, I don't often come down to the centre of Town," she said, trying to retrieve the hand that Frank still held, stroking the back of it with his large thumb while her rubescence deepened its hue on its remorseless march up her throat into her cheeks.

"Well, 'ow you say, don't be a stranger. You must come again. You don't need this `usband to bring you.

These Englishmen, they always want to be in charge, no? Le chef du maison. Now, I 'ave your usual table 'ere Ben. Please seat and I bring the menus."

Frank led the family into a large room off the entrance hall and showed them to a table by the window, drawing back a seat for Lucy. Ben followed behind the small group, ushering George forwards with a hand on each upper arm, trying not to trip on the old man's shuffling heels. He scanned the room for familiar faces, seeking the endorsement of belonging in this choice company. A short, stout and narrow-eyed man the other side of the room waved to him and Ben tacked around a table between them to go over to him, leaving Lucy to finish shepherding the family to their seats.

"Ben, my dear chap, so good to see you here," said the man who had attracted Ben's attention.

"And you, Simon," Ben said, shaking the man's hand warmly, his left hand covering the back of the man's hand in that embellishment of a greeting that emphasises a closeness of relationship. "I'm here with Lucy and the children. Nice for Lucy not to have to cook."

"We're doing the same," said Simon. "A rest from the weekend stove for the girls, eh? This is Annabelle, my wife," he said, indicating an expensively dressed and expansively proportioned woman to his left. "Annabelle, this is Ben Grayson. And Ben, this is Larry and Sue who are visiting us from America," he said, introducing the other couple sitting at the table.

"Hi there," said the man in an East Coast nasal, half rising and extending his hand across the cutlery, "how you doin'?" His wife remained seated, the arms of her seat clutching her ample thighs and capacious hips in a vice-like grip. Ben was reminded of a cow trapped in a crush.

"Good afternoon," said Ben politely, shaking both their hands. "Enjoy your meal. Frank will do you proud. He always does." He turned back to Simon.

"I'll call you in the week and we'll get together," he said as Simon re-took his seat.

"Let's do that," said Simon. "I can book a table here before I leave if you like. Tuesday?"

"Sounds good to me. I'll get mine to ring yours to confirm," said Ben.

Ben walked over to the family's table where Lucy was seating George. She sat down next to her father and placed his napkin on his lap, pulling it up above the waistband of his trousers and securing it on either side under his old tweed jacket. Ben took the remaining seat between the children.

"Who was that?" said Lucy coolly as Ben glanced around the room for other familiar faces.

"Simon Burfield," Ben said over his shoulder without looking at Lucy. "He's Managing Director of our largest client. We're in the middle of a pitch for a large pan-European campaign they have planned. He was rather friendly to me, don't you think?"

"He looks a bit shifty to me," said Lucy uncompromisingly. "Don't trust anyone whose eyes are that close together. Are those his brother and sisters? They're all the same shape." She giggled and winked at the children. George was oblivious to the conversation as he carefully examined his dentures, which he had removed when he had sat down at the table. Finishing his examination he dropped them in his water glass.

"No," said Ben, irritated. "The woman in the blue dress is Annabelle, his wife. The other two are American friends who are staying with them I assume. Perhaps they are clients. Don't stare at them, and children, best behaviour please. That man is very important for Daddy's work, so we want to give a good impression, don't we?"

"Ben, we're not your staff, so can we just be ourselves and not a public relations exercise for you?" said Lucy. "We're here to have a family lunch, so can we ignore clients or impressions?"

As she said this, Lucy glanced at her father who had started to comb his sparse hair with his upper teeth, his lower set retrieved from his glass and now standing sentinel on his side plate.

"Dad!" she hissed. "What are you doing?" Lucy leaned across and quickly took her father's teeth from him. "Put them back in your mouth," she whispered, "you'll need them for lunch."

George returned his teeth to his mouth wordlessly,

and turned his watery gaze to the unintelligible menu, moving his lower jaw from side to side as he tried to arrange the dentures so they were comfortable, his wrinkled face like an unmade bed. A few strands of grey hair protruded through his lips. Ben glanced over his shoulder and was relieved to see his client had not seemed to notice his father-in-law's dental topiary. Lucy noticed his nervous, fleeting look and felt defensively irritated for her father.

Frank approached the table, order pad held reverentially in his left hand, gold pen poised as he prepared to take the family's instructions. Lucy took control of the children and George's selections, extracting from the sophisticated, minimalist and entirely unsuitable menu dishes that would suit the young palates, and that would not asphyxiate her father, who had recently started to exhibit the octogenarian's tendency to choke on food. As she did she wondered what they were doing there and why they could not have gone to a pizza house, or somewhere more suited to a family meal, but of course, she knew only too well why pretentious had trumped practical in Ben's choice of venue.

Frank took the family's order with a theatrical flourish, a man accustomed to accommodating the sybaritic tastes of his clientele. He handed the completed order to a waitress, and bent deferentially next to Ben to better hear his wine choice. Ben selected a fruity Chablis, optimistic of its cold freshness.

While Ben and Frank had been discussing the wine list and Ben's ultimate selection, Lucy had the time to take in her surroundings. Moving through the restaurant to their table she had felt like a shepherdess as she herded the trio that formed her little flock through the maze of tables. She had done so in a constant state of knotted anticipation of some disaster, whilst not sure from which of the three it would emanate. With each safely seated, and the choice of their food completed, she felt secure and able to relax and take in the room and its occupants for the first time.

The restaurant was obviously modelled on Franco-rustic lines. Bare scrubbed floorboards stretched in broad lines to meet the walls that were washed in stressed pale green paint. Rural scenes in large watercolours were on the walls, some with price tags in the bottom right hand corner, giving the impression this was a place frequented by artists and those of more sophisticated leanings. Speakers in the four corners of the room softly played classical music, the mellifluous notes of the piano and its tumbling scales soothing her tensions away like the firm thumbs of a masseuse on her neck. Each table was covered in brown paper in defiance of an urban expectation of soft damask. Large green napkins splashed colour across laps and tabletops, a carefully selected contrast to the green of the walls.

The restaurant's clientele were clearly affluent, dressed à la mode, showing their solidarity as members of a club of sophisticates. Lucy felt detached from them and suddenly out of place, dowdy in her simple skirt and mainstream store sweater. Every inch the housewife and mother with nothing to offer a conversation other than the difficulties of traffic on school runs and the amount of washing two young children can produce. A business discussion between four men was clearly underway at the table to her left. One of the men, tall with startlingly azure eyes, was emphasising his comments with a web of figures, lines and boxes he was writing and drawing on the paper tablecloth. His long fingers held a gold plated pen delicately, tapping the nib on the paper when listening to his companions' contributions to their discussion. The cufflinks in his hand made shirt caught the sun coming through the window, burning flashes of light in Lucy's eyes. His brogue-encased foot tapped an impatient rhythm under the table. A man in a hurry.

Lucy wondered what the man's wife was doing with her Sunday, while he sat at his table in the restaurant, engrossed in his business and in his colleagues, planning and scheming their next promotion, their next coup, Masters of all they surveyed and filled with their own self-importance. Perhaps each was terrified at being passed over, the drive to succeed taking them out of the family home to this annexe of their office. Was his wife also crossing the gender and parental divide, playing mother and father by both cooking and carving, the accepted subtle demarcation of tasks and responsibilities that differentiated the master from the maid and repeated at so many Sunday dining tables.

They were no different to Ben, these Lieutenants of Industry, each striving to become Captains. Ben too would regularly have meetings at weekends. Workshops, he sometimes called them. Did Ben draw on the tablecloth, tap his foot, finish others' sentences in his headlong rush up the slopes of his corporate Everest? He certainly bought into the corporate game, passionate for the hunt and chase that seemed to both preoccupy and stress them all. Lucy often felt an irrational jealousy for his career, his mistress without the complication of sex. Even that she sometimes wondered about, given the bevies of pretty young things the industry attracted and the men insisted on being surrounded by. One of Ben's colleagues insisted recruitment agencies included a photograph of any female applicant to the Agency, with the subliminal message that the unattractive need not apply. She was angry at having to compete with his career for his affection and time. She felt the children missed his company and his influence, and when they did have his attention he was often short tempered with them because he was tired, distracted or on an important phone call, or waiting for one. More importantly he missed their development, years he was too self obsessed to see would never be repeated. To Lucy the blue eyed man with the gold pen and so many material possessions epitomised the corporate vortex that so trapped and captivated Ben and his contemporaries.

Lucy glanced across at Ben, whose attention was still partly held by other diners. Sebastian was trying to show him a couple of cards he had recently swapped in a collection of football cards he had been working on for the past year.

"This one's my favourite, Dad," he said. "He's brilliant and nearly always scores."

"Does he," said Ben distractedly without looking at it. "That's nice." He turned to Lucy.

"We must fix a dinner party soon and invite Simon and Annabelle," he said. "I want them to meet Chris. They'll get on like a house on fire."

Lucy saw the disappointment in Sebastian's face as he put his little cards back in his pocket and looked out of the window.

"Must we," she said, unnaturally reluctant to be co-operative. She glanced at Sebastian again, but he was lost in some daydream.

Before Ben could reply, the small train of waitresses that had emerged from the kitchen bore down on their table with plates of food. In deference to the children and George, Lucy had ignored the issue of starters and only ordered main courses. Simple pasta dishes for the children and George, fish for herself. The family's eyes followed the plates as they were distributed before them. The children picked up their forks in unison like synchronised swimmers, each stabbing at the food like picadors goading their meal. Ben was reminded of the marvel of how two children could make a swarm of locusts appear anorexic.

"Sebastian, Emma, eat slowly," he said. "Remember where you are."

As Lucy turned to pull Emma's hair back before it dragged across the food on her plate, she felt a tug on the sleeve of her sweater.

"I have to go," said her father.

"But Dad, we've only just got here," she said. "We'll go as soon as we've finished eating. Ben and I can have our coffee at home."

George's features wrinkled in confusion.

"No, I need to go. You know. Go. The lavatory, where is it?"

"Oh, I see," said Lucy with a sense of urgency emulating her father's distress. She was only too well aware of the ramifications of delaying her father from any appointment with the porcelain. "Ben, can you take Dad to the Gents," she said quietly.

"Why does he need me to go?" said Ben. "Does he want me to hold it for him or something?"

"For God's sake, Ben, just do as I ask for once. He wants someone to show him where the Gents is, and I can hardly do that, can I? Not here in your precious restaurant in front of your precious clients."

George tugged at Lucy's sleeve again." I want to go," he said, his voice strained by some inner struggle.

"Yes, I know you do Dad. Ben's going to take you, aren't you Ben?" she said, looking at Ben pointedly.

Ben rose from his untouched meal, sighing a farewell to his delicious chilled wine, and went behind George's seat. He helped the old man rise and took his elbow to guide him through the tables. At the men's room, George waved away Ben's hand.

" I can manage," he said as he disappeared into one of the three cubicles, closing the door behind him.

Ben's relief at the cursory dismissal of his services was palpable, and he collided with one of the waiters in his hurry to leave his father-in-law to his inevitably widely dispersed micturitions.

"Where's Dad?" said Lucy as Ben sat down. "Why didn't you stay with him?"

"He didn't want me to," said Ben. "He said he could manage, thank God."

"Well, I hope you're right," said Lucy.

"Lucy, you're the one who keeps telling me he's fine, so if he gets into difficulties in there, it's hardly my fault." Ben felt aggrieved at the implication he had deserted his post at the front-line of his father-in-law's ablutions. "Anyway, how long has he been climbing into other people's cars? Hardly the behaviour of someone who is fine, I would say, would you. It's a bit embarrassing having him returned by neighbours, like a lost parcel. Perhaps we should label him, like Paddington Bear. If found please return to….."

"Don't dramatise Ben. It's only happened a few

times," said Lucy defensively. "And anyway, it's not embarrassing, and it's not all the neighbours. It's only the one car he has got into, and that's only because it's the same colour as ours."

"Well Sebastian said it's been happening a lot," said Ben. "And what was that about hoping he wasn't a continental? What a random question."

"Incontinent," said Lucy, lowering her voice. "He said he hoped Dad wasn't incontinent, not continental. I was so offended. Luckily Dad didn't hear him."

"Well I'm not sure you should have been," said Ben. "It was hardly an unreasonable question, given the state of him. I've seen that chap polishing his corporate dream every week-end, and he doesn't look like the sort who would welcome your father dumping on the upholstery."

"What's Grandpa doing?" said Emma, trying to feed a bread-stick through the inert lips of her doll's mouth.

"He's gone to the loo," murmured Lucy, turning back to Ben. "Well I thought he was rude and a bit patronising."

"Why's he having lunch with those people?" said Emma.

"He's having lunch with us," said Lucy. "He'll be back in a minute, so just eat your meal."

"No he won't," said Sebastian. "He's sitting with them."

Ben had become subliminally aware of a commotion behind him, with raised voices and clattering cutlery. He turned to see George had joined Simon's table, taking a spare seat from the next table. The group at the table formed a tableau of horror around the old man. His trousers were undone and he was clutching his genitals in his left hand. He was staring at them with a confused expression of fascination on his face, like an archaeologist hefting a recently unearthed artefact of extreme antiquity, puzzled at its original use which was now a mystery to him.

The American woman's capacious bosom was trembling in outrage, ripples quivering over its surface as she struggled to stand up from her chair. Each large breast barged into its twin birthed in the next door bra cup, like tugs nudging a liner into its berth on the Hudson. Her husband had ever professed himself to be a breast man in his locker room conversations at his exclusive and expensive tennis club, boasting of her "million dollar chest." Those who knew her agreed, privately assuming he meant in loose change. The simple act of rising might have been easier for her if her hips had not poured themselves through the side openings beneath the arms of the chair. Her champagne cork profile holding her firmly in place, her gaze was transfixed by George's desiccated, and ultimately redundant genitals, which more resembled week old turkey giblets than the source of his genetic heirs.

"'Oy mister, what the fuck d'yer think yer doing wiv that," shrieked Marie, shedding all pretensions of her Franco-origins. She suddenly became not so much La Trinité-sur-Mer as Dagenham-sur-Thames. She stepped back and impaled the foot of the diner behind her under her stiletto heeled shoe. Suddenly off balance and tipping backwards, her arms windmilled to keep her upright, sending the tray of drinks she was carrying flying from her hand like a missile from a trebuchet, covering the occupants of the table next to her in a fusion of House white and House red. Wine glasses and torn, crusted bread rained down like confetti at a wedding.

Ben felt his reputation and career reduced to a midden in one searingly crass act of a harmless but ultimately certifiable old man, marooned on the desert island of his fractured mental state, the once so talented now left at the end of a long life with the solitary talent to embarrass. Lucy sat speechless, shocked into paralysis by the stark evidence of her father's caducity.

Frank bore down on the commotion that had brought proceedings in the whole room to a halt, sidestepping the fleeing and weeping Marie.

"Ben," he shouted. " Get this disgusting old bastard out of here." Clearly Frank was a close neighbour of Marie's in Dagenham.

Frank started trying to pull George to his feet, but the noise had terrified the old man and he was instinctively trying to push his forlorn penis back in his trousers whilst tugging at his zip. Frank got him half to his feet but could not hold his surprising dead weight, and George fell forwards into the lap of the American woman who was still securely contained within the enfolding arms of the chair. She shrieked in disgust, flapping her pudgy hands under her chin. The shock of the piercing noise close to his ear made the frightened George empty the contents of his bladder into her lap.

For one surreal moment, Ben marvelled at his father-in-law's bladder capacity, guessing correctly that the old man had emerged from his visit to the restaurant toilet without doing anything, probably having forgotten why he had gone there. As he leapt forward to pull George upright, Lucy recovered her powers of mobility. She jumped up, pushed Ben to one side and took hold of George's shoulders. The American woman continued to emit piercing shrieks, like a car alarm frantically calling its owner.

"For Christ sake, will you shut up you fat slag," cried Lucy, inches from the woman's face.

The grossness of the insult shocked both the American woman and Lucy into silence. Lucy could not believe she had descended to such fishwifery. The American woman's bosom once more trembled and heaved, a tsunami of flesh building and swelling. Tears cascaded over her cheeks as she started to weep helplessly.

Ben's involuntary reaction was to look at Simon, for once rendered speechless.

"I am sorry," he said. "She didn't mean that. It's just. …."

His voice trailed off as he struggled to find the words that would repair and bridge the inevitable social gulf that now separated them. Simon said nothing and turned to help his guests. Ben helped Lucy lift George off the blubbing woman, avoiding any possibility of eye contact with her outraged husband, or with Simon.

As they moved away from the table, Frank pranced around them like a superannuated rooster, strutting his authority, anxious to have the family out of the debris of his Sunday sitting. He held one of the restaurant's bright napkins in front of George's crutch like a matador's cape as Ben and Lucy guided him through the silenced diners. Sebastian and Emma followed their parents in silence, their unfinished meals congealing on their plates.

In the reception area of the restaurant, one of the waitresses already had their coats for them to take. The silence was absolute, exponentially increasing Ben's discomfort. He turned to Frank as Lucy gently placed George's coat over his shoulders and led him to the front door.

"Frank, I don't know what to say. I'm so sorry."

Frank's stare was unforgiving.

"I think enough has been said," he replied. "If you would leave I can go back and try to repair some of the damage. God knows how much this is going to cost me. The shame..."

Frank peremptorily turned his back and flounced off into the restaurant, where a buzz of conversation and scraping chairs signalled the resumption of social intercourse. Ben had little doubt as to the subject matter, and turned to follow his family out into the street. A club footed pigeon teasing a piece of carrot from a splattering of vomit on the pavement outside the restaurant seemed to Ben a fitting metaphor to sum up his social ruination.

CHAPTER 10

The weak morning sun airbrushed the speckled sky in pastel pink, its hue strengthening and deepening as Ben walked down the deserted residential streets on his way to the Underground Station. Shoulders hunched against the cool air, he leaned forward into his stride, somehow comforted and warmed by the caress of his long blue coat flapping around his calves. The calming anonymity of the train in its tunnel beckoned womb-like as he turned into the station's entrance and went to the ticket booth.

Ben usually drove himself into work, or caught a taxi, but today he welcomed the luxury of remaining hidden from the world for as long as possible. The anaesthetic of sleep had evaded him and he had risen quietly before dawn. Lucy lay on her side, her hair a silken cobweb over her face as she slept on. Ben shaved and showered, the hot stinging needles of water massaging his scalp. He retrieved his clothes from the dressing room and took them down to the kitchen to change while he waited for the kettle to boil. Monday mornings were difficult enough without tea to start the day, the catalyst he needed to start functioning. Lucy used to say his morning cups of tea were the jump leads that sparked him into life, before she began to find his dependence on this part of his morning ritual irritating.

Ben sat under the ceiling lights at the kitchen table in the quiet of the pre-dawn, drinking his tea and turning over the pages of the Sunday papers. He skimmed a lengthy article analysing the long-term impact of South Africa's National Party's win in the elections at the beginning of the summer, a win with which the Party had gained it's fortieth year in power. The hard-line Conservative Party led by P. W. Botha had won twenty-two seats, wresting them from the more egalitarian Progressive Federals, and the author of the article expressed concern at the possibility of a backlash from the disenfranchised majority population if the Conservative gains presaged a tightening of the apartheid controls that were so ostracising the country.

Ben had once visited Cape Town on a business trip. Whilst appalled by the concept of divisions based on colour, or any other prejudicial stratification of society, he had nevertheless been enraptured by the beauty and diversity of the country. On a week end break from the relentless meetings he had had to attend, he hired a car and set off east out of the City, heading along the coast to Hermanus where he watched the whales breaching and cavorting, some swimming close in to the shore, perhaps in response to the whale caller's horn-playing. At a ramshackle restaurant built into a cave on the cliff he sat on a wooden terrace in the glorious sunshine and lingered over a plate of yellowtail fish, coated in honey and grilled over an open coal fire. A glass of South African chardonnay could still take him back to that afternoon of peace and tranquillity in the sun and sea spray. That evening he had stopped at Milnerton, a small place by the bay to the north east of Cape Town, and had sat watching the rich African sun set beside the iconic Table Mountain, whose silhouette so dominates the City. The street lights circling its base flickered into life like fireflies, a necklace of sparkling pearls about its throat.

Putting his empty tea cup by the sink, Ben looked in on the children before going back down to collect his coat from the vestibule by the front door, where the family's outdoor clothes stood sentry against the waiting elements. He had not felt able to go back in to see Lucy, preferring the silence of unspoken words to running the risk of her being awake and reopening the wounds inflicted by the debacle in the restaurant the day before. Only a substantial cauterisation of their bruised emotions would start the healing process, and Ben could not find the words to start building the bridge that was needed to cross the gulf that he felt George had opened between them. The opening gambit eluded him, and with his inclination to feel the injured party, he felt it was for Lucy to make the first move, to apologise to him for not listening, for not seeing the signs of her father's dementia, and for the catastrophic consequences to him of her denial. They had reached an uneasy truce the night before when Lucy had finally accepted, somewhat reluctantly Ben felt, that she should start to look for a home or institution that was better equipped to care for George, where his presence would not impinge on the children and disrupt their lives.

The children's innocent sleep moved him as he stood over them. It always did. In their world, Ben was comfortingly omnipotent, a quasi-heroic figure whose influence guaranteed security. 'Best Dad in the World' the children's last birthday card had said. Their unquestioning adoration of course counted for nothing in the wider world, where respect was earned on a meritocratic basis rather than merely through the gifting of half a person's chromosome quotient. There was never the need to impress with the children, to build a platform of esteem that then came under constant scrutiny as it was in the adult world, where all actions were habitually judged and measured against unrealistic benchmarks.

Sebastian lay on his side, arms wrapped around a muddy football, tousled hair a stranger to the caress of a hairbrush. In her room, Emma stirred when Ben bent and kissed her lightly on the forehead. She rolled over, pulling the duvet up so only the top of her head showed on the pillow. The duvet had slipped sideways and her small feet were showing. Ben covered them and slipped quietly out of her room. He hesitated momentarily on the landing, half turning to go back to where Lucy slept, but the moment passed and he turned back to the stairs, aware of his cowardice in deferring the moment.

The Underground train pulled into the station and Ben stepped back to let two builders step off it, marvelling at their ability to appear for work in the morning apparently in the same state as they had left it the day before. He boarded and sat down in a corner, leaving his hands plunged to the depths of his coat pocket. A tramp at the other end of the carriage was haranguing his reflection in the glass of the connecting door between the carriages. He shouted obscenities and threats at it as he lurched and swayed with the movement of the train in the tunnel. A bottle of cheap sherry hanging in his grimed hand had clearly fuelled his courage, and he closed his eyes as he lifted it to his lips and drank from it. The sinews in his emaciated neck stretched, like rope tethers straining in the wind.

Ben turned his eyes to the advertising cards above the seats opposite him. The banality of some of them left him wondering at the creative process that was their origin. One eulogized about the properties of an exotically named aftershave and implied that the smallest application would cause pheromones to issue forth, making any male sexually irresistible, creating a constant state of musth. Unfortunately the look on the faces of the two girls either side of the male model, clearly directed by the photographer to gaze longingly at the man with their interpretation of an air of sexual anticipation, left Ben with the impression that the model had halitosis that could strip the paint off a car at fifty paces. The girls' thespian skills were not quite up to the task. Looking down the length of the carriage, he was relieved to notice that none of the Agency's clients appeared to be represented in the line up of posters in front of him.

The train pulled into the station that was close by Ben's office and he disembarked, leaving the dishevelled tramp accusing the image of having sex with his wife. A large cut above his left eye had bled and the blood congealed into a brown stain that stretched down his cheek to the corner of his mouth. His mangled nose headed east from its bridge before turning south to run down under his left eye. Ben wondered at the times it must have been broken, to have repositioned itself so far from where the man's mother would have remembered it being when she first cradled him in her arms, squawking his impotent fury at being evicted unceremoniously from the comforting shelter of her womb.

Ben walked through the high atrium at the front of the office building, the top floors of which were occupied by the Agency. The heavily moustached security guard greeted him, pleased to speak to someone after his solitary vigil through the night.

"Good morning, sir," he said, pushing up at his bosky upper lip with the back of his index finger like the army sergeant he had been. "Good weekend?"

"Yes thank you Sam," said Ben. "How was yours?"

"Very good, thank you sir," said Sam. "All quiet on the Western Front."

Their Monday morning ritual was unchanged,

neither particularly interested in the detail of the other's life but each socially aware some recognition of the other's well being was required, and taking comfort from the status quo. It was permanently quiet on Sam's Western Front apparently, and Ben wondered what it would take for Sam to acknowledge a disturbance or commotion there. His Corps of Commissionaires uniform, with its white peaked cap and polished leather belt across his chest, his medals ribbon and the jacket's shining brass buttons denoted a man of a military air. Sam ran his small domain at the front of the building with metronomic precision and an authoritative rhythm.

Ben took the lift to the fifth floor where his office was situated. It was still too early for anyone else to have arrived, and he sat down at his desk, to plan the day and to prepare for the inquest that would follow the inevitable discussions over the previous day's embarrassment.

As Ben sipped his first coffee of the morning in the office, Lucy became aware of a pressure in the small of her back. Reaching behind, she felt a pair of small feet pressed hard against her. She turned onto her back and straightened her legs under the bedclothes, arching and stretching her back somnolently, a sensually feline act that greeted the morning light filtering through the window. Emma was fast asleep, clutching a dishevelled furry object that was once a teddy bear, but which now looked more suited to being a bacterial propagator. She must have climbed into the bed after Ben had left to go to work. Lucy had been aware of him getting up but had feigned sleep rather than face the strained politeness that would inevitably follow the previous evening's arguments.

Ben had been furious when they came home from the restaurant. Sitting in the back of the car fighting back her tears, Lucy had felt his anger boil and build its head of steam within him, a palpable pressure of self-righteous indignation that would inevitably seek relief in release against her. On getting home, Ben had got out of the car silently and walked into the house, leaving Lucy to help George out of the car. She ushered him up the steps to the front door as the children followed.

"I'm still hungry Mum," said Sebastian.

Lucy realised no one had eaten anything worthy of being called a meal.

"I'll make you a sandwich as soon as I get in," she

said, her maternal instincts automating the prioritisation of her duties. She settled George into an armchair in the room set aside for the television and then busied herself in the kitchen, welcoming the distraction of mundane tasks.

Leaving the children eating their sandwiches in front of the television, Lucy went to find Ben, who had buried himself in the Sunday papers in the drawing room. As she came in, he realised he had read an entire article without taking in one word of it. Lucy sat down on the edge of the sofa opposite him, knees pressed together, her clenched hands resting on them.

"Ben, I'm sorry," she said, reaching high for the olive branch that would trigger the rapprochement she needed. "I..."

"Well, now will you listen?" Ben said tersely, ignoring the fledgling dove of peace she had released and instead fixating on the memory of the restaurant which became high octane petrol to the flames of his anger. "You just would not accept it, would you?" he continued, cutting across Lucy, who was about to acknowledge that perhaps she had not wanted to face what was in front of her, and to ask whether that was so difficult to understand, and for a bit of forgiveness.

"I just assumed....." she started

"You assumed everything was fine, that we would all just carry on making allowances for good old George," Ben said, spreading his hands palm up in supplication. "You wouldn't listen to me. Everything's fine, you said. It's your imagination you said. Well, it's not in my imagination and it's over, he has to go and the sooner the better."

"If you would just let me finish, Ben, I...."

"No Lucy, no more. This isn't something about which there can be any more discussions. Face it Lucy, your Dad is senile and he should be in a home where there are people better qualified to look after him. I'm sorry to be blunt, but those are the facts. We can't have him going around embarrassing the shit out of us. What's the old goat going to do next, try to shag the neighbour's dog? The poor children, how do you think they felt?" Ben's voice rose through the octaves to the treble of righteous indignation.

"Don't blame it on the children," shouted Lucy. "Don't drag them into this to cover up for yourself." She stood up and started walking up and down in front of the sofa. "It's never your bloody fault, is it? Whatever happens, you have to find someone else you can shift your guilt onto, to blame. Why not just be honest for once? It was you embarrassed in there, more than any of us. You in your precious pretentious restaurant, heaving with people like you, filled with their own self-importance. God, it's pathetic..."

"I thought we were discussing your father," shouted Ben. "I don't care what you think of my world just at the moment, the one that pays for all this." Ben swept his arm in a circle to take in the room. "I want to know what you are going to do about George, not tomorrow, not next week, but now."

The silence between them was broken by the door opening as Emma tentatively came into the room, index finger on her right hand held vertical, a plump tear quivering precipitously on the top of her cheek before its inevitable plummet to the floor.

"'Bastian broke my finger," she wailed.

The time for talking passed and Ben and Lucy had

no other opportunity in the evening to speak. Now, in the cold light of day, Lucy knew Ben was right. It was going to be impossible to keep her father at home without being trapped there with him, watching his every move. Clearly he could no longer be trusted and was not capable of looking after himself. If only Ben could have been more sympathetic, more understanding of her feelings of guilt at the prospect of abandoning the old man to some home or institution. If he could just have been kinder, less callous of her father.

Lucy got up and showered. As she dried herself, Emma sleepily slid off the bed and went downstairs to join Sebastian in front of a cartoon on the television, leaving Lucy alone to watch a blue heron perched precariously on the chimney pot of the house that backed onto their garden. She smiled to herself at the memory of their neighbour proudly telling them he had bought a stone heron to stand guard over his fishpond in his garden. He had eulogised about an article he had read in some pond-keeper's weekly about the effectiveness of a stone heron in keeping the real predator away from the fish. He had been so proud of his purchase when he took them into his kitchen to view it down the garden.

The fact that a live heron had chosen that moment

to fly down into the garden, strut over to the pond and mount the stone facsimile somewhat devalued his argument. The aroused bird was clearly attempting to impregnate its new mate with a generous portion of heron-semen, and Lucy was not sure whether it was that act of violation of the stone pet or the humiliating loss of face that so enraged her neighbour. She still remembered the sight of the apoplectic man rushing down the garden, flapping his arms and shouting. Given the bird's delayed reaction it was obviously quite difficult for a tumescent, pre-orgasmic, and ultimately frustrated heron to take off on a short runway. The poor bird was probably rendered a lifelong impotent through this one moment of coitus interruptus, forever condemned to glance over its shoulder for an intruding chaperone at the first stirrings of arousal.

Lucy dressed and went downstairs. Felicia, the Spanish au pair was arranging breakfast for the children. She had been away for the week end and must have come home late in the night, after the family had all gone to bed. Lucy made a cup of tea for herself and left them to finish the meal. She went to Ben's desk and opened the local telephone directory at the section on Homes for the elderly and infirm. She wrote down numbers and addresses of those that seemed to be within a reasonable driving distance. She would make the calls before going to her yoga class and the girls' lunch she was suddenly looking forward to. She felt in need of a sympathetic ear. She had arranged to meet Sue and Jane, knowing Felicia had no English class on Mondays. She would ask her to stay in until she got back so George would not be left at home alone. Sue and Jane were two of her oldest friends and she looked forward to their regular meetings over lunch. Jane was ever cynical about the male ability to commit, and revelled in her newfound freedom after her divorce from Stephen, her serial philanderer of a husband. Sue was softer, comfortable in a happy, rambling marriage with John, one of Ben's colleagues. Their chaotic lives seemed quite ordered and normal to them, but Ben often said he could not live in such chaos, which Lucy took to be a subliminal instruction to keep their lives under structured control.

By mid morning Ben had already had a call from a journalist from one of the media based papers, enquiring about rumours the Agency's largest client, for which Ben was ultimately responsible, was putting the account up for tender. The journalist was known for his ability to smell a story, and for his complete disregard for the interests of any characters involved in whichever plot he was working on. To Ben the man epitomised everything he despised in the hack journalist, and yet he had courted him over the years to nurture a relationship through which he could exert influence. Sometimes there is no alternative to dancing with the Devil. This morning's call revealed to Ben that the relationship had been a one-sided pursuit, that his well-being and career were a matter of complete indifference to a man whose only master was the scoop. The man was like a prostitute, wielding power with complete irresponsibility, and Ben felt he might just as well have expected to curry affection from the piranha fish at the aquarium to which he had once taken Sebastian.

It was becoming obvious to Ben that the journalist bottom-feeding for his story was not the only issue that was facing him this Monday. Alison, his secretary, had slipped a note onto his desk while he was on the phone.

`Carter – 11.30' it said, the black ink stark on the white A4 sheet.

It might just as well have been an invitation to a condemned man's leaving party on the scaffold except he was clearly the condemned man without whose presence the party could not start. The Agency's Managing Director was a distant figure, aloof and recovered well from the compassion by-pass operation he must have undergone in his youth. Ben didn't think old Carter was asking to see him to enquire into his health. He got up from his desk and walked out of his office and down the corridor to an office at the end, entering the open door without knocking. A large man in shirtsleeves sat behind the desk, his back to the window. Ben sat in the chair in front of the desk and waited as the man finished a telephone conversation he was having about a copy deadline. He closed off his conversation and rested the phone back in its cradle, sitting back in his chair, fingertips together under his lips. John and Ben had forged a close relationship through their shared experiences, their victories and defeats, through campaigns they had worked on together and through the many shared drinks in wine bars in the evenings after work. John was the one person Ben felt was not a rival, competing for attention or position. The fact that John's wife, Sue, was a good friend of Lucy's was a bonus in cementing their relationship. Like many physically large people, he seemed to have no fear of anyone, his size giving him a presence, a carapace of invincibility.

"How are you?" John said. "I heard about yesterday from James. Funny on one level of course, but not for you I suppose."

"No, it was bloody awful," said Ben. "If only Lucy had listened to me instead of pretending her father was just being a bit forgetful, I wouldn't be sitting here facing an inquisition with our great leader in twenty minutes."

"He's asked to see you?" said John.

"Yes, at eleven thirty. I don't suppose he has asked me for a chat about my promotion, do you?"

"No," said John. "No, I don't think Carter will list relatives masturbating in restaurants in front of clients as career enhancing activities. He's probably dusting down the genital clamp as we speak."

"The old fool wasn't wanking, he'd just forgotten to do up his flies for God's sake. If that bloody waitress hadn't overreacted, we could have sorted it all out quietly and nobody would have known. I blame Frank for employing imbeciles."

"Don't think Carter will quite see it that way myself," said John. "How's Lucy taken it?"

"I was a bit hard on her I'm afraid, but I had no option," replied Ben. "I told her she has to get George into a home. We just can't look after him at home anymore."

"That'll be hard for her, with the father and daughter thing, and all that. She's devoted to him and they were very close. Do you think she'll do it?"

"I don't know," said Ben. "We didn't really finish. It all got a bit heated, and I didn't see her this morning before I left. I was in here early. Preparing my defence I suppose."

The phone on John's desk rang. Ben looked at his watch and quickly stood up.

"Better get on and face the music," he said.

"Let me know how it goes," said John as Ben left the room.

He looked back, but John had picked up the phone and swivelled his chair around to face the window, his feet crossed on the low windowsill. A sense of isolation came over Ben. This really was a journey he had to make alone. There was no sharing this, no spreading the pain of the humiliation that faced him in the office on the top floor, with its picture windows and views over the surrounding buildings below. Perhaps this is what facing death felt like for the condemned man as he left his cell for the last time, that final step through a door with the unknown but well-imagined horror beyond.

Ben was reminded of a film he had seen of a Cape Buffalo being attacked by a pride of lions. The struggle was titanic, a testimony to the monumental strength and durability of the buffalo and its passionate will to live, its indomitable spirit tangible. A huge male lion hung from the buffalo's head, its jaws clamped around the buffalo's nose, claws hooked into its flanks and neck. Blood poured from the buffalo's nose, running down onto the face of the lion. Two lionesses were attacking its haunches, whilst a third was already eating into the soft tissues around its backside under its tail, pulling out the beleaguered animal's intestines, like unravelling a slippery hose reel from its housing.

And yet the image that stayed with him was not so much this desperate fight for life, or the overwhelming odds the buffalo faced. What had burnt into his mind was the sight of the rest of the herd, standing close by in a semicircle around the tragedy before them with its almost inevitable conclusion, motionless as they watched. Were they capable of thought? Was each glad not to be the victim, silent tricoteuses, each relieved they were not the subject of the predators' natural desire to eat, so brutally fulfilled in their combined assault? Was that how the staff in the Agency saw him now, with vicarious horror or even pleasure at the fate that awaited him, and relief that it was not them facing the confrontation with Carter? Perhaps the staff were his own group of knitting onlookers, happy to see old scores settled for them. Ben retrieved his jacket from the back of his chair and headed for the lift, the tumbril in the centre of the building.

Lucy left the Underground Station, crossed the road and went into one of those small gardens in a square that appear unexpectedly in London. The restaurant occupied a corner building the other side of the small square, and she always liked to walk through this garden when going to it, especially in the Spring when the daffodils and tulips were in full bloom. A pair of pigeons trotted line astern ahead of her, the one at the back stopping every few paces to dip its head, as intent on its relentless courting as the one in front was intent on ignoring it. It seemed to Lucy the sexual imperative was as much a constant in pigeons as in sentient thinking primates. It was easy to anthropomorphise the male pigeon's comical and inexorable pestering of the female, and transpose it to the everyday existence of the human race where sex seems to be the engine that drives life. No matter the number of rejections he received he persisted relentlessly until the only option available to the female other than bored submission was to fly off, impatient of the unwelcome attention, leaving the male to hide his rejection in a face saving and nonchalant preening of a wing.

Sue and Jane were already seated at a table by the window, and Lucy joined them, taking the remaining seat. A glass of white wine the others had ordered for her in anticipation of her arrival sat on the table in a damp spreading pool formed by the cold rivulets of condensation running down its side and stem.

"It won't end, you know," said Jane, her dark eyes narrowed and fixed on Lucy's face.

"What won't end?" said Lucy, frowning slightly as she looked from Jane to Sue.

"The world, dear," said Jane. "You look awful. Boyfriend playing up again?"

Lucy laughed. "I don't have a boyfriend," she said. Jane's habitual irreverence and anarchic attitude to life was a cathartic release of the tensions and conflicts she harboured within herself.

"Dad's not good. I've got to get him into a home. It's so sad." Her eyes welled with tears.

"He's had a good life," Sue said gently, leaning across the table and putting her hand over Lucy's. "I'm sure he will be happy somewhere where he can be cared for. And have company all the time. He'll be fine. My mother went through the same when we had to find somewhere for her. And now, in the end she is much happier."

"Oh, I know. You're right, but I just feel I'm letting him down. Throwing him out before his time, like so much rubbish."

"Hardly," said Jane. "There just comes a time when

an institution is the best, and right option. What does Ben say?"

"That's another story," said Lucy. "There was a bit of a disaster with Dad in a restaurant yesterday, and Ben's so angry."

"What happened?" said Sue.

"Dad came out of the loo and had forgotten to do up his trousers. Things were hanging out a bit."

"How much is a bit?" said Sue.

"All of it, if you must know," said Lucy.

"George flashing," Jane interrupted. "How wonderful. I wouldn't have thought it of him. There's life in the old dog then."

"Oh no, it was worse than that," said Lucy. "Much worse. One of Ben's clients was there with his wife and some guests, and they all got a bit upset about it, especially when Dad peed in the wife's lap."

Jane shrieked with laughter as Sue put her hand to her mouth, eyes wide with mock horror.

"I suppose it is quite funny," said Lucy, smiling for only the second time that day. "But Ben doesn't see it like that. He's absolutely furious. He's more concerned about the bloody corporate image. I just wish he'd understand and be a bit more supportive. And poor Dad. He doesn't deserve to sink to this. Whatever happened to dignity?"

"None of us deserve to lose it like that," said Sue.

"What did Ben say?" asked Jane.

"He just yelled that I should have listened to him and seen that Dad was getting worse. Of course I yelled back, which didn't help. He went to work early this morning and I haven't spoken to him since."

"John called me just before I set off for here," said

Sue. "He said Ben had been summoned to see Carter. He mentioned there had been a problem at the week end, but he didn't say what it was. I had no idea. Poor you."

"Oh God," groaned Lucy. "He'll be furious with Ben and that's really going to help us when he gets home."

"Is everything OK between you?" asked Jane.

"Well, I don't suppose you could say we've been getting on too well lately, but he's just never there, and even if he is his mind's on work or some client's problems. He's become obsessed with it all. I feel I'm bringing up the children alone. Even Sebastian has been commenting on it. It's not exactly what I married for. I could have achieved single motherhood with a one night stand if that was what I wanted."

"We're all single mothers," said Jane. "Men just aren't suited to being at home. It's only society and its artificial rules that forces men to conform to the stereotype of the chap at home, helping with the kids, faithful to his wife, and happy with all that. It's not a natural state for them. They want to have nothing to do with it. What they want to do is get out with their spears for some hunting and a bit of good old rape and pillage. Thankfully they can't be doing all that, so instead they end up in the pub and other women's knickers."

Jane's views of the genesis of the fallibility of the male were well known to her friends. It was a view developed and matured as her own marriage had slowly disintegrated in the face of her husband Stephen's and her own indomitable wills. Each was quite unprepared to concede their respective positions in what had become more a conflict than a relationship. The fact each one's victories were ultimately pointless, in that the marriage inevitably crumbled and failed on the rocks of their obduracy, never deflected either of them from winning their point. In the tears and emotional turmoil of their break-up, Jane regularly expounded her theory that men were incapable of being faithful, and generally had the sexual morals of a rabbit. Expecting them to be monogamous was in Jane's view chasing a false dawn of hope. The most that could be hoped for from them in the domestication task women took on when marrying them was they would successfully train them to remember to put the lavatory seat down after peeing.

Stephen's opposing view however was a long held conviction that women were biologically ruthless, clinically capable of separating the irrational emotion of love from the cold logic of their innate need for someone who would be likely to give them strong healthy children, security and an obese bank account. These were the excuses he conjured for himself as he unwittingly pursued, and ultimately fulfilled all the attributes of Jane's stereotypical male. He justified his proclivity for multiple sexual relationships with the theory that women were on the verge of perfecting their preference for a parthenogenetic and less messy alternative to the standard way of populating the world, and he wanted as much as he could get before the shutters came down.

"I suppose I must be lucky," said Sue. "John's not like that at all."

"Exactly," said Lucy. "Why can't Ben see it? He always said he didn't really want the children to change his life, but I didn't really believe it. It's not that he doesn't love the children. He's just become a bachelor who happens to have a family. Can't John talk to him?"

"I don't think you can relate our marriage to yours, or anyone's for that matter," said Sue. "I'm not sure John would want to get involved. It's a very personal thing. I think he would find it all horribly embarrassing."

"No, you're right," said Lucy. "It's just I'm getting a bit desperate. I feel I'm being made to choose between Ben and Dad. Whichever choice I make, I lose."

A waitress came to their table and handed each a simple menu. They fell into silence as they studied the choices and made their selections. Jane and Sue chose quickly and fell into a lively conversation about some show they had seen together in the West End. Lucy had been unable to join them because Ben had been working late that evening, even though she had agreed with him earlier that she would be going and thus wasted her ticket. While she vacillated over what to eat, she realised she had little to offer to the discussion. She suddenly felt an overwhelming sense of exclusion and isolation. Perhaps, she thought, when reduced to its basics, life was about being alone, each of us an emotional island where our lives interconnect with family, friends and acquaintances like the interlocking pieces of a jigsaw. But at the end of the day, each piece is still a solitary unit in the box, waiting to be slotted into its rightful place, and once in its place, still separate from all the others in the picture. Perhaps people only connect on the periphery of their emotions.

The meal finished, the three women said their farewells and Lucy hurried home to relieve Felicia, and to finish the calls she had started making in the morning to the list of residential homes she had drawn up from her hurried enquiries.

CHAPTER 11

George stared rheumy eyed through the back window of the car, his bony, age-spotted hands clutching a cheap, worn out canvas shopping bag on his lap. He sniffed at a large drop hanging pendulously from his nose. It disappeared like a frightened rabbit retreating into its burrow, only to re-emerge immediately to recommence irritating its host. Damp explosions on the shopping bag marked where its predecessors had succumbed to gravity. Hertfordshire hurried past his uncomprehending gaze.

Ben swung the wheel of the car to take it through a large set of gates, and up a long drive to an imposing, asymmetric Queen Anne building, its tall chimneys rising out of its roof like cocktail sticks. A gardener with a wheelbarrow full of implements stopped by the side of the drive to let the car pass on its way to the parking area in front of the building. Ben parked in an space designated for visitors, and he and Lucy got out. Lucy opened the back door on George's side of the car to let him out.

"I'm not staying here, you know," George said loudly, his voice wafting across the drive.

Ben ignored George's protestation and lifted a battered leather suitcase out of the boot of the car. The case was trussed by two broad leather straps, insurance against the tarnished brass locks giving way. Faded stickers from long forgotten sea voyages decorated its side, and the initials G.H. drew the eye to the centre of the lid. He walked to the front door of the building as Lucy helped George out of the car.

The double wooden doors of the building were pinned back to reveal a glass vestibule with an intercom box on the right. Ben pressed the button and stooped to speak his name into the box. The glass door opened and he stepped into a reception area with a desk, behind which sat a smartly dressed woman in her late twenties.

"We're here with George Harkness," Ben said, sitting on one of the two seats that faced each other in front of the desk.

"Good morning," the woman said, running a long red fingernail down a short list of names.

"Ah, yes," she said, her finger stopping at the third name down on the list. "We have four new residents joining us today," she said breezily as the front door buzzer went again. She glanced up at the door and reached under the desk to press a button. The front door opened and Lucy came in with George, guiding him gently forward with her hand under his left arm. She led him to the second chair and pressed on his shoulder so that he sat down. She remained standing behind him with a reassuring hand on each shoulder.

As Ben was completing the registration formalities, a door at the back of the reception area opened. A large young man in dungarees came through. He picked up George's case with a hand the size of a piece of agricultural machinery and stood wordlessly, stooped forward, arms hanging by his side. His acromegalic jaws worked on some object in his mouth in a slow, relentless circular motion. He slowly lifted his free hand and expressionlessly plunged a salami-sized finger up a nostril. Lucy stared aghast as he retrieved his hidden treasure and examined it closely before wiping it on the seat of his trousers. She wondered if he had scraped out his brain through his nose.

"Jim here will take you along to your room," said the receptionist, nodding towards the Neanderthal youth without actually looking at him. "Matron will see you in there. Welcome to Mount Pleasant, Mr Harkness," she said, leaning across the desk towards George. "I hope you'll be happy with us Mr Harkness." She spoke to him loudly and slowly, as so many do when speaking to the elderly, unaware of the patronising affect of their assumption of deafness.

"Why should I be?" said George. "I don't want to come here. They're making me." He turned to Lucy. "Why's that woman shouting at me?" he asked.

"Dad, we talked about this," said Lucy leaning down to him and putting a protective arm around his bony shoulder. "You agreed it was for the best."

"No I didn't," George replied doggedly.

Ben stood up impatiently and started walking towards the inner door, following the shambling Jim who had already turned and gone ahead through it. Lucy helped George to his feet and steered him through the closing door.

A long corridor led to a staircase that the young

porter with George's case had started climbing, doggedly slapping his large feet on each bare step. The small party emerged at the top of the stairs into an identical corridor on the first floor. Doors at regular intervals along the corridor opened into rooms, each door bearing a card with a name. Most of the doors were open, revealing institutionalised inmates lying on beds or sitting in wing-back chairs that faced windows that looked out onto a small neatly tended garden. Lucy felt the cards on the doors were like ante-mortem memorials to the occupants, each comatose in death's waiting rooms. Ben had walked ahead with the young porter and was standing by a room near the end of the corridor. Lucy followed with George and as she reached the room, Lucy could see a card on the door with her father's name on it.

Lucy ushered George into the room and sat him in an armchair by the window as she busied herself with the task of unpacking his case, tidying shirts and underwear in drawers and hanging faded corduroy trousers on wooden hangers in the solitary cupboard in the corner behind the door. There was a washbasin behind the armchair and she arranged the meagre contents of George's wash bag on the glass shelf above it before hanging his old dressing gown on the back of the door. These minor domestic tasks occupied her hands and mind, suppressing the sadness she felt at the opening of this ultimate chapter in her father's life, a life that was once dignified and elegant, but was now that of a child once more, helpless and under the absolute control and whim of others. The seventh age of man, as helpless as the first. Her sense of guilt at his eviction from home she could not assuage.

Ben glanced at his watch and caught Lucy's eye, nodding his head towards the door. Lucy stooped to hug George, reassuring him she would be back to see him soon, and they left the room as one of the staff crouched down in front of him to talk to him. George's bemused gaze was fixed over her shoulder on the door as Ben and Lucy walked out into the corridor. She turned at the door and was torn by the frightened look on the old man's face as he sat all alone in his chair, afraid of his new surroundings, his eyes beseeching her to stay with him. She could not linger or go back to him because Ben was striding quickly down the corridor, a step ahead of Lucy as he hurried to leave the building. Ben's secretary had found the Home, carefully following Ben's brief, paying particular attention to his instructions concerning cost. Lucy's enquiries had drawn up a shortlist, but her choices had been somewhat pre-empted by Ben's insistence that they should see Mount Pleasant as soon as possible as it was one of the few

Homes with places available.

When he and Lucy had visited it to assess its suitability, he had been quite effusive about it and Lucy had been swayed by his assurance that George would be happy there. Now Ben seemed fixated on leaving the place as quickly as possible. His packed suitcase in the car heralded a two-day conference he was going to, and as she tried to keep up with him in his headlong charge for the front door of the building, Lucy wondered whether Ben would ever voluntarily visit her father. She resolved to return to the Home to check her father had settled in once she had dropped Ben off at the station.

Ben's conference was being held in a hotel in the Oxfordshire countryside. By some quirk of chance, it was the same hotel he and Lucy had stayed in for the first two days of their honeymoon, a gift to the impoverished newlyweds from Lucy's older brother Hugh. Hugh was a stockbroker and had 'done rather well for himself', as his mother fondly told her friends in her ignorance of the implications of insider dealing. Hugh had continued to do well for himself, and no doubt for his clients, as he cavalierly rode the rodeo of bull markets and two divorces. Having acquired all the material trappings of success, the trophy of a mistress had been an unwelcome addition to the collection as far as his first wife was concerned, who bewailed the fact he could never just have one of anything as she opted for a sizeable portion of his assets and freedom for herself.

The mistress, who stepped forward in the queue to fill the vacancy and become his second wife, only gloated at the capture of her prize for as long as it took her to trip over the evidence of his further liaisons. It had been the sexually incontinent Hugh's misfortune to conduct a brief affair with someone who listed jealousy as one of her hobbies. On realising he was not going to leave his second wife for her, she had expressed her feelings one afternoon by aerating the marital waterbed she had just vigorously occupied with him. Hugh had filled the vacuum created whilst his wife had been out for the day and night being pampered at a health farm. As he and his mistress reclined entwined after their tender moment in the afternoon, she had raised the subject of a longer term future with him, and a question about when he was going to tell his wife. Hugh's response was to look surprised and let her know that was not going to happen in a way that hinted he questioned her sanity. Perhaps it had after all been a bit rash of him to follow that up immediately with the suggestion of another bout of the vigorous stuff, which rather left his inamorata feeling jilted and suddenly frigid. Waking up to reality, it dawned on her she was no more than a semenal spittoon, the lot of so many misguided and delusional mistresses of married men. Surprised and somewhat irritated at the rebuff, Hugh went out to buy cigarettes for some post-coital relaxation, giving the spurned woman the opportunity to attack the waterbed with the largest carving knife she could find in the kitchen.

Explaining to his wife the presence of a couple of hundred gallons of water in the drawing room below had challenged Hugh's ingenuity. She found his description of a small leak to be somewhat improbable given the evidence of some frenzied activity in the bedroom. His wife agreed he was quite correct in saying there had been a leak, but had taken issue with his definition of small and felt 'shredded' would have been more apposite. The fact that the lunatic woman had also cut out the crutch of every one of his underpants left Hugh in a cold sweat, and not a little hurt at the implication of his inadequacy.

The aggrieved second wife consoled herself in her grief with the balm of a leaf from her predecessor's book and a sizeable portion of his acquisitions and portfolio. Taking inspiration from the pained mistress, she completed her own emotional recovery with the demolition of his entire wardrobe of Jermyn Street shirts with the aid of her pinking shears. The removal of the left trouser leg and right sleeve of each of his suits helped her to lay the ghost of his memory, enabling her to recover quickly in the arms of an even larger bank account belonging to another Managing Director of the World in the City.

The taxi delivered Ben to the conference hotel in time for him to fit in a swim before dinner. He checked in at the reception desk and followed the porter to his room on the top floor of the hotel. He stood at the window looking out over a golf course that lay in front of the building. The afternoon sun created long shadows across the manicured fairways. The hotel was part of an exclusive Country Club, and the Company had decided to use it for the first time for the annual conference, breaking its traditional use of City-based hotels. Ben walked around the bedroom and into the bathroom, as he always did when in a new hotel, marking the limits of his territory and establishing its boundaries. He opened one of the small complimentary bottles of shampoo and waved it gently beneath his nose, taking in its scent before rubbing some of the hotel's choice of moisturising cream into his hands. He went back into the bedroom and turned on the television for background company as he unpacked his clothes and hung them in the wardrobe. Having done that he put on his swimming trunks and the thick and luxurious towelling robe that hung behind the bathroom door and headed for the lift to take him down to the swimming pool in the basement.

As Ben stood in front of the lift entrance, somewhat self-conscious in his bathrobe, he became aware of someone by his side. He was not feeling particularly gregarious, perhaps more guilty after his evident relief at having ejected George from the house and into the institutional life that was now to be the last chapter in his life. He focused his attention on the cabinet by the lift doors. It contained the hotel restaurant's dinner menu and Ben started reading slowly through the items listed whilst praying the lift would arrive soon. He assumed everyone found lifts excruciatingly embarrassing vehicles, judging by the habitually fixed stares always borne by fellow passengers, as they too carefully studied the numbers counting the passing floors, each unable to find the words to break the silence, each eager for their chosen floor to arrive to release them from the tension of their confinement within each other's comfort zone.

"Going for a swim, or is this a fashion statement?"

Ben turned and smiled at the pretty girl standing by him. She too was dressed in a bathrobe and had a bright pink pair of rubber sandals on her feet, her toes hiding underneath a large plastic flower on each foot. Her blond hair was tied back, and Ben was aware of a slender neck and wisps of hair that had escaped from the ponytail hanging down her back. She had remarkably blue eyes, and her face was alive with an impish smile on her full lips. Ben noticed she wore no lipstick and yet her lips shone with a slight wetness. He wondered if she had had a drink before leaving her room.

"Sally, I didn't realise it was you," he said. "I was hoping to sneak down to the pool without anyone seeing."

"I can see that," she said, tugging at the sleeve of his dressing gown.

"You're a fine one to talk. Have you seen yourself?"

"Er, yes," Sally said, "and I'm trying not to think about it."

"When did you arrive?" Ben asked.

"About an hour ago," Sally replied. "I wanted to get here early. I thought I would go in the sauna and have a quick swim before the evening started. I'm not sure anyone else is here yet."

"No, I think we're the first," Ben said.

Sally had been with the Agency for just over a year and had worked on some of the accounts in Ben's sphere of responsibility. Intelligent and vivacious, she had clearly taken to her first job after graduating from University, a marketing natural. Ben knew very little about her, but was aware she seemed popular and was a regular part of any group from the Agency congregating in the bars after work.

The lift door opened and Ben stepped aside to let Sally in. They both stood at the back of the lift with their backs to the back wall. The doors closed and the lift dropped one floor where it stopped and the doors opened. A large group of elderly people were waiting for it, and they all moved forwards in unison, momentarily jamming themselves in the entrance. As they filled the lift, Ben moved to the corner to make room, and Sally moved to his side. With the press of people in the now full lift, Ben became acutely aware of the pressure of Sally's young body against him. She seemed quite unselfconscious about the physical contact, and of the awakening of desire in Ben's mind. He stood perfectly still, wishing the lift had to travel a hundred floors to prolong the moment. Instead it quickly reached the ground floor, the doors opened and the elderly occupants again filled the entrance as they tried to move out as one, slowly moving off in the direction of the hotel foyer and reception desk. The doors closed and the lift continued down. Ben noticed Sally had made no attempt to move away from him. The lift quickly reached its destination in the basement where they left the lift and turned right for the pool complex.

CHAPTER 12

Lucy parked the car in front of the house, turned off the engine and sat staring ahead through the window. She felt tired, more tired than she had ever been, and closed her eyes to rest. She awoke with a start, realising she had fallen into one of those deep sleeps that come to the truly exhausted. She thought it had only been momentary but in truth had no idea how long she had been asleep. The noise of a lawn mower being started had brought her back to consciousness, but the depth of the brief moment of sleep made her thankful it had not happened when she had been driving. She had come home from Mount Pleasant with the window of the car open, relying on the flow of cold air to keep her alert for the journey home. Leaving her father again had been painful, and she had driven down the Home's long drive almost overwhelmed with sadness, so much so she had pulled into a small lay-by half way down the drive to collect herself, but only after weeping into a small handkerchief. She could not believe a long life, that had been filled with the usual quota of joy and sorrow, success and failure, should end like this, alone in a room staring blankly out of the window at an alien scene.

`Perhaps elective euthanasia is the best way after all,' she thought. She leant over to the passenger seat to pick up her handbag and glanced up at the house. Felicia was standing at the window with Emma, who was waving to her, a small soft toy tucked under her other arm. Lucy smiled and waved back, lifted by the child's innocent joy at her return. The front door of the house opened as she reached it and Emma ran to her, babbling words in her eagerness to tell her mother about her day.

"Hello Emmy," said Lucy as she gathered her up and hugged her. The trusting depth of the small child's affection, evident through the squeeze of her small arms around her mother's neck, brought tears welling into Lucy's eyes, and she started to cry again.

"Why are you crying mummy?" asked Emma, leaning back but with her hands still clasped behind Lucy's neck.

"Oh, I'm just so happy to see you," she said.

"But why does that make you cry?" said Emma. "You should be glad."

"I am glad," said Lucy, "but I'm also sad because I had to say good bye to Grandpa today."

"But we'll see him again won't we?" cried Emma, her eyes too filling with tears at the shared thought of loss.

"Of course we will," said Lucy as she put Emma back down and took her hand to walk down the hall. She smiled wanly at Felicia who fell in behind them as they walked to the kitchen.

"Let's start making supper shall we?" said Lucy, recovering her composure, determined to paper over her real feelings for the sake of her daughter.

Felicia laid the table for the evening meal and then helped Emma colour in a book whilst sitting with her in a two-seat sofa in the corner of the spacious kitchen. Lucy busied herself with the simple task of cooking the meal, heavily relying on the auto-pilot those who are obliged to cater for a family must use to avoid the natural depressive slump awaiting anyone foolish enough to stop and think about the banality of domestic catering. She sometimes wondered if there was such a thing as repetitive strain brain injury, caused by the sheer boredom of producing very ordinary meals with monotonous and relentless regularity. This evening, the familiarity of the movements around her kitchen were a comforting distraction, preventing her thoughts dwelling on the unpalatable realities crowding into so many aspects of her life.

The meal ready, Sebastian was summoned from his bedroom, and the four sat down to the ritual of the meal. The children chattered between mouthfuls, Felicia massacred the English language and Lucy wondered if the other three also thought the meal tasted like cardboard. When they had finished eating, Lucy washed and cleared while Felicia took the two children upstairs for a bath and to get ready for bed. Sebastian protested going up the stairs that he was old enough to bath himself, and did not want to bath with Emma, and for the sake of a peaceful end to the day Lucy reassured him that he could use the water after his sister, and could play in his bedroom until he was called. Lucy had spoken to Felicia a few days earlier, aware of the onset of physical shyness in her son, and they had agreed he should be allowed his privacy.

After the children had gone to bed, Felicia went out for the evening and Lucy settled down to read a novel she had bought and started the week before. She enjoyed contemporary authors, and this was this author's second book. It was a right of passage novel, the story of a young boy moving into adulthood at the turn of the century. Knowing the savagery and horrors of the Great War that lay ahead of the pubescent character, his innocent aspirations and dreams seemed so futile to Lucy. Perhaps, she felt, all our plans are futile, and if there is a God, and He or She has a sense of humour, people's plans must be a great cause for amusement to Him or Her. She wondered if this supreme but probably fictitious being, relentlessly promoted by the religiously fervent as so caring and so loving, took pleasure in wrecking plans and ambitions with sudden and unexpected moves on the chessboard of life. In a human, such a sadistic trait would be deemed to be distinctly unsavoury, and yet in this God of the faithful it was viewed as wisdom. Was such sycophantic forgiveness granted to this God for fear of His or Her capacity for eternal retribution? 'Love God or be damned for eternity' did not seem to Lucy to be the basis for a balanced relationship.

Lucy's embryonic cynicism about the foundations and subliminal agendas of all religions was born of a searching mind that refused to accept without question the fundamentalist preaching to which she and her generation had been subjected. The more strident the preaching, the more she came to believe that all religions were founded in the desire of a few for autocratic control over the unwashed masses. She believed the concept of Hell and eternal damnation were fiction, conceived by the higher orders of Man as the ultimate sanction, whose purpose was to control the lumpenproletariat's behaviour. Without the fear of an extreme, unbearable and eternal punishment, meted out on the evidence of the record of a person's earthly conduct, Man would have no incentive to conform to any moral code.

Building an image of a choice between everlasting pleasure and pain, in an afterlife whose existence became accepted as a matter of dogma, seemed to Lucy the definitive confidence trick that had taken in the majority, irrespective of the religion of choice or birth. She felt the concept of another, and potentially better life to which we move is reassuring to those who cannot imagine or comprehend a vacuum, or of themselves as ceasing to exist in any form. Having resolved the fear of dark finality, it was surely a simple step to expand and refine the theory over successive generations, to create an entirely new celestial world that had Hell as its oubliette for the recidivists unable to conform to the rules of society, or to the will of the majority. Thus was created a structure on earth that gave authority to a select band with the motivation to seek a way to the pinnacle of power embodied in religions' ruling classes.

Lucy awoke with a start, the open book resting on her legs, her feet tucked sideways beneath her on the sofa. She closed her eyes again, her dream still vivid in her mind, and rested her head on the back of the seat as she tried to become fully conscious. She glanced at the clock, realising she had been asleep for nearly an hour. Her neck was stiff from where it had arched as her head had sunk forwards and the side of her mouth was damp where she had dribbled slightly through her open lips. She wiped them with a tissue, stretched out her stiff legs and winced as the blood rushed into them and set off the exquisite tingle of pins and needles.

Lucy had been tempted earlier to phone Ben but remembered he had said he had a full evening of meetings followed by a working dinner. Now it was too late and so she decided she would call him in the morning when she woke up, before his day at the conference started. She closed up the ground floor for the night, checking Felicia could open the front door when she came home, and went upstairs to look in on the children before going to bed.

The alarm startled Lucy, interrupting her dream in which she somehow floated over a house, with no apparent means of support, drifting with the ease and grace of a raptor on a thermal. Sebastian and Emma ran out of the French windows and through the garden beneath her, into a field of wheat on a farm where they had holidayed a couple of times. The farmer was cutting and baling the hay at one end of the field, his dog barking at the wheels of the tractor as it moved slowly over the ground. Floating high above the rural idyl, Lucy watched her children running through the uncut wheat as it danced in the light breeze, catching the evening sun's rays, the ripe golden crop forming ever changing shapes and patterns. A skylark hovered in the sky, twittering and chirping at the top of its voice to no one in particular and careless of that, just singing for the joy of it. The sense of peace, freedom and open space she felt in her dream lasted mere seconds when she woke and the harsh, unpalatable reality of the present returned to flood her mind.

Lucy rolled onto her back, her forearm across her eyes, and ran her tongue over the roof of her dry mouth. She slowly got out of bed and went down the stairs as she put on her dressing gown. In the kitchen she laid the table for the children's breakfast as she waited for the kettle to boil and her tea to brew. As she poured the tea into a mug, she glanced at the kitchen clock and decided to call Ben in his hotel. She remembered he had said his meetings would start quite early and a call now would catch him before he disappeared into his irresistible vortex of work for the day.

Moving Emma's colouring book and crayons to one side, she sat on the small sofa in the kitchen and dialled the hotel. As she listened to the ringing tone, her mind slipped back to the start of her honeymoon at the hotel, to the hopes that filled her breast that day as she gazed into her future of a marriage and family, her very own grown up dolls and dolls' house the visual evidence of her emancipation.

As he had walked her proudly down the aisle earlier that afternoon all those years ago, her father had tightened his guiding arm against his side, squeezing her forearm against him. It was a comforting private paternal expression of love, a father's affectionate farewell to his little girl at her final step into womanhood. The bond between them had never felt stronger to Lucy than at that moment, a rising surge of filial passion for a man whose love had always been unconditional.

At that time he had still been a man full of his faculties, a figure of authority, independent of spirit and in control of his life. They had sat up together the night before the wedding. Lucy huddled on the sofa in her parent's drawing room, a hot chocolate drink tucked under her chin. Her father was stretched out in an armchair opposite, his feet reaching for the open fire he had kept alive through the evening, its dancing flames providing the only light in the room. Her mother had gone to bed earlier, exhausted from the tension of anticipation, but it was clear to Lucy her father was in a contemplative mood and not ready for sleep. The evening had reminded her of when she was little and the many times she had curled up in his lap before the same fireplace, his clean masculine smells strong in her senses. She always felt supremely protected by the strength of his omnipotence over her world. He would put his arm around her and she would snuggle as closely and tightly as she could, her head under his chin, her ear pressed to his chest where she could hear the calming metronomic beat of his heart, a rhythm that steadied her life.

On that final evening of her spinsterhood, they had talked of relationships; of paternal love and letting go; of the excitement of a new life. He had reminisced about her youth, surprising her with the detail in his memories. Lucy had never really thought of her father as a passionate man, and yet that evening he had talked openly to her of the intensity of his emotions, his fear of crying in the Church when he passed her hand to Ben and when she finally left for her honeymoon. Perhaps that evening had been his final act of passing responsibility for her life to Lucy.

In the end, none of his fears were realised and his tears remained unshed. He was intentionally the last person she said good-bye to as she and Ben left after the reception. As she hugged his neck she whispered her congratulations for holding his nerve in his ear. They shared a private smile that excluded the guests and her hand slid from his as she climbed into the festooned and decorated car. She had looked over her shoulder as Ben drove away from the house. He was standing by himself to one side of the wedding guests and separate from them, his right hand half-raised, a quizzical smile on his face. He seemed so alone in his isolation, suddenly small and vulnerable, and Lucy resisted a strong urge to ask Ben to stop the car so she could run back to him and hold him one more time, to tell him she would be back. That she loved him.

Her reminiscent daydream was interrupted by the receptionist answering the phone, and she realised she had been quite unaware of just how long she had been waiting for her call to be answered. The receptionist apologised for the delay, explaining the hotel was short staffed due to some illness, and she had been checking out an early leaver who had a plane to catch. She asked Lucy to hold while she connected her to Ben's room.

The phone fell silent as the connection was made, and then she heard it being picked up as Ben came on the line.

"Hello," he said, somewhat hesitantly.

"Hi, it's me," said Lucy.

"Oh, hi," he replied.

"You don't sound too pleased to hear me," she said, frowning and worried that Ben was still angry with her.

"No, no," he said quickly. "I'm just half asleep,

that's all. How are you? Did you sleep well?"

"I'm fine," said Lucy. "I thought you had early meetings to go to. Won't you be late for them?"

"Oh, no, I should be fine. The alarm has just gone and I'll grab a quick shower. How are the children?"

"They're fine," said Lucy. "At least I think so. They're not awake yet. I thought I'd call you before they were up and before you went to your meetings. I just wanted to chat to you without them arguing with each other. It's so hard to concentrate..."

"Yeah, I know," said Ben. "Look, I'd better get on or I'll be late. I'm on second at the seminar this morning and I need to read my notes. I'll try and call you in the day, or tonight if I can't get away. Is that OK?"

"Yes," said Lucy. "Yes, of course. I'll give the children your love."

"Great," said Ben. "Speak to you later. Must run. Bye."

He put the phone down and stayed sitting with his bare legs over the edge of the bed, where he had swung them when he had answered the phone."

"Was that your wife?" said Sally, her hand stroking his naked back as she ran it down his spine.

"Er, yes. Yes, it was," said Ben with his back to Sally, who was lying in the bed next to where he had been.

"That's fine," she said. "I mean, I don't mind. I knew you were married. I'd expect a wife to call in the morning before the day starts."

She sat up and moved over to him, kneeling behind him and putting her arms around his waist. He smiled and leant back into her nakedness, luxuriating in the sensation of her bare skin and perfectly formed breasts pressed into his back, exhilarated and slightly shocked at his audacity on the phone to Lucy. He had not planned this, although there was no denying he had not been excited by Sally's proximity in the lift the evening before when they had gone for a swim. The pool had been full, and as he swam and then sat in the sauna, he had been surprised by the sudden and unexpected attraction he had felt. From his seat in the sauna, he could see the pool through a small glass window in the door of the darkened little room. He found himself waiting for each pass Sally made across its frame as she swam out her lengths in long lithe strokes. Her lean young body slid effortlessly through the water. He felt a surge of annoyance when a large man came into the sauna and momentarily stood in the doorway, blocking his view at the moment he estimated she would next come into view.

On returning to his room, he had showered and dressed for the evening, aware he was carefully selecting clothes he felt were understatedly sophisticated, and in which he felt most confident and attractive. He joined the growing collection of colleagues in the bar before dinner, unable to avoid intermittently glancing towards the bar entrance, conscious of the tension in him over the anticipation of Sally's arrival. In the event, he missed her quiet entrance, which coincided with the moment he turned to the bar to order more drinks for their party.

He only became aware of her presence shortly before they moved into the room reserved for their evening meal. Making his excuses to the others, he walked obliquely to another group next to the one Sally had joined and as the meal was announced, stepped sideways to stand just behind her.

"Hi," he said, feigned surprise in his voice, as though he had not been expecting to see her.

As the group moved forwards, they fell into step beside each other as he carefully cut her out of the flock, and it seemed quite natural they should end up sitting next to each other when they reached the table. As the wine flowed through the meal, the noise levels rose and the evening became raucous, inhibitions and office hierarchy forgotten in the liberating atmosphere of alcohol and jocularity. The game of life commenced as Ben and Sally sat and talked, leaning in towards each other when they laughed at shared flirtations, their heads nearly touching when he whispered in her ear. He occasionally laid his hand on her forearm to stress points in conversation, and was pleased to notice she did not move her arm away. Indeed, she responded in kind when she too wished to emphasise an issue. He was careful to turn and talk to others, covering his aroused tracks but only long enough to let any casual observer feel he was sharing his attention, and never long enough to break the web of desire he was spinning around her, which she seemed to be so willing to wrap herself in.

By the time the meal ended, any inhibitions and marital fealty Ben felt had been washed away by the copious amount of wine he had drunk. The diehards pushed back their chairs and headed straight to the bar. Those committed to a spouse or a career bade their farewells and gathered at the lifts to ascend to their rooms. More drink flowed for those less encumbered by a long ago promise or by ambition, and the group became raucous and boisterous until it finally dawned on some that they had a full day of workshops and functions ahead of them. As the conversations had flowed, Ben had carefully torn a beermat into small pieces and then, like Hansel and Gretel, had laid them out on the bar to make the number of his room, sweeping them up into a small pile when he felt sure Sally had noticed. Now the evening was closing, Ben and Sally joined the others in the lift and got out on their floor with two others. They all wished each other a good night and parted and Ben made his way to his room and let himself in. He turned the lighting down low and switched on the radio as he awaited Sally's knock on the door. This would not be the first time he had been unfaithful to Lucy in their marriage, but it felt one or the more alluring of his infidelities.

Now it was the morning after and the excitement of the evening was still with him. Turning around he took Sally in his arms and pulled her down onto the bed next to him.

"You're going to be late," she giggled.

"Who cares?" Ben said pulling her closer to him.

"Clearly not you," Sally replied relaxing back into the pillows.

Later, as he shaved before going down to breakfast, he was surprised to realise that not once through the whole evening had he thought of Lucy or the family. Like a predator focussed on its prey, his attention had been singular, to the exclusion of extraneous distractions. More surprising to him was the lack of guilt he felt about his infidelity, unlike on previous occasions. It was as though he had crossed an Alpine ridge after a strenuous, energy sapping climb, and was now free to ski down to the floor of the valley of opportunity and temptation, a temptation he no longer felt inclined or duty bound to resist. He was suffused with a sense of liberation and quickly concluded that he would not have been enticed by Sally's feminine charms and allure if Lucy had not driven him to it, thus conjuring for himself instant justification and absolution. As he finished dressing he wondered what

Sally might be doing in the break for lunch scheduled in the day's programme. Like a small boy desperate to return to the sweet shop for another helping out of the Lucky Dip jar, to Ben the charms of her soft, naked young body were irresistible.

CHAPTER 13

Winter - 1987

The residents sat around the perimeter of the Day Room, their backs to the wall or the windows, facing into the centre of the room like Scouts around a camp fire. Some slept, heads slumped forwards, nodding gently in peaceful rhythm with the rise and fall of their chests. One woman lay with her head back against the antimacassar covering the back of her chair, mouth open to reveal pink toothless gums. Her wig had slipped over her right ear, allowing a catch-light to glint and glisten on her bald head as the sunlight fell through the window behind her. Baggy support hose lay collapsed around her ankles and calves and her thin hands lay in her lap, dark blue veins showing through dry, tissue paper skin.

George fiddled with the edge of the old tartan rug that lay over his knees, his nervous fingers pulling at loose threads and small bobbles of wool. He repeatedly glanced at the door into the room, his face both worried and expectant. In between these glances he glowered at the ring of vacuous faces arranged before him, like a punter frowning at targets in a fairground shooting gallery. His once luxuriant hair was now thin, a silvery gossamer halo floating above his scalp. On the small table next to him lay a pad and pencil and his glasses, and at regular intervals, sighing deeply, he reached out and arranged them carefully in a row, each time placing them exactly where they had just been. He glanced at the woman sleeping in the chair next to him and surreptitiously leaned over to take a paperback novel that lay on the table next to her chair. He slipped the book onto his lap under his rug and rearranged the cloth over it to hide it. He hummed tunelessly to himself, once more rearranging the objects on his own table.

The door to the room swung open and a family came in hesitantly. A woman in her early forties ushered in three children in front of her, her arms stretched out before her, palms to the room and their backs as she shepherded her charges before her. The children stopped and stepped back in unison as they came into the room and saw its rank of occupants with their front row view of death. The woman bumped into them, toppling over them as they pushed back against her. The youngest, a little girl of about three with blonde hair in bunches at the side of her head quickly moved behind her mother's legs and peered around them.

The compact little group stood in the doorway as the woman ran her eyes around the room. A quick look of recognition crossed her face and she moved the children forwards towards an old man fast asleep in his chair by the window. His lower set of false teeth protruded through his lips, pink, white and wet from his saliva, which drooled down onto his chest like a limp mooring rope. The children crowded self-consciously onto a stool in front of him as the woman sat on a chair at his side. She leaned forward and put her hand on the old man's where it lay in his lap. He slowly stirred and lifted his head, blinking, clearly confused at his surroundings. As recognition dawned he tried to speak, but merely coughed and fired his teeth into his lap. The woman quickly picked them up and handed them to him. The children each involuntarily hunched in embarrassment, looking around the room to see if anyone was watching as he pushed them clumsily back into his mouth.

As the woman leant forward to speak to him, Lucy came into the room behind two other groups of visitors. She quickly spotted George and walked over to him smiling.

"Hi, Dad," she said, leaning over to kiss his baggy cheek. She pulled the empty seat by his chair closer to him and sat down, leaning forward with her elbows on her knees. She reached up and tucked her blonde hair behind her ears.

"How are you?" she said.

"They're stealing my things," he replied in a conspiratorial whisper.

"Who are?" said Lucy. "What are they stealing?"

"They are," George replied, nodding at the immobile and comatose residents. "They're taking all my things. I want them to stop."

"Dad, are you sure about this?" said Lucy, frowning perplexedly.

"Oh yes," George replied.

"I'll talk to the staff about it for you," said Lucy. "Before I go."

"Yes," said George, "and ask them to make them stop doing it all the time, it's disgusting."

"What is?" said Lucy, her confusion building. "I

don't know what you mean."

"It," said George. "You know. It. Sex. They're doing it you know. I hear them all the time, at each other like rabbits."

Lucy controlled the urge to laugh.

"Who are?" she asked seriously.

"Them, over there," said George indicating two sleeping nonagenarians on the other side of the room. "They do it in the room next to me. I've seen them."

"Oh Dad, I don't think they can be," said Lucy, her thoughts focused on how to move the conversation on. "The children sent their love to you," she said. "And Ben too."

"How is he?" George asked. "Does he still like his walks?"

Lucy ignored her father's confusion. Shocked at the

deterioration of his mind since his arrival at the Home, she tried to suppress a growing feeling of guilt at the thought that this might not have happened if she had continued to care for him within the family at home.

The room was now filled with visitors, most of the residents' seats facing a small semi-circle of family, each little unit engrossed in their conversation. The murmured conversations were interjected with louder questions or statements directed at the elderly inmates. At one or two chairs, visitors unwrapped flowers and put them in vases, arranging the display and fussing over the stems, breaking them off to shorten them where they flopped over the edge too much.

Unnoticed in the far corner of the room, a tall and clearly once elegant resident stirred and threw back the rug that covered his legs. He was wearing striped pyjamas and had slumped low in his seat, which was covered in a plastic sheet. He had obviously slipped down on the plastic and was now struggling to get up. He reached under himself and pulled off his pyjama bottoms and threw them on the floor next to his chair so he was naked from the waist down. He lifted his legs off the floor towards his chest, raising them like two huge thin sticks of pale celery. His genitals hung over the front of the seat of his chair. He pulled fruitlessly on the arms of the chair as two nurses walked into the room, his legs waving in the air like an upturned praying mantis trying to right itself.

"Oh, God," said the older nurse, "he's off again. Lionel, stay where you are!" she called.

The nurses rushed over to him, quickly trying to cover the old man's lower half with the discarded rug. As Lucy watched the commotion at the end of the room, she became aware of someone standing close by and next to her. She glanced up at a man who was clearly another resident. He stood silently before her and George, wrapped in a thick dressing gown and with a pair of large corduroy slippers on his feet. Without saying a word, he opened the front of his dressing gown like bat wings and exposed himself to her, slightly wiggling his hips as he did so. He was completely naked under his gown and from a distance of two feet, Lucy had a front of stalls view of waving and flapping offal, making her wish she had been a bit further away up in the Royal Circle.

As Lucy automatically recoiled, the man closed his gown, and mutely moved over to the woman and three children who had come in earlier and who were on the other side of the room. This time the man stood behind the family as they sat in front of the elderly resident who was facing both them and him. Once again the man lifted the two sides of his dressing gown, giving his aged fellow inmate the full benefit of his naked body. The look of horror on the old man's face made the woman turn round and she let out an involuntary cry of disgust. The children leapt off the stool they were sitting on and shrieked in harmony with their mother. The two nurses, still trying to dignify the old man who had tried to get out of his seat, looked up, instantly aghast.

"Mr Benton!" the older nurse cried out as they hesitated in the No Man's Land between the seated would-be escapee and the flasher at the other end of the room. Perhaps through telepathy, or just long practice at the art of containment, they peeled off and the elder nurse rushed over to the exhibitionist Mr Benton. She closed his dressing gown, tying the belt in a double knot, and then led him by the arm out of the room. He meekly followed, staring down expressionlessly at the other inmates and their visitors as he passed them on his way to the door. Lucy turned back to her father who seemed agitated at the commotion.

"It's OK Dad," she said stroking his forearm, aware how thin it was under the sleeve of his dressing gown.

His frailty, mental and physical, seemed palpable to her, and she felt an overwhelming sadness as she looked at his confused eyes. His hands fluttered over the rug, and he turned his head to stare out of the window, retreating into a silent world in his mind where she could not follow.

Lucy quietly got up and went out of the room, leaving behind her the chaotic scene. She walked down the corridor that led to the nurses' station. Three nurses were standing beside a desk, engrossed in conversation and laughing at a shared comment while one of them checked the contents of a wheeled medicine cabinet, making notes on a list on a clipboard resting in the crook of her left arm. The nurses looked up warily as Lucy approached them, subconsciously moving together, closing ranks in a form of protectively supportive herd instinct. Lucy's anger rose within her, a surge of vicarious indignation for her father and the frustration of his incarceration in what had all the hallmarks of an ammonia-scented lunatic asylum. She realised a flood of tears was threatening to engulf her, and she struggled to remain in control of herself.

"I'm sorry to interrupt your little meeting here," she said, "But can I speak to you about my father. He says someone's stealing his things and it's upsetting him.

Can't someone control what's going on here? It can hardly be difficult, given the average age of your residents."

Lucy felt she had somewhat blurted her complaint, and in doing so it had lost its impact, but she felt relieved to have said it.

"I'm sorry," said the most senior looking of the three nurses, seemingly choosing to ignore the implicit sarcasm in Lucy's question. "What's your father's name?"

"Mister Harkness," said Lucy. "George Harkness. He's in the Day Room at the moment. And what's more," Lucy went on, glancing over both shoulders and slightly lowering her voice, "he says there's a couple who have been having sex in the room next to his."

Lucy was now blushing in embarrassment, and folded her arms defensively across her chest.

"Oh," said the nurse who had spoken as she stepped forward. "I'm Sister Steer. Can we go up to your father's room to see if you can see what's missing?"

Lucy and Sister Steer made their way silently to

George's room. On going into it, Sister Steer bent down and lifted the valance surrounding the bed, reached under and pulled out a small radio, a ladies' hairdryer and a pair of pink fluffy slippers.

"Are these your father's?" she asked without preamble.

"No," said Lucy, confused.

"No, I thought not," said Sister Steer. "You see, er, Mrs…..? "

"Grayson," said Lucy. "Lucy Grayson."

"I think you'll find it's your father that is doing the stealing Mrs Grayson," said Sister Steer coldly.

"It can't be," said Lucy. "He just wouldn't. He's never done anything like that." As she said it, she knew in her heart the nurse was right.

"I'm afraid it is Mrs Grayson," said Sister Steer.

"This isn't the first time we have found other residents' things in Mister Harkness' room."

"But what about the goings on next door, in the next room?" said Lucy. "My father says there's a couple having sex in there, although I struggle to believe it. Perhaps that could have something to do with it. Could someone else be putting these things in here? It's just so out of character."

"I don't think so," said Sister Steer. "I can assure you, no one was having sex in the next room. We found your father in there the other night. I think you'll find he has confused himself over that. He was extremely excited and started asking us to get the couple in the room next to him to stop, but I'm afraid there was only one resident in there. He had woken her up and she was shocked to see him standing naked by her. When he started getting into bed with her she rang the alarm bell and we came up and took your father back to his room where we gave him a light sedative."

The empirical evidence of her father's mental degeneration confirmed to Lucy what she had been so afraid to face, and she sat down on the edge of his bed, tears slowly running down her cheeks. Sister Steer put a hand on her shoulder, a gentle and reassuring pressure.

"I know it's hard to face," she said, softly. "We see it all the time, and it's never easy when you see a loved one get old like this. I'll leave you to compose yourself, but do come and see me if there is anything you want. Are you alright? Can I get you some tea?"

"Yes, I'll be fine," Lucy replied. "Thank you, and I'm sorry he's been so much trouble to you."

"Don't worry, I can assure you we get much worse. It's what we're trained to deal with." Sister Steer replied.

She left the room in a rustle of starched linen, and Lucy slowly calmed herself as she sat on her father's bed. Her gaze wandered around the room, taking in his few possessions. There were a few photograph frames on his bedside table showing photographs of her, Ben and the children. A black and white one of her mother as a young woman, pretty and laughing at something the photographer had said, was larger than the others, and in its old worn red leather frame, it dwarfed one of her brother and his first wife next to it. To Lucy this seemed so little to show for a lifetime of memories, and suddenly she needed to leave the room. She returned to the Day Room to say good bye to her father, but from the door of the room she could see he was now fast asleep, the rug slipped from his knees and a paperback book in his hands. She turned and left him, hurrying to the front door and the fresh air. An elderly resident was sweeping up leaves with a domestic pan and brush and tipping them into the large letterbox attached to the front of the building. Lucy closed her eyes and stood with her face lifted to greet the breeze, letting it dry the wetness on her soft cheeks.

CHAPTER 14

Ben leaned back in his chair, his feet resting on the bottom drawer of his desk. He distractedly fingered the report that lay in his lap, realising he had read the last two pages without taking in one word that had been written. With a resigned sigh, he turned back to the beginning to start again, looked at the battalions of paragraphs lined up to engage his mind and instead lay the papers on his desk. He swivelled around in his seat, moving his feet from the drawer to the low windowsill and looked down into the busy street below. A small car was making its way down the road and then turned left into a one way street, going the wrong way. A few seconds after it had turned and disappeared from view, Ben became aware of the growing sound of sirens. Suddenly, the small car reappeared, weaving backwards at speed out into the main road, a huge red fire engine with lights blazing feet from its bonnet. He laughed spontaneously, enjoying the schadenfreude moment of the shock the car driver must have felt at the sight of the urgently unstoppable coming at him, no doubt filling his windscreen with a festive display of twinkling blue lights, expressive faces and abusive gestures.

A fine drizzle drifted down from a nondescript sky,

dampening the pavement and road. Umbrellas moved up and down the street like mobile mushrooms as the people huddling beneath them hurried about their business. Ben felt a sense of detachment as he watched the comings and goings below. So many unconnected lives, each oblivious of the parallel lives about them, each immersed in the issues affecting their own world. He had had the same sensation after visiting his father-in-law the day before.

As he and Lucy had driven away from the Home, Ben had felt acutely conscious of its existence as a self-sufficient micro-world. It was an environment independent of the wider world about, insensitive of the goings on outside it's walls. Equally those outside its confines remained unaware of the lifeblood and daily rhythms within, even where there may be a tenuous connection, as there was with George and his penultimate incarceration. Perhaps it was merely an example of humanity's tendency for introversion, a survival instinct where self-interest becomes the dominant force when we are faced with overwhelming issues, engendering a selfish disinterest in the difficulties facing others. Ben was aware of his sense of relief, of escape when he had driven out of the Home.

For some time Ben had theorised that people were

nothing other than domesticated animals, where clothing was the visible evidence of a social veneer that was nothing but that. A thin veneer, discarded effortlessly and without guilt when self-preservation became the ascendant emotion. Centuries of civilisation had superimposed social standards on humanity, but it was only a gossamer facade, and did not supplant the basic animal instincts with which we are all imbued from the moment of impregnation. The inescapable conclusion to Ben was that the unwritten rules that are the engine of a smooth running society produce an unnatural state, rarely replicated in the lower mammalian orders. To him, many of the accepted and sacred social attributes of a polite society were themselves the root cause of the stresses that fractured relationships. The expectation of a monogamous commitment seemed to him an aberration, flying in the face of the male's instinctive drive to recreate himself in as many forms as possible, through the widest range of hosts. Ben felt that to expect the male to undertake to commit to a lifetime of fidelity was a utopian dream that flew in the face of logic and blindly ignored the inexorable urges all men feel. As far as he was concerned, especially now with his new inner and unspoken sense of liberation, any coerced or enforced commitment to fidelity was doomed to failure from the start, and arguably unnecessary.

And yet successive generations persisted in perpetuating the myth that the simple act of appearing at an altar and making promises that for many would prove to be impossible to keep, would for once cleanse the male of all his natural instincts. The marriage ceremony was not so much a confirmation of love as a rebirth, where an old skin is shed and is followed by a baptism into a new and perfect monogamous order. Perfect to women, that was. Perhaps subconsciously men only went through marriage and its attendant ceremonies because society said that was the only acceptable way for them to produce offspring. The enticement to accept the contract is the tempting promise of unlimited and free sex. Without the empty promise of faithfulness, the opportunity to produce a new generation, that primordial urge in all men, would be denied and so the male is prepared to pay lip-service to the charade, so strong is the urge to procreate.

Ben thought that women played the percentages, knowing that some would indeed stay the course and not stray, but that without the bribe of the implicit promise of fatherhood, none of them would. Within the constraints of a marriage women at least had a chance of striking lucky with a man prepared to stick to the unwritten rules. And therein lay the unspoken bargain. The sublimation trade off, where both parties to a marriage feel there is sufficient profit to be gained from the long-term commitment for it to be worth making. To Ben, marital monogamy was the consideration in the contract, at the heart of which was an unspoken struggle for dominance between the sexes. For the man, there was the promise of the chance to pass his genes to a new generation, and of course all that free sex. For the woman, the price she extracted was the security of a provider and protector, whilst taking from the man the genes she needed for the healthy and strong children she craved. Each party essentially had parasitic intentions from an outwardly symbiotic relationship that purported to be socially altruistic, but at its basest level was ultimately selfish.

Ben felt that in this game of life, women ultimately called the shots, and in doing so revealed a biologically ruthless streak with an analytical ability to separate the emotion of love from the pragmatism of the compromises they need to make to land the correct rather than perfect partner. Men were more led by their sex drive, and in being so were blinded to the subordination of their needs to those of women's.

Ben was convinced that nature cannot be interfered with. Men would inevitably stray in response to a basic need they made no attempt to understand, instead blaming their hunting ancestors and genetic imprinting.

In doing so they would merely endorse and affirm women's conviction that they are essentially unreliable. He was certain that in time, their pragmatism and objectivity would bring the realisation that they really had no further use or need for men. Looking around at colleagues and acquaintances older than himself, he detected a pattern of men being rejected at a time when they were probably contemplating a retirement with their long term partner. This had puzzled Ben, who had always subscribed to the axiom that if couples had been together for many years, there seemed little point in parting at the point where they would have the luxury of more time in each other's company. But the cynic in him proposed the logical thought that women would examine what was in it for them in the twilight of their husband or partner's life. Many would surely come to the conclusion that they would be presented with an obstacle in the path of the vacuum cleaner, someone who wished to live his life through them, thus interrupting an independent life they had created for themselves as a matter of necessity outside their husband's work. The less than attractive prospect of the autumn of their life as an unpaid carer would most certainly make them revisit the cliched plan, and decide to opt out of it.

That they would be able to do so was predicated on a number of certainties. They would have no need or capability of further children, their nurturing instincts satiated by the arrival of grandchildren. This would have the added benefit of dispensing with the messy and now somewhat tedious business of sex. As a couple they would have accumulated a certain material wealth. The comfort of an equal share of this asset base would invariably be considered to be sufficient to guarantee financial independence, so the other great tenet of male superiority as the supreme provider would crumble in the face of reality. Perhaps women who did not opt for this course of partition were held in the stocks of their marriage by an insufficiency of assets rather than by any feelings of loyalty. For the rest, the realisation that they could indeed at last achieve their own sovereignty would be the signal they needed to release their partners, turning them out to roam the landscape predatorily as nature intended, much as old buffalo are pushed out of the herd, but with only a decaying pool of the blue-rinsed and needy widowed from which to select a companion for the years left to them.

Ben was not normally given to moments of self-analysis, but was subliminally aware his own upbringing had developed in him a muscular habit of self-interest and self-preservation. The cynical metaphorical glances over the shoulder he had been accused of at times were no more than a defence mechanism against being let down or left behind, and an instinctive distrust, even of those he should have no reason to doubt. The pleasure in his embryonic affair with Sally, which he had every intention of propagating, nurturing and continuing, provided the confirmation he needed to justify to himself his extra-marital liaison, whilst conveniently glossing over the transgression that Sally was a colleague, and technically a junior to him in the hierarchy of the Agency.

The door of Ben's office opened noisily, startling him out of his reverie and momentarily disorientating him. He had no idea how long his thoughts had been wandering. He had been daydreaming and, like so many dreams, its detail floated away and became instantly impossible to recall. John strode in waving a piece of paper.

"Have you seen this latest bit of lunacy from Carter?" he said. "He can't be serious. The man's not got enough to do." John's normally equable temperament seemed to have deserted him.

"I've not seen anything yet today," said Ben, holding out his hand for the paper.

John had walked purposefully to the window, and was looking out across the roofs of the buildings on the opposite side of the street, his hands clasped behind his back, crumpling the memo between them. Ben got up and went over to him and took the paper from him, reading it's content as John carried on speaking.

"He's come up with this idea that junior Account Executives should only be allowed two door cars. Four door cars are for the likes of us, and main Board Directors of course. Apparently one of the juniors has ordered a car the suppliers can only get in the four-door version at the moment. Some problem with the production line apparently. Carter's asked me to get in touch with the supplier and ask them to weld the back doors shut."

Ben laughed involuntarily. "Can I be there when you call?" he said.

"Ben, I can't do that. They'll think I'm calling from some asylum. The whole four-door, two-door issue is crazy anyway. What sort of inspirational incentive initiative does he think that is? Does he really think anyone is going to work harder, or be more efficient, or whatever he wants them to be just so they can add an extra couple of doors to their car?"

"Well, the corporate dream machine is a pretty

emotive issue for most people," said Ben. "For a lot of people an upgrade in car seems more important than a salary hike."

"I know that," said John, "but this is ridiculous."

"Well, I think you should embrace this new management encouragement programme," said Ben, laughing. "You could really go for it. Suggest to Carter that only executives should be allowed to put the loo seat down. All lesser mortals in the Company would have to sit on the porcelain."

"Piss off," said John. " I should have known I'd get no sympathy from you." The door to Ben's office opened and Sally walked in.

"Ben, about tonight...." she said, before suddenly noticing John by the window.

"Oh, hi," she said hesitantly. "I'll come back."

Sally quickly turned and left the room, feeling a slight flush rise up her face. There was a momentary silence that clattered around the office like a pebble in a shaken tin can.

"So, this thing you two have got going," said John. "Is it serious?"

"What thing?" said Ben, a cold hand squeezing his stomach.

"Well, I assume you two haven't been discussing knitting patterns or competitive reviews during your little tête-à-têtes. Cosy dinners à deux get noticed."

Ben felt himself flush slightly. "I hadn't realised you had noticed," he said.

"I don't think there's anyone here who hasn't," said John, "or at least who doesn't know about it."

"You're kidding," said Ben.

"Er, `fraid not," said John. "Come on Ben, you know what people are like. They love a story, a gossip. And if it comes with a helping of scandal, well.... what can I say? They're on to it like dogs at a bone."

"How long have you known?" said Ben.

"Was your night together at the conference the first time?" asked John.

"Yes."

"Well, from the beginning then I suppose. Quite a few people noticed, and it just spread from there. Does Lucy know?"

"God, no," said Ben. "No, she doesn't. And I don't want her to, so don't say anything to Sue, please. You know what women are like. The sisterhood. She'd be straight round to Lucy."

John moved away from the window and sat down in the seat in front of Ben's desk.

"Of course I won't," he said, "but how long do you think you can keep this from her? It's bound to come out. That's why I asked if it's serious. It's none of my business, but when Sue eventually tackles me about it, which she will, what do I say? I don't like having to lie to her. She'd see straight through it anyway."

"No, it's not serious," said Ben. "It's just, you know, well…a bit of fun really. I mean, I don't want to settle down in a cosy life with Sally or anything. She's just fun to be with and makes me feel wanted."

"I'm not being judgemental here, mate, but I do

think Lucy and the kids want you too you know."

"Well, it doesn't feel too much like that at the moment," Ben replied. "Lucy's so wrapped up in her bloody father, I may as well not be there. I just feel I'm only good as a walking chequebook. As long as Cheque-book Charlie pays the bills he has some use. A Trappist monk has more sex than I do and there's not much bloody appreciation for working my arse off here to give her the lifestyle she has."

"I really don't want to get into this too deep," said John. "I just wanted to know what to say to Sue when she brings it up."

"Just deny you know anything. That's the best thing to do."

"I can't," said John. "It's not how we are together and as I just said, Sue would see through that straight away."

"Well, you could just say there's nothing in it," said Ben.

"If you think that's the case," John replied.

Ben fell silent for a moment. "I just don't know," he said. "I know I should end it, but it's such fun. She's fun. I haven't had too much of that lately. We connect somehow. Perhaps I could persuade Lucy to let me carry on seeing Sally. They could share me."

"I can't believe you think that's possible Ben. Are you crazy? It would never work and even if they both did agree to such a weird arrangement, it would never last. Everyone wants more. As for Sally being fun, of course she's fun," said John. "She's young, she has no responsibilities, and you have a bigger bank account than she does. You can afford to show her a good time, better than anything boys her age she knows could."

"It's not like that," said Ben. "She's fond of me."

"Really Ben? Are you sure? Anyway, I really don't want to get into this," John said, standing up. "Just be careful because this is likely to end in tears."

"I will be," said Ben. "We're being very discreet."

"Discreet enough for the entire company to know about it," said John over his shoulder as he went out of the door.

Ben leaned back in his chair again. He was fully aware of how he was being pulled between his duty to Lucy and the thrill of what he perceived as an enigmatic relationship. He had somehow revelled in the knowledge that his friends would hardly believe him capable of the sheer effrontery of it, admiring his chutzpah if they found out. He had felt the affair had given him a certain élan and he had revelled slightly in what he had believed to be its anonymity. John's revelation that it was not the secret he had thought it to be alarmed him slightly. In the excitement of the affair he had naively given no thought to its consequences. If he were honest with himself, he would accept he had pushed out of his mind any glimmer of a thought about the morality of his actions, subliminally aware that letting any such scruples come to the fore would have terminal consequences for his assignations, and he didn't want the good times to stop.

The phone on his desk rang, startling him. He picked it up as he swung his chair around to his desk and put his elbows on the papers spread across it. A newspaper lay on the desk at Ben's elbow and its headline once more caught his eye as it blazoned its vicarious interest in the fallout from the recent crash in the stock markets. Its editorial stance, which Ben had read on the way in to the office, seemed to be that the unthinking public had been duped by the Government's siren call of wider share ownership. The politically motivated exhortations for all to benefit from the divestment of Nationalised Industries were in truth a thinly disguised inducement born out of the Government's need to fuel its short-term obligations. Having responded to the lure of quick gains, the generally inexperienced fledgling capitalists were now abandoned by that same Government, and left to learn the hard lessons of a market economy and the concept of *'caveat emptor.'* Ben felt the Government had acted like prostitutes, purveyors of a volatile commodity they had sold to the uninitiated and innocent public without acceptance of responsibility for the moral implications of their actions. The article mused on the hypocrisy of the retribution the regulatory framework the Government had put in place would have visited upon any company that had perpetrated such an obvious fraud on the public but as ever in the seat of power, accountability and acceptance of responsibility for mistakes were not part of the Westminster moral code.

"Ben hi, it's me," said Sally. "I'm sorry I interrupted there. I didn't know John was in with you."

"Not a problem," said Ben, smiling a comfortable smile of desire. "We were just going through some internal issues he's got stuck with."

"I've just seen him go to his office, so I knew it would be OK to call now. Is tonight still on?"

"Oh yes, definitely," said Ben. "I'll pick you up from your flat at eight."

"OK," Sally said. "See you there. Looking forward to it."

"Me too," said Ben, holding the phone until he heard the click of it being put down. He put his receiver down as well, and it rang again almost immediately.

"And have something cold and ready in the fridge before the hot and sticky," he said into the receiver.

There was a momentary silence before Lucy spoke.

"What do you mean?" she asked.

"Oh hi," said Ben, his thoughts racing. "I was just asking the temp here to stock the fridge for what's likely to be a difficult client meeting we've got later this evening."

"Sounded pretty familiar for a temp," said Lucy, forcing a laugh.

"Yeah, she's one of those crazy ones. Probably does temp work because she couldn't hold down a permanent job."

"I'm sorry to interrupt," said Lucy, "but I've just come from Dad and he's not good. I want to go back tonight to talk to them about him. Can you come?"

"Oh, I'm really sorry," said Ben. "This client meeting's going to be a late one, and then we'll have to have a bit of a post mortem about it afterwards. I really can't get out of it and might even book into a hotel here as it's an early start tomorrow. Can't we go at the weekend?"

"No, I want to go now. It's awful there, and I'm worried they'll ask us to take him away if he gets any worse."

Lucy began to cry softly. She was sitting hunched forward on the edge of the sofa in the drawing room, her elbows on her knees, her forehead in her hand as she held the phone to her ear. Tears ran down her nose and dripped onto her shoes. She reached down and wiped the wetness with her fingers.

"Well, it's just impossible," said Ben firmly. "This

is important here, and I'm sure they're not going to throw George out. That's silly. Ring them up and tell them we'll come in on Saturday morning. Look, I must get on. I've got to get ready for this meeting. I'll try and call you this evening. I'll be very late and I'll eat here, so don't wait up."

Ben put the phone down quickly, eager to cut the connection. He got up and strode out of the room, with no particular idea where he was going, but feeling the need to exercise to calm the slight tremor in his hands, perambulating off the adrenaline that had surged into his system. As he walked he was aware the phone call from Lucy had been a close shave, and he felt a curious mixture of relief and excitement at having got away with it. The risk he was taking with his liaison had been pulled sharply into focus by his slip on the phone with Lucy. As he walked through the building he felt calmer and, taking a deep breath and exhaling sharply through his lips, he returned to his desk to attend to the report he had been meaning to read all morning.

In the silent house, Lucy frowned at the receiver as she slowly placed its stillness in the cradle. Something had changed, and her feminine intuition detected subtle undertones in Ben's voice, despite his assured performance. Perhaps she was putting too much pressure on him with her concerns about her father, but her need for help and companionship in dealing with the issues the old man cultivated was at times overwhelming. Did the elderly all propagate problems in a seemingly uninterrupted torrent? George seemed to have the ability to produce a new crop daily, like a magician pulling a stream of bunting from a child's ear, and Lucy had begun to fear what might greet her when she visited him. She felt out of control, and Ben's seeming indifference hurt. She folded her arms and hugged herself in a foetal response to her sense of solitude as she walked through to the kitchen to go through the motions of preparing the children's evening meal.

CHAPTER 15

Returning to the empty and silent house after dropping the children off at their schools was always a moment of pleasure for Lucy. Felicia habitually went out to her English classes in the morning, although Lucy suspected the majority of the classes were conducted in the arms of some other foreign student who was probably hirsute and seductively swarthy, someone more interested in the study of female anatomy and gynaecology than in English as a foreign language. Lucy couldn't help but feel that Felicia's talents were probably equal to any young Lothario's desires, a sign of her rebellion against a strict Catholic upbringing in a village where old ladies with beards, facial warts and halitosis hired themselves out as chaperones to young girls on dates, a bromide as welcome and distracting to their suitors as itching-powder in a condom.

Unwittingly, of course, those shaggy harridans ran the risk of a task too well done, giving a stark glimpse into the future for the young men. How many chose the Church and the refuge of celibacy rather than face the rigours of sex in later life with a woman with a face like a bad tempered camel with ruptured haemorrhoids? Under the protective shelter of an ecclesiastical umbrella the fugitive young men could pursue and satisfy their clandestine physical needs in the wider community, without taking on the commitment of companionship and fatherhood, with its attendant daily glance into a Dantean future.

Felicia clearly had a smorgasbord of choice in her range of lovelorn swains, judging by the phone calls for her, and by the steady stream of breathless and clearly priapic young male visitors wearing a furrow in the path to the front door. Ben referred to them as the Tom Cats, likening the cigarette ends they left on the doorstep to feline territorial marking. The most persistent was a young Argentinean called Carlos, who Ben called the Copious Copulator, an alliterative reference to the alarmingly tight jeans he seemed to favour. The ever present and disconcerting bulges in them were an unsubtle visual clue to what was on his mind. Even Lucy had to admit he was a vertical expression of a horizontal desire, and she shuddered to think what Felicia's parents might say at the thought of this sexual gourmand's eager finger on their doorbell, and potentially in their daughter.

In her heart, Lucy knew she should speak to Felicia,

to give maternal warnings of the indifference the likes of Carlos would show to her fate if she were to become pregnant. Fatherhood and its close companion 'responsibility,' those twin antidotes to a career bachelor's desire, were unlikely to be long term objectives of the likes of Carlos.

Lucy feared for Felicia's life in the illiberal environment of her village back home if she were to return with a child but without a husband. The truth of the matter was Lucy did not feel she had the energy to take on one more problem, particularly now, and so she had avoided the issue, assuaging her sense of guilt with the knowledge that what she didn't see she didn't know. She had tried to reason away this patent naivety with the thought that Felicia wasn't her responsibility and as an adult must make her own decisions, but Lucy knew this was a cop-out and so she just blanked the concern from her mind.

While she waited for the kettle to finish boiling, Lucy cleared away the breakfast implements that had been drying on the draining board while she was out. She poured the boiled water into a cup of strong coffee and took it to the small armchair in the corner of the kitchen with the morning's newspaper. Bright sunlight shone through the window across the room. Lucy was in the habit of taking a snatched moment each morning to relax, read the paper and gather her thoughts before the day ran away with itself. As she settled down with the paper on her lap and the warm cup clasped to her chest in both hands, the phone next to her rang. The unexpectedness of its shrill tone exploded into the silence of the house and made her jump. Angered by the fright, and irritated at the interruption, she picked it up quickly.

"Yes", she said sharply, quickly aware of the asperity of her tone.

"Lucy? Is that you?"

"Yes," she replied hesitantly.

"Hi, it's James. How are you?"

"Oh my God! James! Oh, I'm sorry, I was miles away. I must have sounded so grumpy. I was just sitting here with a cup of coffee and the phone gave me a fright."

Lucy was conscious she was gabbling, words rushing out in an uncontrolled and animated stream and that her cheeks were reddening.

"Where are you? It's been so long. What are you doing?" As she spoke, Lucy was aware that she must sound almost incoherent.

"Time for coffee, eh?" said James, teasingly ignoring the stream of questions. "Tough life, is it? I can just see you sitting there, with your legs tucked under you and the cup under your chin."

"Yes," laughed Lucy, "I am. How did you guess?"

"That's how you always sat," he replied. "I can still see you in the bay window of that hotel we went to in Fowey, the morning sun shining through the window on your hair. You were looking out over the bay...."

"Yes, I remember," said Lucy. "That was such a good weekend."

"How are you?" said James. "I'd love to see you. I'm back in the UK now. Have been for a couple of months. I've bought a house in London."

"I'm fine," said Lucy. "Well, sort of. Dad's really bad. He's in a home now and has pretty much lost his mind. It's so sad. I'm going up to see him this afternoon."

"I'm sorry," said James. "He was such a nice guy. I liked him. Do you want me to come with you?"

"Oh, that would be great," said Lucy, flushing again. "But you don't want to come all that way. He won't even know who I am, let alone you. It's years since he last saw you."

"It's not a problem," said James. "And I could see you and catch up with all your news on the way. I could come round. I've got your address. I got it from Sue."

"That would be great," said Lucy. "I'll be going just after lunch. Why don't you come here for a bite to eat first, and then we can head off. It'll just be a salad if that's alright?"

"Perfect," said James. "I'll be there for lunch. Looking forward to it."

The phone went dead. Lucy replaced it and picked up her coffee mug again, her wedding ring clicking against it as she hugged it to herself. The noise of the ring on the china mug startled her abruptly into the present and out of her memories. Flustered, she got up and busied herself about the ground floor of the house in a flurry of tidying.

CHAPTER 16

The slightly overweight waiter walked effeminately to the table with a cafetière on a small silver tray. Ben had noticed during the meal that the man seemed to cross his feet in front of each other as he moved about the room, like a catwalk model. The affect was to give his buttocks the appearance of a couple of cats squabbling in a sack, which Ben felt was probably not exactly the image the plump man had in mind. The waiter put the coffee on the table and minced off to the kitchen, a crisp white cloth over his limply held arm and pouting a moue with his full, soft lips at the guests at the tables as he passed. Ben picked up the hot coffee and filled the two cups in front of him.

"What have you said to your wife about this weekend?" said Sally as she picked up a lump of Demerara sugar between her long fingernails and dropped it gently into her coffee. Ben watched the feminine delicacy of the movement with fascination, subconsciously comparing it with the inelegant opencast mining style he would expect from a male companion.

"Well, Lucy is pretty much preoccupied with her

father at the moment, so I doubt she'll notice I'm away," he replied. "I've told her we've got a new business pitch to prepare for and we're all going to be at it over the weekend in a hotel."

"Delicately put," said Sally.

"You know what I mean," laughed Ben.

"Do you think she suspects?" said Lucy. "About us, I mean."

"God no, she has no idea," replied Ben. "As I said, she's so bloody focussed on her father you could be living with us and she wouldn't notice."

"I can't believe that," said Sally, raising a quizzical eyebrow.

"You haven't seen her with George," Ben said. "It borders on the obsessional. I come a long way down the pecking order at the moment. I sometimes feel I'm just a walking chequebook, but of no great interest to her apart from that. I work my butt off while she swans about doing her classes, having stressful coffee mornings and lunches with her muckers and going to see her father, who she tells me doesn't know who she is. I asked her what was the point in going?"

"What did she say?" asked Sally.

"Nothing. Well, nothing I can remember," said Ben.

"Aren't you just being a bit jealous?" said Sally.

"What do you mean?" said Ben. "What's there to be jealous about?"

"The attention she's giving him, perhaps?"

"That's ridiculous." Ben almost spluttered his indignation.

"Is it?" said Sally. "Why shouldn't she see him? He is her father, and from what you say, he can't have long to go."

"God, 1 hope not," said Ben. "Our lives just seem to be on hold for him at the moment, and they're difficult enough as it is without having to play second fiddle to someone who's off with the fairies. George really is the perfect example of the need for a bit of State sponsored euthanasia."

"That's dreadful," said Sally. "How can you be so callous?"

"Well, I mean, look at him. He's no use to anyone, doesn't know anyone, costs a fortune to keep, contributes nothing. Just a drain. If he were an Eskimo, they'd put him out for the Polar Bears. In fact, thinking about it, I can see a business opportunity in there. EXIT Tours. Imagine it. The business could always undercut the holiday travel opposition because clients wouldn't need to buy a return ticket. Their ends could be wildly exotic, and they could choose whether that be by general squashing, chewing, an ivory enema or just some vigorous pulling apart. Natural waste disposal would save money on an expensive funeral. I think it's a brilliant idea."

"Are you serious?" said Sally.

"Of course not," said Ben. "It's probably against the law, apart from anything else."

"No, I mean about your father-in-law."

"Oh, that," said Ben. "Well, his life is pretty pointless, isn't it? It's got no quality, and it's such a strain on us all."

"Perhaps that's more the issue," said Sally. "Perhaps that's what any mercy killing is about, getting rid of an inconvenience. Like capital punishment. Still sounds pretty callous to me."

"Well, it's not going to happen," said Ben, weary of the subject of his father-in-law and eager to move on to more comfortable ground. He reached across the table and put his hand over Sally's. "Let's go up to bed. We've got an early start on the golf course in the morning, and I'm tired. We can have a drink in the lounge before we go up."

He pushed back his chair from the table, threw his crumpled napkin next to his plate and pulled the table out to let Sally out of her seat. She took his arm as they moved through the tables to leave the room.

At her table the other side of the dining room, shielded by a large rubber plant, Jane watched the couple walk out of the room over the top of the napkin she held over the lower part of her face, ready to raise it if they turned around to look in her direction. She felt a seething resentment rising in her.

"Men are such bastards!" she said to her companion. "Who do you think she is?"

"I don't even know who he is," said the man opposite her, "let alone her. And in any case, it's none of my business. Nor yours, for that matter."

"It is when he's two timing my friend," said Jane.

"How do you know he is," said the man. "They could be having a business meeting, or something completely innocent. You can't just jump to conclusions."

"I don't think she's running over spreadsheets with him," said Jane, "just spreading herself on them. Did you see them? Couldn't leave each other alone over their bloody cosy little candlelit supper. God, I can't believe he's doing that to poor Lucy, not now."

"Stop working yourself up into a lather. It isn't going to help, and it still isn't any of your business. Just drop it and let's finish our meal."

"Chris, that's such a typical male response. Brush it under the carpet. Pretend nothing's happening, help the brotherhood. Well, I can't just 'drop it' as you say. Lucy really needs help now, and seeing him here with his bit of floozy is just so unfair. I just knew he was up to something. It makes me so angry....."

"Jane. Jane. Can we move on?" said Chris, knowing as he said it the naïve futility of his request.

They finished their meal to the accompaniment of small talk, and decided to have coffee in the lounge rather than at the table. Settling into the deep cushions in one of the armchairs, Chris put his head back and closed his eyes to enjoy the languorous postprandial moment, the smoke from the cigar in his hand drifting across his face, tiredness from the day sweeping down through his body. An involuntary jolt woke him to the realisation that he was falling asleep in the chair, and also to the fact that Jane was striding purposefully across the lounge to a secluded alcove at the far end of the large room where Chris could see a couple were snuggled up on a small sofa, heads together and absorbed in each other. With a feeling of dread at what the occupants of the room were about to be entertained to, Chris realised the love birds on the sofa were the couple from the dining room whose assignation had so infuriated Jane. Knowing her fiery temper and fondness for speaking her suffragist mind, Chris could only sit in trepidation at the inevitable pyrotechnics that must surely follow. He glanced around for the exit as he considered the allure of a cowardly retreat from the coming conflagration.

On reaching the romantic little corner, Jane stood staring down at the unsuspecting couple for a moment, until Ben became aware of the presence of an intruder and looked up with a frown of annoyance on his brow.

"You bastard," Jane said. "You complete bastard. What the hell do you think you're doing?" Her voice worked up the gears through the decibels, and stirred coffee cups fell silent in the room behind her.

Ben's shock was palpable, his face ashen, his mind mysteriously transported back years. For some unaccountable reason, the memory of his first serious attempt at a sexual encounter with the young assistant matron at school came flooding back with the same bad taste in his mouth. Now, with the incandescent Jane in front of him and the numbness of a crumbling life behind him, Ben sat speechless, his mind frozen in horror as it was overwhelmed with the reality of the consequences of his dalliance becoming public and how much he had to lose.

"How could you, and now of all times?" she shouted. "You should be ashamed of yourself but no, you wouldn't know what shame is would you?"

Ben was still dumbstruck, staring at her. She

turned on her heel and marched back across the room to her seat where she wordlessly picked up her handbag and headed imperiously for the door. Chris struggled to his feet and followed her, protesting he must pay the bill before they could leave the hotel, cursing the couple for cancelling his evening of pleasures of the flesh. Jane was definitely not going to be too receptive to any tender moments of their own but he consoled himself with the thought that the other man was probably in the same boat. Coffee cups clinked in the room behind them as their owners stirred vigorously, filling the uncomfortable silence.

CHAPTER 17

Ben sat staring at the phone on his desk, the fingers of his right hand nervously spinning a pencil as he listened to the ringing tone of the unanswered phone in his left ear.

"For God's sake Jane, pick it up," he muttered aloud. "Where the hell are you?"

He had already rung the number three times since arriving at work, and was now convinced Jane was not answering on purpose. He had arrived home the morning after the shrapnel of his exploding weekend tryst had clattered about him. Sally's interest in energetic moments under the bedclothes was less than enthusiastic after the confrontation with Jane. She had come to the conclusion that whilst younger men might have pygmy expense accounts, they were less likely to come with the baggage of guilt from stolen moments. Ben watched her as she packed her things in her bag, and as she angrily and silently disentangled some of his clothes from hers and threw them into his overnight case. She called for a taxi that would take her to the arms of eager and more taught-fleshed, firm-thighed youths, who would be unencumbered by the distractions and inconvenience of a marriage certificate in their overnight bag, or for that matter by deranged acquaintances who appeared through the furniture and potted plants at compromising moments, evangelising about fidelity, to her thinking an outmoded commodity.

His sense of loss and abandonment were soon supplanted by the practical problem of how he was going to face Lucy. He was in a restless frenzy and had been unable to sleep, pacing the room in the hotel. He rehearsed two scenarios that might greet his homecoming, the more difficult one if Jane had called Lucy and the other if she had not. His quandary was how to get hold of Jane before she spoke to Lucy, and to do that he had to go home to find her telephone number in Lucy's address book.

After his peripatetic night in the room, Ben showered and shaved, and called room service for a cup of coffee to be brought up. He felt unable to face anything to eat, and certainly unwilling to be seen by any of the other guests in the dining room, some of whom would have witnessed his denouement the evening before. He had nervously called Lucy when he knew she would probably be up, and was relieved to hear in her voice that Jane had obviously not called.

"I've finished a bit early, so I'm going to come home now," he said.

"That's fine," Lucy had said distractedly. "Will you be back for lunch?"

"Yes. Yes, I will," said Ben.

"O.K. I'll see you when you get back then," Lucy said. "Drive carefully."

"I will," said Ben, before realising he was speaking to an empty phone.

Lucy had rung off. She had seemed somewhat distant. Ben wondered if this was a bad sign. Perhaps Jane had called and Lucy knew. He decided on balance that Jane had not made the call, but that he had better get back as soon as possible to run interference on all the calls into the house.

As it turned out, there had been no phone call from Jane, and Lucy was not a good enough actress to have hidden the knowledge for a whole day if Jane had told her, breathless with the excitement and righteous indignation of her news scoop. He had come home to the usual family greeting. A quick kiss from a busy

Lucy, a cursory "Hi Dad" from Sebastian and from Emma a warm hug around the neck. He had unpacked his weekend case, throwing his dirty linen into the clothes-basket in the bathroom, carefully rubbing some of his aftershave onto his shirts to hide any lingering scent from Sally's perfume. Hoping he had covered his tracks, Ben came down to the normality of a Sunday at home. There had only been two phone calls during the rest of the day, and to Ben's relief when he answered the phone, each had been from mothers of friends of the children, calling to synchronise diaries with Lucy for the coming week's extracurricular activities.

Never before had the customary rhythms of a Sunday stood out in such sharp focus for Ben, and he felt an exquisite pain at the prospect of the loss of all that was about him at home if Lucy found out about Sally. He knew the sensible thing to do was to tell Lucy before she was called by Jane, to throw himself at her mercy and beg her forgiveness. She would be hurt and angry, but surely she would understand. But then again, would she? She would have to. After all, it was her fault he had taken up with Sally. It was she who had redirected her affection and attention to George, leaving Ben out in the cold and tempted by Sally's charms, which he still missed as he mourned the loss of having the best of both worlds.

Now, in the middle of this bleak Monday morning, Ben felt a hunted man, in the sights of a stalker roaming at large, permanently in the cross hairs of an emotional gun, one with an irrationally deranged and angry woman's finger on the trigger. In the end, his courage had failed him and he had not said anything to Lucy. He had instead opted for a roll of the dice, gambling that he could talk his way out of the situation with some carefully selected and credible explanations. Jane held his future in her unsympathetic hands. The years fell away and once more he felt hopelessly in the power of a greater force, one that was able to manipulate and dictate his life at will, and without reference to his own feelings or wishes. The loss of control of his destiny unsettled him deeply, shaking the foundations of his being. His mind continuously rehearsed and honed the conversations he might have with Lucy, in which he justified his actions by transferring the blame to her. He had now convinced himself the affair would never have happened if he had not been neglected. What did she expect?

It wasn't until midday that Jane finally answered the phone.

"Where have you been?" said Ben. "I've been calling you all morning."

"I know," said Jane coldly.

"Why the hell didn't you answer?" Ben's tension overflowed in an uncontrolled torrent.

"I don't think you're exactly in a position to pontificate to me, do you? I suppose contrition is too much to expect from a man, but a bit of civility wouldn't go amiss." Jane was clearly not going to be intimidated by anyone, let alone by one she considered a philanderer.

"I'm sorry, but you can imagine how I feel" Be said.

"Actually, Ben, I can't, so please don't drag me down into your sordid little world."

"Are you going to tell Lucy?" Ben blurted, unable to take the suspense in which he was floating, leaving him feeling vulnerable and defenceless.

"Ah, we get to the heart of the matter. Why do you ask?" said Jane.

"I just don't want Lucy hurt…"

"Well you should have thought of that before you

set off for your dirty weekend away" said Jane, "so I don't buy that. You're just worried about you in all of this, not Lucy."

"It wasn't a dirty weekend away," Ben replied. "We were at a conference and had agreed to have dinner together to go over a joint presentation we were giving next week. Lucy wouldn't understand and would read more into it than exists so I just don't want her being unnecessarily upset and......"

"Ben, Ben," Jane interrupted. "I know what I saw and I wasn't borne yesterday. Colleagues tend not to rub feet against legs under tables, hold hands on tables and cosy up to each other in private booths. So, let's cut the crap. How long has it been going on? Is it serious?

Ben hesitated, realising he was probably sounding ridiculous, a small boy caught with his hand in the sweetie jar and pretending he was just tidying the contents.

"Only a few weeks," Ben replied. "And no, it's not serious. In fact, it's over."

"Hardly surprising, I suppose," said Jane. "I wouldn't imagine your little floozie felt much like having a romantic moment with you after my little intrusion into your cosy dinner together."

"So, are you going to tell Lucy?"

"I don't know," said Jane. "I haven't decided yet. How could you do that Ben? Just when she needs you most. You do know how worried she is about her father, don't you?"

"But that's it," said Ben. "There's no room in her life for me. It's all about George. George is wetting himself. George has lost his teeth again. George has been caught in bed with someone again, George….."

"Ben, if you could just hear yourself. That's so bloody selfish."

"Well, it's true. But it's not the issue. What's the point in upsetting Lucy? She doesn't know about this, and if you tell her, it'll be your fault that she's hurt. It's over, and it's not going to happen again, so why not just leave it at that? Forget it happened. I will. You and I are the only people who know about this. If Lucy doesn't find out no harm is done. Where's the profit in hurting her?"

The phone was silent, but Ben knew Jane must be

listening as there was no cut-off tone.

"Jane, are you there?" he asked.

"Yes," she said.

"Well, what do you think?" he asked. "You're not going to say anything, are you? It would achieve nothing."

"I'm just coming to terms with it being my fault if Lucy gets hurt," Jane said. "That's breathtaking, Ben. It really deserves a medal in responsibility dodging. Anyway, you think about it and stew in it for a while. If nothing else, not knowing my decision and having to guess will make you keep your nose clean."

The phone went dead in his hand and he replaced the handset pensively. It immediately rang again as the girl on reception called to tell him his lunch guests had arrived and were waiting for him.

CHAPTER 18

As Lucy hurried about the house after dropping the children off at school, tidying up after the family and superficially cleaning the worst of the damage from the weekend, she began to regret agreeing to let Felicia take a few days off to go to a rock festival. Apart from the concern that a large percentage of those days were going to be spent in a sleeping bag with one hundred and fifty pounds of erectile tissue called Carlos, she really didn't need the extra chores at the moment. James had offered to take her to see her father again, and he was on his way round. She felt her hair was a mess, even though she had brushed it three times since getting up, and she didn't want to be clearing up when he arrived, and then just rush out. It would be nice to sit down with a cup of coffee to carry on catching up on the past. In her heart she knew they had unfinished business between them. She felt guilty she hadn't mentioned to Ben that James had called and had taken her to the Home, but Ben was so preoccupied, and there just didn't seem to have been the opportunity. In any event she knew he would be difficult about it and she didn't feel like making things worse between them. Ben was being difficult enough as it was, and was acting rather strangely. Work must be stressing him she assumed but while he was being so defensive, James was a conversation she didn't want to open up.

Seeing James again had been a shock. She had not expected to be excited, and it was unsettling. And yet, now that he had reappeared in her life, the need to see him once more was a powerful urge in her. She had read once that relationships that do not end acrimoniously are not properly laid to rest, and run the risk of resurrecting themselves in the future. James had been a special boyfriend in so many ways, her first real love, and it still bemused her as it had bemused their friends at the time that they had not made something permanent out of their time together. There had been no particular cataclysmic separation. It had been more continental drift than volcanic eruption. James had wanted to work abroad and travel, and she had found the tie to her parents too strong and so, without ever seriously discussing it, there came about an unspoken acceptance that they would part, without severing or burying the relationship they had developed. Hence the unfinished business. They had never quite laid to rest the ghost of their past together.

He had, of course, come into her mind now and again over the years since they had gone their separate ways. At first the memories came quite frequently and she would wonder in an idle moment alone where he was and what he was doing. Was he happy and with someone who loved him and made him happy? It was a bitter sweet thought. She hoped he was but was jealous of his new relationship. As time passed and the family and the responsibilities they brought took over her life, he came into her mind less often, as happens with all memories that subordinate themselves to the urgencies of the present.

Lucy was surprised at the ease with which they had slipped back into their comfortable conversations together, aware of a slight pang of conscience at the pleasure his voice and presence brought her. She knew she was flirting with him, her moth drawn irresistibly to his flame, but she didn't want it to stop. Not yet. He had always been easy company, chatty and attentive, and she could not help but compare it with her relationship with Ben, and where that had gone. How different would her life have been if she and James had married? The stark contrast frightened her, and she pushed it from her mind.

Now, sitting next to the sleeping form of her confused husk of a father, Lucy glanced across to James sitting patiently on the other side of the old man. She caught his eye and smiled, even as a small tear escaped from the corner of her eye. She felt that tear encapsulated all her sadness, her loneliness, and she realised there was little point in them remaining as George was clearly not going to waken. There had been no spark of recognition when they had arrived and before he had drifted off to sleep, and the nurse on duty had confirmed they had concerns for him now. He was no longer eating, and had withdrawn into himself completely. As she looked at his lowered head, Lucy wondered where he had gone. Was his mind taking him through the optimism of his youth, running through the fields of freshly mown hay he used to tell her about when she was a small girl and had gone for walks with him in the country. She had loved those stolen moments when she had him to herself, walking next to him with her small hand enveloped in the warmth and comforting softness of his. He had told her how he and his brothers used to play around the hay bales, and about the haystacks they climbed on and lay in, and which he later courted against. Perhaps in his dreams he was there now, lying in the healing warmth of the summer sun on top of a haystack, a piece of straw in the corner of his mouth, a pretty girl's head on his shoulder, wisps of her long blonde hair across his face, watching a red kite circling above in its relentless hunt for food. At least he would be at peace.

Lucy signalled to James with her head, and they

stood up and left the room. James put a comforting arm around her shoulder as they walked down the corridor together, and she involuntarily and quite naturally laid her head on his shoulder and let the tears fall silently, realising she was not mourning her father alone but a missed opportunity and a life now empty in so many ways. There was so much more to her grief, so much more to mourn, and it seemed all the more terrible for that.

"I'm so sorry, Lucy," said James. "It must be so hard for you to see him like that. I wish there was something I could do."

"There's nothing any of us can do. I know that," said Lucy. "We just have to sit and watch nature take its course. It's just so hard. So unfair. Thank you for being here."

"I know," said James. "It makes me appreciate my parents, if that's any consolation," he added, laughing briefly.

"I'm glad," said Lucy. "And you should. You don't know it's there until it's taken away, and now there's no chance of getting it back. There's so much I wanted to say to Dad, and now it's too late. I so wanted to tell him how much he means to me, to thank him for everything he has done for me. He was everything to me, the constant in my life, the beacon I always sailed home to, where I could rest and heal, and I never told him. And I can't. It hurts."

"I think he probably knew that," said James.

"But I didn't say it. I didn't tell him. Not directly. That's really hard."

"He understood, I'm sure," said James, feeling inadequate at the little consolation his few words held for Lucy. They reached the car where they parted to move either side of it, until that moment both seemingly unaware that James still had his arm around Lucy, and she hers around his waist. It had seemed so natural.

CHAPTER 19

"'Ow many we got today then Stan?"

Jim mopped his sweating face with a large, grubby red and white neckerchief, reaching behind with his other hand to extract the seat of his capacious trousers from between his buttocks where the cloth appeared to have burrowed and taken refuge, like a large bed sheet being forcibly pulled though a wedding ring.

Stan consulted a clipboard in the crook of his arm, running a stubby, broken-nailed and nicotine stained finger down a column of names.

"Six today Jim," he said, pushing back the peak of his greasy flat cap in a gesture of studied exasperation. "Fucking six of them! You'd think they'd 'ave the bloody sense to spread 'em out. We'll 'ave to do the last tomorrow. I'm not staying late again, not me! Arsenal are playing tonight."

Stan was of Eastern European extraction, short and swarthy, with a luxurious moustache modelled on a Mexican bandit he had once seen in a cheap Latin

American film that somehow contrived to involve Jesse James meeting Frankenstein's monstrous creation. Jim's mastery of geography was limited. His cartographic knowledge was restricted to the streets of the borough in which he lived, its pubs the trig points that guided him, and so he had never been able to ascertain exactly where his colleague had been born and had lived before he had moved to England. He had certainly never been able to pronounce his co-worker's full name, Stanislaus, and so had quickly settled on the diminutive. For his part, Stan had immediately felt accepted by its easy familiarity. To him its use represented the essential badge of the camaraderie and brotherhood of the workplace.

"Nor me, mate," agreed Jim, hitching the large leather belt slung beneath his overhanging belly. He reached out and took the clipboard from Stan. His brow creased as he stared at it, his pendulous lips moving as he slowly read the words on the page.

"Look at the size of number two!" he snorted. "That one's going to take half the day to do by itself! I'm going to see the Guv'nor about this. It ain't right."

Jim tucked the clipboard firmly under his arm and set off for the door. Stan quickly fell in step behind him, his short steps forming an unchoreographed dance as he hopped from side to side behind the large form that loomed above and before him, fussing in Jim's wake like a tender bouncing in the disturbed water behind a yacht.

The crematorium manager was seated at his desk, his attention focused on the cheap pornographic magazine that lay open before him. Breasts were his weakness and the magazine specialised in the outsized, regular featuring Maureen the Mammary Marvel who had become something of an old friend of his. The morning sun shone weakly through the grime-smeared window behind him, catching the dust floating and dancing in the air like mayflies in the slanting evening light above a trout stream. The door to his office burst open as the small delegation pushed officiously and unannounced into his cramped and untidy office. Files lay scattered over a table in the corner, their contents rupturing out of them and spilling over the surface and onto the floor beneath. A metal spike on the desk impaled a small tower of invoices, and a heavily stained coffee mug sat half empty by the old bakelite phone. Jim and Stan's unexpected entrance startled the manager and he quickly snatched some papers to cover the magazine, aware that both visitors were staring at it with lascivious smirks on their faces. Glancing down to follow their gaze, he saw one of Maureen's prize winning over-inflated breasts peering out from under the hastily thrown camouflage, and he quickly covered it with his hand in a deliberately nonchalant movement.

"It ain't good enough," said Jim, tossing the clipboard onto the manager's desk and adopting the position of spokesman, his large feet apart and his fleshy hands on his hips. His overhanging stomach stood proud, like the prow of a ship, greasy stains smearing the front of his blue checked shirt.

"What isn't?" said the manager, irritably tapping the papers by his hand with the pencil.

"Six bleeding toastings in one day, that's what," said Jim. "And look at the size of number two. That one's going to take half the bleeding day by itself."

"Half the fucking bleeding day," said Stan, eager not to be sidelined.

The manager marvelled yet again at his staff's ability to detach from their jobs, to depersonalise the objects of their attention. He supposed this was part of some basic survival instinct, to remove emotion from an emotionally charged event, but their callousness never failed to surprise him.

"The new ovens will easily cope," said the manager reassuringly.

The crematorium had recently modernised its equipment, replacing the old ovens with the latest models that were computer controlled and lauded by the manufacturers as the most efficient waste disposal systems available. They automatically weighed the corpse entrusted to them, calculated the length of burn required to complete the task, and generated significantly greater heat than the older models they replaced. The new versions started the cremation process with an all round deluge of intense flames from numerous gas jets that turned off at the appropriate temperature to allow the corpse's own body fats to continue burning and finish the task. In this way they used less fuel, and presented a substantial cost saving to the crematorium over the course of a year.

"I wish we still 'ad the old ones," grumbled Jim. "This new fangled computer stuff does me 'ead in."

"No fucking good," added Stan for emphasis.

"I know they're new, but you'll get the hang of them," said the manager, wincing at Stan's inarticulate contribution. "It'll be less work for you," he added soothingly.

"Yeh, and then you'll get rid of us," said Jim. "Well, we ain't `aving any of that. I ain't losing me job to some bloody machine."

"No one has said anything about losing jobs," said the exasperated manager. "There's only the two of you. How do you think we'd manage with just one?"

"Well, don't even think about it, that's all," said Jim hitching his belt authoritatively.

The manager decided to ignore Jim's comment, seeing little profit in engaging with him. Having made his point, Jim turned and walked out of the office to prepare for the arrival of the first funeral party. Stan hurried after him, his little steps eager to keep up. The manager returned to perusing his magazine to fill the time left to him before he had to go out to meet the first funeral cortège.

As the crematorium manager fantasised over the naked bodies lying on his grubby desk, Lucy sat at her small dressing table and brushed her hair slowly. Her ashen face stared back at her, sad and drawn. The black jacket of her suit only served to highlight her pale cheeks, and with a deep sigh she decided she must apply some more make-up to bring some colour to them. As she did so, Sebastian came into the room and stood by the door watching her solemnly. Lucy relaxed her shoulders and rested her hands in her lap as she looked at him in her mirror.

"Are you alright?" she asked.

Sebastian nodded, biting his lower lip as he held her gaze. Wordlessly he stepped forward and put his arms around Lucy's neck, hugging her tightly.

"It'll be alright, Mum," he said. "You'll feel better in the morning."

"Yes, I know. I will," she said reassuringly, holding his slim forearm in her hand and stroking it comfortingly. She hoped she had spoken with enough conviction to hide the uncertainty and loss she felt. "How's Emma?" she asked.

Sebastian kept his face buried in her hair behind her ear, his voice muffled by it as he answered.

"She's playing," he said. "In the kitchen. Felicia's

with her."

"Why don't you go and see if she's alright," said Lucy. "I'll be down in just a moment. I've nearly finished here."

Sebastian kissed her cheek and turned and left the room to go down to the kitchen. Lucy watched his slim boyish back in the mirror as he walked slowly down the corridor, his arm out to his side as he ran his fingers down the wall. He disappeared around the corner on the landing and she heard his steady footsteps on the stairs. Her little man was growing up fast, changing before her eyes. Looking at herself again in the mirror, she took a deep breath and smoothed her skirt on her lap, aware that she had dreaded this day. In her heart she wished her father's funeral could be a private affair for just her, Ben and the children. The call from the Home had been a shock, even though she had known the moment could not be held off indefinitely. Her father's health had declined so rapidly and she could see what strength he had haemorrhaging out of him as the dam that held his will to live was breached by the corrosion of his exhaustion.

Lucy had picked up the phone when it rang as she was writing a small shopping list. Her mind was distracted by the minutiae of family catering and she was only half listening to the caller's voice.

"Mrs Grayson??"

"Yes," she said distractedly, the phone held between her shoulder and ear as she steadied the slip of paper on the table and added ice cream to the list, remembering Emma's request for it.

"It's the Matron at Mount Pleasant Mrs Palmerston. I'm afraid I have some bad news." The disembodied voice was solicitous and yet businesslike, it's Irish lilt softening its edges.

"Oh," said Lucy. "Is it Dad? Is he worse?"

"I'm afraid he has passed away Mrs Grayson," said the Matron. "We checked on him in his room just now — we had decided to leave him in there this morning you see, rather than take him down to the Day Room with the other residents. He had been fast asleep in his chair when we took in his breakfast, and there didn't seem any point in disturbing the poor soul. When we went in to collect his tray, he had slipped away. He moved on gently in his sleep there Mrs Grayson. It was very peaceful."

Lucy sat silently, numbed by the news, the phone now in her hand, her other hand at her mouth. Part of her mind perversely thought about the ridiculous euphemisms the Matron had used for telling her that her father had died, words more appropriate for ships leaving harbour or for someone moving house. She wanted to scream at the woman to just say, "Your father has died," but she said nothing.

"Are you alright there Mrs Grayson?" asked Matron. "I'm sorry to tell you over the phone but I felt you would want to know as soon as possible."

"Yes. Yes, thank you, I'll be fine," Lucy replied. "Thank you. It's just a bit of a shock really. I know we were expecting it, but somehow I had put it off...."

Her voice trailed off and she sat staring at the words written on the list in front of her.

"We never seem ready for this moment Mrs Grayson," said Matron. "It's always a shock...."

"I'll come over this morning," Lucy interrupted. Suddenly she wanted the conversation to end, to be alone.

"Of course," said Matron. "Come whenever you want. We will have Mr Harkness' things ready for you when you arrive. We can attend to the formalities then."

After sitting quietly for a while, Lucy rang Ben at his office, but was told he was out at a client and could not be contacted. Without thinking, she then called James, who offered to leave his work and come with her to Mount Pleasant. Lucy readily accepted his offer and they drove out to the Home together. As they neared the Home, Lucy felt an overwhelming wave of sadness come over her as the reality of her father's eternal absence from her future washed over her. Silent tears fell down her cheeks and James put his hand across to rest it on hers. She grasped it eagerly, holding it tightly, as a drowning swimmer grasps a lifebelt in a stormy sea.

James parked the car in front of the large building and took Lucy's arm as they walked through the front doors and up to the reception desk where Lucy announced herself. After a short wait the receptionist escorted them down the corridor to the Matron's office. She stood up as they walked in and came around to the front of her neatly organised desk.

"This is obviously a painful time for you Mrs Grayson." she said taking Lucy's hands in hers. "Please take a seat. It's a sad part of our work here and the only comfort I can give you is that he died peacefully in his sleep. In the meantime, there is some paperwork we must complete, but we can be attending to that in a while. Your father is still in his room. Would you like to see him?"

Lucy started slightly and looked quickly at James. She had not imagined her father would still be at Mount Pleasant, or that she might have to see him. She had automatically assumed he would have been collected by the undertakers. She didn't know quite what to do. James leaned forward and put his hand over hers where it lay in her lap.

"You must do as you feel," he said gently.

Lucy looked back at Matron, biting her lower lip.

"Yes, I think I would like to see him," she said.

"He looks very peaceful," Matron said. "I'll take you up."

Lucy and James got up and followed Matron along the familiar corridors to her father's room. Matron opened the door to his room and stood to one side to let

Lucy and James pass. George lay on the bed, the sheet drawn up to his chin. He was on his back, his knees bent up under the sheet such that he lay in the same position he would have been in when sitting in his chair, frozen in place by rigor. He had obviously been moved from his chair to the bed. A piece of bright pink lavatory paper lay over his face. Matron moved around Lucy, went up to the bed and removed the paper from George's face.

"There now, doesn't he just look the peaceful one?" she said in her Irish lilt.

George's clenched teeth grimaced through the rictus of his parted lips. His nostrils were pinched closed. Standing by the side of the bed, Lucy gazed down at her father's yellowed waxen face, unable to recognise the sentient being she had once known in this ivory mask before her. For the briefest moment Lucy expected him to roll his head to the side to look at her with his old smile. It was a surreal sensation to her as she realised this would not happen. She realised he had gone, that he had deserted the sinking vessel that had carried his essence all these years, and this husk was all that remained of her memories of him. She watched his motionless form for a moment longer, transfixed by the stillness of his chest, and then turned and left the room, hurrying for the fresh air and freedom.

Now the pain of the funeral ceremony lay before her and she shivered as she broke her reverie. She made a quick final adjustment to her make up, pushed her hair behind her ears and stood up from her dressing table to follow Sebastian down the stairs. The undertakers had sent a car to take the family to the crematorium for the funeral service and the driver hovered solemnly in the hallway. In the kitchen, Ben was on the telephone and from the one-sided conversation Lucy could hear, he was speaking to his office. She went into the drawing room where Felicia had taken Sebastian and Emma. They were sitting solemnly on the sofa staring at the tall undertaker who was standing in his long black overcoat in front of the fireplace. Like all undertakers he exuded a sense of calm respectfulness and solicitude. Each family's grief is unique to them and whilst he had witnessed the scene and emotions before him a thousand times before, his professionalism refused to allow him to appear to be blasé or casual. He was a class act of the caring and empathetic companion in a moment of bereavement.

"Good morning Mrs Grayson," he said in a hushed and reverential voice. "We can leave whenever you are ready."

"I'll just get my husband," said Lucy. At that moment, Ben came into the room.

"I'm sorry, that was just the office," he said sheepishly, looking back over his shoulder to indicate the telephone in the kitchen. "Are we ready to go?"

The family followed the undertaker to the large limousine waiting in the street outside the house. The children were excited about the fold down jump seats in the stretched back of the car, and squirmed vigorously at the novelty of them. Ben leant forward to calm them, glanced at Lucy next to him and then settled back into his seat for the journey. He somehow felt he should feel guilt at his relief, indeed delight, at George's death, but he rationalised his feelings with the justification that Lucy could not have taken the strain of her father's failing health much longer. Whilst she would mourn his loss, she would surely get over it and have time back to herself in which to get on with her life, and bring the focus of her attention back to the family, and perhaps him. Ben also wrestled with his conscience over his conversation with the Matron at Mount Pleasant a couple of days before George died. He had just come out of a meeting and was collecting some papers to take with him to a client when the phone on his desk rang. His secretary told him that she had the Matron from Mount Pleasant on the line for him. When he tried to get his secretary to put her off, the reply came back that it was urgent and that she really must speak with him.

"Mr Grayson," Matron asked. "Would that be you?"

"Yes Matron, it's Ben Grayson. Matron, is this call really necessary? I'm very busy you know, and I have a taxi waiting to take me to a meeting. Could we not speak later? Next week perhaps?"

"Oh, Mr Grayson," Matron replied. "I'm sorry to be troubling you there, but it is an important matter I have to discuss with you. It's Mr Harkness you know."

"Well, I didn't think you'd be calling to discuss the weather Matron," Ben said.

The phone went silent and Ben waited for Matron to continue, but there was silence.

"Matron? Are you there?" Ben's irritation was palpable.

"Oh, yes Mr Grayson. I'm here fine, thank you."

"Well, what is it you want? I really am in a great hurry."

"It's Mr Harkness, Mr Grayson." The phone fell

silent again.

"What about him," asked Ben.

"Oh, we need your permission Mr Grayson."

"Permission for what Matron?" said Ben. "Could you just come to the point please."

"It's for the drip, Mr Grayson."

"What drip Matron," said Ben, glancing at his watch. His exasperation was beginning to get the upper hand and he struggled not to shout at the obtuse woman at the other end of the phone.

"The drip. We need to give Mr Harkness a drip because he's not taking too much of the fluids at the moment, what with his dribbling when he drinks and all, but because we consider it an invasive surgical procedure, we need permission."

"Why can't you just do it?" Ben asked impatiently.

"We are a Rest Home, not a hospital Mr Grayson, and so strictly we need the permission for things like this. You know, the invasive procedures. Well, your man can't give it, poor lamb, not with his mind off with those fairies like it is, and I cannot get hold of Mrs Grayson so I'm ringing you. May we go ahead with the drip?"

"Well, is there any point?" said Ben. "I mean, it's just going to prolong his agony, and for what Matron? He hardly has what I'd call a quality life, and all we'd do is drag it out. Hardly a kindness I'd say."

"Well Mr Grayson," said Matron, her voice revealing her surprise, " it wouldn't be normal like, not to give it, if you get my meaning. He wouldn't last long without it there, he wouldn't, that's for sure."

"Well, that would probably be a great kindness Matron," said Ben. "I know my father-in-law wouldn't want it. He never wanted to be in this position and I promised him I wouldn't let it happen, so no, I don't think there should be any intervention like this."

"As you wish, Mr Grayson," said Matron. "But if you should be changing your mind will you call me?"

"I certainly will Matron, thank you for calling," replied Ben, eager to get off the phone. "Oh, and by the way Matron," he added. "There's no need to mention any of this to my wife. I'll tell her tonight and I think it would only upset her to discuss it further."

"As you wish, Mr Grayson," said Matron. "I understand."

The phone went quiet as the receiver was put down, and Ben slowly lowered the phone to complete the severance of the connection. He felt a surge of guilt, aware that he had played God, but quickly pushed it to the back of his mind, justifying his callous decision with the consoling thought that he had acted in George's best interests. Whilst George had never actually said he would not want his life prolonged in these circumstances, he had never said he wouldn't, and he had often commented that people lived too long in the second half of the century, thanks to modern medicine and science.

As Ben stared out of the window of the limousine, his conversation with Matron came back to him. George had indeed only lasted a short time after Ben's refusal to grant permission for the drip to be given to him, and Ben could not deny he had felt elated to hear of his death. He glanced across at Lucy who sat next to him, tense and rigid in her seat. She looked at him and smiled thinly and without any conviction before turning back to the road ahead, lost in her thoughts.

The organist at the crematorium shifted his numb buttocks on the hard wooden seat of the organ, once again ruing the fact he had forgotten to bring a cushion. The fourth funeral of the morning was under way, and at least this lot had not asked for 'Smoke Gets In Your Eyes' as the second session had, probably thinking it was both novel and funny. He had the menu from the local Indian takeaway on the music sheets in front of him, and as he pushed out by rote the well-memorised notes of the hymn the congregation behind him were torturing, he gazed at the restaurant's offerings, trying to decide what he would order for his evening meal.

At the furnace behind the chapel, Stan stood in front of the computer screen to the right of the oven doors. He scratched his head, perplexed by the figures in front of him, and somewhat alarmed at the fact most of them seemed to be coloured in red. The oven was making a rather disconcerting roaring noise, and smoke seemed to be seeping out from the seal around the door. He and Jim had had some difficulty pushing the coffin into the oven, as it was the oversized second funeral they had complained to the manager about earlier that morning. The automatic rollers that loaded the coffins into the furnace chamber had struggled to take the strain of the weight of the occupant. Stan and Jim had had to push hard to get the coffin to move, but they had finally managed to get it in. Now, things didn't seem to be quite right and Stan began to worry. The burners still seemed to be going at full steam when they should have turned off, and the temperature readings were climbing quite alarmingly. Jim had gone to the lavatory, and Stan hopped from foot to foot, flapping his arms in agitation as he waited for him to come back.

When he did, Stan ran over to him and clutched at his sleeve, pulling him towards the ovens.

"Jim, she's fucking burning up," he said, pulling at Jim's check shirtsleeve.

"She's meant to be, Stan," said Jim, laughing. "They don't come here for a shower mate. We don't fuck about here."

"No, Jim mate," said Stan. "She really fucking burning. It's fucking smoking."

"Fuck me," said Stan seeing the smoke coming from around the door.

"See," said Stan pointing at the obvious.

Jim hurried his bulk over to the oven and started to push at the unfamiliar buttons of the computerised controls without any clear understanding of what they did.

"'Ow d'you turn this bleeding thing off?" he said to no one in particular, stabbing a meaty finger at some of the buttons on the control panel. "Blimey, the old cow's really going!"

Behind him, Stan had pulled a handkerchief from his pocket and was flapping it at the smoking door, from behind which the roaring was now reaching ominous proportions, like a wounded animal growling a warning from the depth of its lair.

In the chapel, the organist played on as he surveyed the menu before him. His salivary glands sprang into life as he contemplated the evening meal that he could almost smell. The service was almost over, and it would be followed by a break for lunch when he would pop over the road to the pub for a couple of pints of beer that would sustain him through the afternoon. It was not often the crematorium had a day as busy as this, and he welcomed the coming opportunity for a quiet moment to himself. As he played, the screen doors opened to let George's coffin pass through. He was somewhat alarmed to see a large puff of smoke come through the doors and around the coffin, and it occurred to him this new stage effect was perhaps a little too theatrical and progressive for your average mourner.

From her seat in the front pew, Lucy watched as her father's coffin began its last slow journey. The finality of the moment was almost overwhelming, and she stared at the disappearing shape unblinking. As she did, the solemnity of the moment was shattered by the strident shriek of a fire alarm and her father's coffin flying back out of the small door through which it was passing, a large meaty hand pushing it out. The congregation gasped and looked at each other for enlightenment and direction as to what to do. A door in the corner of the austere chapel burst open and a small man in baggy trousers and with a large moustache rushed in, flapping his arms and jumping around like a frog legs in a blender.

"Everybody fucking out!" he yelled, hopping about and waving towards the doors as though shooing a clutch of chickens through a hatch. "The old cow's burning."

The congregation stood up as one and moved quickly to the exit, spilling out onto the gravelled drive in front of the building where they started to mill about and look back. Some stepped back onto a lawn that was covered with lines of bouquets of flowers from the mourners of the earlier funerals. The cortège for the next funeral was already turning in through the gates of the crematorium. There was a large, square brick chimney at the back of the building, and it was belching black smoke into the air and emitting a threatening deep throated roar.

As the growing sound of the sirens of fire engines could be heard, Lucy gazed up at the chimney and the thick smoke pouring out of it. Tears were falling down her cheeks and yet she realised she was laughing.

"There you go, Dad," she whispered quietly to herself. "At least you went out with a bang."

Arriving back at the house later, Lucy had busied herself with the niceties of serving drinks and food to the funeral party of friends and distant family. Like many old people who have stayed the course longer than their contemporaries, very few of her father's friends were there but she felt duty bound to his memory to welcome them all and thank them for joining her in his farewell. Slowly people drifted away, back to their lives in which George or his memory would play no part.

Late afternoon the next day, when Ben was at the office before going out to a client dinner, the Funeral Director rang the doorbell and presented her with an urn containing her father's ashes. George's coffin had been retrieved and taken to a nearby crematorium that had not been busy and his cremation had been completed there. Lucy thanked the man for his thoughtfulness and shut the front door as he turned and walked back down the steps into the gloom of the evening. As she watched his stooped receding back moving down the pavement through the drawing room window, she wondered if undertakers slept in their uniform long black coats. There seemed little room for individuality in their choice of clothes. The Director, who went by what some would call the apt name of Mr Fry, had said he would personally deliver George's ashes, which he had just done.

"I mean, Mrs Grayson, after the unfortunate little incident yesterday, it is the least we can do for you," he had intoned in his sepulchral voice.

Lucy was fascinated at his definition of an 'unfortunate little incident' and she was left wondering what would have to happen for an incident to be moved up the range of disaster classification. Perhaps undertakers rated the success or otherwise of their jobs according to some obscure scale. Dropping the coffin would probably rate higher than going to the wrong church, but not as high as the central player in the show knocking on the inside of the coffin to be let out.

Perhaps burning down the crematorium was less heinous as it was mitigated by the fact that at least it got the job done, although somewhat Pyrrhic in its outcome.

Lucy turned and started walking towards the kitchen with the small casket containing her father's ashes, intrigued at the weight in her hands. She felt strangely comforted in holding his remains and she was surprised at her equanimity. She was placing them on a high shelf in a cupboard in the kitchen when the phone rang.

"Mrs Grayson, would that be yourself?" The Irish voice was unmistakeable.

"Hello Matron, how are you. How nice to hear from you," she said.

"Well look at you, recognising me and all," said Matron. "I was just phoning to see how you are. After the terrible goings on down at the crematorium. Mr Fry rang me to tell about it. Wasn't that an affair? You poor soul. It put me in mind of a hospital I worked in once in Limerick, it did. Oh, there was a terrible fire. They had to get all the poor souls out, but one didn't make it. He'd been having a little smoke in his bed and fell asleep, so that's where the fire started. He didn't have a chance, poor man. The brave firemen brought him out on a stretcher and there were the bits of him falling off all over the floor. What a mess it was Mrs Grayson...."

"Yes Matron, I can imagine," interrupted Lucy, marvelling at the insensitivity of the woman and eager to change the subject. "What can I do for you Matron?"

"Oh, as I said, I was just after ringing to see if you are alright, after the fire and the difficult decision and all. It must be a lot for you to bear there."

"What difficult decision?" asked Lucy.

"Oh, the drip," said Matron. "I must say," she ploughed on, brooking no interruption to her flow. "I was a bit surprised there, when Mr Grayson said we shouldn't be giving it to Mr Harkness. I mean, there's no doubt he'd have been with us a few days more but I can see Mr Grayson's point of view. Mr Harkness was not enjoying the best of life, I can see that. Mind, I'd not be wanting to make that decision myself if you see what I mean..."

"I'm not sure I understand what you mean," Lucy interrupted again, frowning her confusion. "Are you saying my husband told you not to help my father. Not to give him a drip or something?"

There was a long pause before the hesitant reply came.

"Well, I suppose you could be saying that Mrs Grayson," said Matron. "He said he would speak to you about it that night. It was a sort of thoughtful decision if you like, and I'm sure it was difficult for the poor man, him being in a hurry for his meeting and all when I called."

Lucy stood silent, transfixed.

"There was a taxi waiting, and all," continued Matron. "My but he's a busy man, your husband, and I rang just like that Mrs Grayson, out of the blue so to speak as I could not get you, though I tried there, that I did. The poor man was on the spot, he was...."

Matron was gabbling to fill the vacuum of the silence on the phone, a silence that discomforted her enormously. She felt an almost uncontrollable urge to end the conversation to escape the searing embarrassment that accompanies any perceived faux pas.

Her wish was realised when the phone went dead in

her hand as Lucy put the receiver down.

CHAPTER 20

Summer 1988

The late afternoon sun fell across the sea onto the beach, setting the surface of the water alight with a dancing hypnotic light, a stroboscopic affect to mesmerise and dazzle the scattering of sunbathers relaxing on the sand. A game of football was in full swing on a makeshift pitch marked out in the sand, crumpled beach towels marking the goalmouths. A family of uncertain middle-European origins, led by the restlessly dominant father of three sons, had challenged all comers to a game. They were now in the process of annihilating the cosmopolitan opposition, every goal scored a World Cup Final winning achievement to be marked by a mindless rushing around the sandy pitch yelling at the top of their voices. The more observant onlooker would have noticed each of the three sons taking their every lead from their father, his all-consuming competitiveness an omnipotent threat to every trip or mistake. He berated and belittled every off target pass from them, and poached the ball at the goalmouth so he could glory in the inevitable scoring moment, ululating his achievement in a victory dance modelled on

Bayern Munich's finest. The fact that the opposition goalkeeper was probably about to celebrate his seventh birthday seemed not to diminish his accomplishment.

Slowly, the allied opposition lost interest in the game, disenchanted with a score-line that read like a telephone number, and one by one they drifted off. The game withered on the vine and the three sons set off for their towels, unaware of their father mapping out a volley ball court in the sand for the game he dragged them back to play. Lucy watched his first serve, a full blooded stroke that hit the youngest son full in the face at the other end of the court before he could lift his hand. She saw the small boy's shoulders sag under the weight of recrimination from his father as a tirade of instruction on the art of returning serve deluged him, like a wave bursting on the shore, but not delivered before the father had loudly celebrated his outright winner.

Lucy shifted on her large towel on the soft sand, aware that by some osmotic process she could feel the small boy's discomfort. She wondered at the inadequacies that drove a man like that to win at all cost, and then to pour those same inadequacies into anyone subordinate to him. Not for the first time she realised that we enjoy, or perhaps endure and survive, upwards of twenty years of education and upbringing, a tutelage designed to make us complete beings, housetrained, able to hold down jobs and contribute to society. An upbringing intended to make us more interesting and rounded people. And yet for the biggest, most difficult, and arguably most important role of all, parenthood, there are no lessons, no training. No lessons, that is, apart from those we imbibe from our formative years, the examples set by how we are treated. Perhaps we all follow an invisible path that is laid without our knowledge or connivance, a path that we so often use to absolve ourselves from the mistakes we inevitably make with our own progeny.

As the impromptu teams fragmented and went their separate ways, Lucy noticed Sebastian turn and walk down to the water's edge. He sat down with his legs spread flat on the sand before him, letting the waves wash their death throes over his feet. He had been watching the game of football in its progress, not pushing himself forward to join in. Lucy could see he was aching to do so. She worried about him since she and Ben had separated. Their parting had somehow affected him at a deeper level than she could fathom. Like many robustly masculine boys, his carapace of sturdiness protected a sensitive core that bruised at the slightest fall. Ben's departure from his daily life had opened a void that Lucy felt impotent to fill. How could she? She was a mother, not a father. There was an implicit blackmail in his introversion, that it would be removed if she would let Ben back into her life, and by association into Sebastian's. So his new-found self-sufficiency was of her doing, and it was in her gift to change it, but was she prepared to pay that price?

In her more rational moments during the last year, Lucy had marvelled at the male ability, even at this young age, to shift blame and transfer guilt. And yet she knew she had been complicit in accepting this guilt, because she knew that parting from Ben had left a void in Sebastian's life, a void that Emma did not seem to feel so deeply. Or perhaps like many of the female sex, Emma was more robust, her resilience a common and shared genetic strand that supported all womanhood, leaving her confident in her ability to control and maintain her relationship with her father at will, without reference to the quantity or quality of their time together.

Lucy had found it impossible to explain to Sebastian why she had ended their marriage, and thereby the security of his home and his life as he had known it. How can children in broken relationships not become collaterally damaged by the familial conflict raging around them, and which they have no control over? Looking back now, nearly a year after she came back from the weekend away that had allowed Ben the time to clear his things from the house, she could still feel her anger surge within her. Would she ever be able to stop these raw emotions from welling up within her? Would she ever be able to find it within herself to forgive him? She was left hurt and exhausted, flushed with an adrenaline-fuelled fatigue.

The thoughts and feelings came of their own volition, unasked and unannounced, often catching her unawares, a confusing amalgam of grief and rage, forced up from her subconscious like magma thrusting to the surface as it rides the intolerable pressures from beneath, no matter how she tried to push them out of her mind. Her instincts told her that she somehow had to come to terms with the past if she was going to have a future, or a future worth having. As she watched Sebastian pouring wet sand through his fingers to form ragged fairy castles, as Ben had taught him, she questioned for the countless time how she had ended up in this position.

The conversation with the Irish matron of the Home had shocked her, but it had also opened her eyes to so many things. She remembered the conversation with startling clarity, and she remembered the coldness she had felt, the frightening detachment from emotion. The anger would come later. It was as though their love, their marriage and their lives together were a balloon, and the Matron's words were the knitting needle thrust into it that destroyed its form. It was no more, and it's shapeless, wrinkled remains no clue to the filled and robust form that moments before sat proud for all to see.

After putting down the phone to the Matron, Lucy had sat quietly for a while, and then picked up the receiver and called Ben at his office. His secretary had tried to put her off, telling her he was in a meeting, but Lucy had said it was urgent and that she must speak to him. The phone had gone to that Limbo where all phones calls go when put on hold, a silent place that hinted at the horrors of sensory deprivation. Eventually it had come alive, slightly startling Lucy as the secretary announced she was putting her through. Lucy felt she had been granted an enormous favour

"Lucy, hi, what's wrong? Is one of the children hurt?" Ben's voice was rushed, a mixture of impatience and concern, irritated at being interrupted but hesitant before full commitment to anger in case it was important.

"I want you to come home," said Lucy, her voice flat and calm.

"I'll be home on time this evening," said Ben. "I'll see you then."

"I mean now," said Lucy firmly.

"I can't just come now, Lucy. I'm in an important meeting which I've come out of to take this call. I'll see you tonight."

"No Ben, you won't. You'll see me now. I don't give a fuck if your meeting's with the Queen. Get home if you want to find someone there when you arrive!"

The receiver slammed in Ben's ear and the line went dead. He was shocked at Lucy's language. She never swore and something extraordinary must have happened for her to speak to him like that. A cold dread squeezed his stomach as only one explanation presented itself to him from the menu of options that sprang to his mind. Jane must have told her about Sally. What a bitch! Why did she have to do that? And why now, of all times?

"Selfish, interfering bitch," he muttered, kicking shut the half open drawer of a small mock mahogany filing cabinet by his desk. Ben picked up the phone and pressed the button that put him through to his secretary.

"Lara, look, I've got to go home and sort something out. Can you go in and sit in for me. Make my apologies will you. Just say I've got an urgent problem to deal with. Keep low on the detail for the moment. It's just a status meeting and I've given my briefing, so just note what's said and let me know when I get back. I should be back in a couple of hours."

"Sure," replied Lara in that efficient, can-do voice that would take her to the top floor as secretary to the Chairman when the present incumbent's drinking regime brought her to the office late once too often. "I'll postpone your meeting this afternoon as well, just in case. It's only a creative brief and you can do that in the morning. Tomorrow's quiet."

"Oh, God, I'd forgotten that," said Ben. "Thanks. And oh, Lara, one more thing, could you order me a taxi to take me home too please. What would I do without you?"

"Sure, no problem. I'll get reception to call you when it's here. See you later."

"Yeah, see you," said Ben, but the competent voice

was already gone. No doubt his secretary was multitasking her way through an algorithm of arrangements whilst planning a contribution to the status meeting and a seductive recipe for the evening for some lucky boyfriend who was probably sitting at a desk somewhere in the City, making fortunes whilst fantasising about the illegal practices he intended enjoying with the deliciously fragrant Lara on the hearthrug that evening. Ben regularly empathised with her boyfriend. The rest of the time he envied him.

In the taxi on the way home, Ben tried to guess at Lucy's intentions now she knew about Sally. Like any woman unable to differentiate between love and lust, she would initially be hurt and angry. He could hear her voice asking him "How could you do it?" and he'd have to put her right on that. But for her bloody father and all the time and emotion she spent on him, all of it wasted in these last months, he wouldn't have been tempted by Sally, or anyone else for that matter. Not that there was anyone else at the moment, apart from the one nighter with a client's secretary a few months ago, but you couldn't count that as they'd both been pretty drunk and he could hardly be held responsible in the condition they had got themselves into that night. The clinches and feverish groping in the lift and a stationery cupboard with that pretty temporary secretary a week after finishing with Sally could not be considered a sexual encounter so didn't even rank on his guilt spreadsheet.

After the initial hurt and upset, Ben reckoned Lucy would calm down and see sense. It was hardly the end of the world, and he'd been discreet so none of her friends knew. Apart from the ever-bloody helpful Jane that is. Lucy would rant a bit and sulk for a while, and there would no doubt be some tears, but in time she'd come round and they could get on with their lives. She could join some clubs and do some good works, which would help fill the vacuum left by her father's death. Ben conceded there would be a bit of a gap, but he'd have to make sure she didn't make a meal of it. The old bugger had had a good innings and none of us go on forever, so turning mourning into a career was not going to help much.

As the taxi swung north up towards Camden, it stopped at some lights that were red for a pedestrian crossing. Ben glanced to a large mirror-fronted building occupied by one of the Agency's larger clients. The revolving doors of the building sprang into life and Sally popped out onto the pavement, like a pea shelled from its pod. Ben realised she must have had a meeting at the client, remembering that she worked on that account. He had not seen Sally since the night of the debacle in the hotel, apart from a casual nod whenever they passed each other in the office. They had spoken briefly on the telephone when they were both back in the office. There had been no recriminations in her voice, just a finality that closed a door firmly.

"Ben, I can't do this any more," she had said. "I don't want to be a secret or hidden part of a man's life, tucked away out of sight. I don't want to be sitting at home waiting for a phone call or for you to drop in for a snatched couple of hours, leaving me feeling I'm just a sex object. Saturday evenings are boring and lonely alone, waiting. I want more, and let's face it, I'm not going to get it with you."

"But I'm sure we can work something out." Ben was aware he was pleading, but he didn't want to lose the excitement of the relationship.

"The only way of working it out is for you to bring me fully into your life, introduce me to all your friends, your family." Sally was resolute, and unyielding to his fear of losing her.

"But I can't. Not yet anyway...."

"Not ever Ben," Sally interrupted. "Why not just be honest about it. And anyway, I think I have met someone else and I'd like to give that a chance, which I can't if I'm seeing you. It wouldn't be fair. And in any case, it's not what I want."

"Who are you seeing?" Ben blurted. "When did you meet him? How..."

"I don't want to go into all that, Ben," said Sally. "Anyway, it's not really relevant or frankly any of your business. I just want this to end so I can get on with my life. A complete life, not as someone else's secret sideshow of casual sex, where I begin to feeling I'm just being used. You can go and buy that. I had fun, and thanks for that, but there's no going forward for us. You just have to accept that."

And that had been the end of the affair. It had hurt him to lose her, and he knew his pride was badly dented by the appearance of someone else in her life, but the finality in her voice was clear and Ben knew the relationship was over.

Seeing Sally now, unexpectedly, brought back those same hurts, and the memories of their moments together. As she stood on the pavement looking around, Sally suddenly smiled broadly. Ben leaned forward to open the taxi window to call out to her when a young, tall and good looking man of her age walked nonchalantly up to her and folded his arms about her. They embraced with a lingering kiss. Her arms were up around his neck, and her head was thrown back as she looked up into his eyes, their bodies moulded together into one. The sunlight sparkled in her eyes, and for a searing moment Ben realised she had never looked as happy when she had been with him. Yes, she had enjoyed herself when they had been together, but this was unbridled pleasure and the rapier of jealousy ran him through.

Sally and her man turned and started to walk away as Ben sat back in the shadow of the cab, their arms around each other. As they did, the young man reached down behind her with his right hand and put it between her buttocks and squeezed, crumpling her skirt so Ben could see the familiar line of her abbreviated panties. It was an act of pure eroticism, an act between two people who know each other's bodies intimately, no place in their delicate folds a secret. Sally looked up at the young man and laughed. She said something to him that drew their bodies even closer as they hurried off in unison, hugging tightly as they stepped around a corner and out of Ben's sight. The taxi moved off and Ben leaned forward and looked down the street where they had gone, catching a glimpse of their diminishing backs before they were lost to him behind the buildings.

Seeing Sally like that, happy in her new life with her new partner, depressed Ben. He knew he should be happy for her. Happy that she had found someone nearer her age who could share the interests of the young with her. But the feeling of rejection was overwhelming and hard to bear, and that was all he could focus on, a selfish wallow in his rejection and misery. He stared disconsolately out of the window, the overflowing stalls of Camden Market an untidy jumble of colour as clothes hanging from the metal supports of the stalls danced in the breeze that blew down the street, each jigging its own interpretation of St Vitus' ill-choreographed steps. Their syncopated flapping and jerking reminded him of flying kites when he was young. The kite at the end of the line was like a fish hooked in the river after taking the fisherman's fly. It fought on the end of its tether, fought to be free and away, jerking, feinting left and right before diving. And yet, if let go, it would lose direction and ultimately fall to the ground, useless and suddenly inanimate. So holding it a reluctant captive was a shackle of kindness that restrained it from self-destruction.

Perhaps, Ben thought, we are each like that kite. Perhaps we all fight on the end of the line in a relationship, fight to be free of the tie. To do what we will without reference to anyone. And yet, if freed, if the tether is cut, how many fall to earth, lost, detached from their purpose in life? Anchorless and drifting. Surely, Ben felt, that longed for freedom proves nothing more than that most people find that sort of self-determination agoraphobic, a life incomplete. Before long, most are back in some new relationship that is often no different to the one so recently vacated. Why otherwise would those who are bereaved so regularly find new partners, and often so soon after the death of the former love of their life, the love so often and so recently considered irreplaceable? Ben often felt it would be easier to form no emotional attachments in life. In that would lie the certainty of never being hurt. But freedom is an illusion, a utopian dream.

Ben had read a dog-education book he had been obliged to plough through as background information when the Agency pitched for a client that manufactured some appalling dog-food, which the client was convinced all dogs would select if given a choice. The book hypothesised that a dog held on a leash became aggressive and would bark and snarl at other dogs, straining to get at them. Off the leash, that same dog would join in ritualistic circling and bottom sniffing, with an air of stiff-legged uncertainty before retreating unharmed and without a direct physical encounter. So the leash is a source of Dutch courage, a security blanket that allows the restrained to express their innate aggression with no fear of coming to harm. To Ben, marriage and all its commitments and responsibilities was that leash and no wonder he strained to get away, to be free. How much less emotional damage would there be if men in particular were free of these unnatural shackles. There would be lower expectations of them and less of a sense of desperation to break free. Lucy must see this before she did anything rash or made a hasty decision, and Ben resolved to make sure she did. She must see the affair with Sally meant nothing and was merely a symptom of the situation he found himself in. Now with George dead she could find time for him again.

The taxi swung into his familiar street, lined with trees whose desiccated autumnal leaves fluttered on the branches in the breeze, some floating off in the air, skipping and sinking before coming to rest with the growing throng on the ground. A young lad with a large bin on wheels was sweeping one of the pavements, piling the leaves in front of him, unaware that a new carpet was already forming behind him. Ben turned and watched him as the taxi passed where he was working and wondered if the young man was happy in his life, a life that seemed so uncomplicated from where Ben sat. No clients to upset, no mortgage or school fees to pay. No irate wife to face. Just the wage packet at the end of each week, to be spent in the pub and at the bookies, and another pavement of uncomplaining leaves to sweep in the morning. The simplicity of the life Ben saw was appealing, it's attraction masking the realities of a life on the breadline, eked out on the strength of the mind-numbing tedium of clearing detritus, whether from trees or from people's hands. The taxi stopped outside Ben's house and he delved into his pocket for the fair.

"Cheer up mate, it probably won't happen," said the cabbie suddenly, watching Ben's face in the mirror.

"What?" said Ben.

"Whatever it is making you look sad mate, that's what," said the cabbie. "I hope you don't mind me saying so, guv'nor, but I couldn't help noticing you had a face like a wet `addock on the way here. Now I've got a missus that's got a face that looks like that all the time, that's when it ain't looking like her arse that is, not that there's much difference, if you know what I mean sir, so I can recognise a wet `addock face when I see one, and yours is as wet an `addock as I've seen in a long time sir. My granddad, he was a fishmonger sir, down West Ham, and I used to go down his shop Saturday's to help out, when I was a nipper like, and those `addock of his, well, they weren't exactly the Marx Brothers were they? So I hope whatever's troubling you sir ain't that bad. Do you want a receipt for that sir?"

The seamless transition from his wife's face and arse being interchangeable, through the psychological profile of his grandfather's marble slab and its connection with Ben's well being, to the mundane offer of a receipt bemused Ben. He felt he should be affronted by the intrusion into his life but the blatant honesty and kind concern of the man was strangely refreshing. Ben did wonder whether, when taxi drivers in London took the Knowledge during their months of learning the streets of the city, they took evening classes in psychology and the formulation and delivery of opinions. They invariably had an opinion about any subject you could throw at them, and some were so full of opinion they were forced to offload them onto their unfortunate fares, trapped and imprisoned in the back. Perhaps this off-loading was necessary to make room for the inevitable flow of more that followed behind.

"No, thank you," said Ben. "And thank you, I'll be fine. Just a difficult day, that's all."

"There you go, mate, that's the spirit. You see, you're up to a catfish already sir, what with them always looking like they're smiling, and before you know it sir, you'll be off the slab like a leaping salmon and on your feet. Thanks, and here's you're change."

The metaphors seemed to come from an arcane tome blending the sea with the psychological, and Ben stepped out of the cab and held the door for a new passenger standing patiently waiting for it to come free. The man stepped into it and Ben heard the cabbie greeting him.

"Morning guv'nor, and where to today. If the bleeding council haven't dug up the streets, I should get you there in no time. No better than bloody politicians those councillors if you ask me, if you'll excuse me adjectival sir. If I had my way...."

Ben closed the cab door and stepped up onto the pavement and went up the steps to the front door. He wondered at what point in the journey the cabbie would stop long enough to find out where he was supposed to be going.

The front door swung open and as he stepped through it, he tripped slightly on the mat that lay behind it. He walked through the house calling out Lucy's name, glancing in at the drawing room, which was empty. He walked into the kitchen where Lucy was sitting silently at the table.

"You're there," said Ben. "I've been calling you."

Ben could see Lucy had been crying. Her hands lay still in her lap.

"How could you?" she said suddenly.

"Now look, before you start, it's over," said Ben quickly.

Lucy was startled. She had not expected Ben to end their marriage, and certainly not in this way, peremptorily and so dispassionately.

"What do you mean, 'It's over'?" said Lucy.

"I mean it's over. I'm not seeing her anymore," Ben replied.

Lucy sat quietly in the completely silent room, frowning her confusion. "I don't know what you're talking about?" she said. "Seeing who?"

A cold dread gripped Ben, and he shifted his feet in discomfort, aware that he was still standing, but uncertain as to whether he should or could sit down. His mind froze, immobilised like an engine out of oil, and he was lost as to what to say. Anything more could incriminate him further if he had got it wrong and Jane had not made the call. What did Lucy know? Why had she called him home? Perhaps it was nothing to do with Sally, but it must be. Surely Jane had told her by now.

"Wasn't that why you called me?" he said eventually.

"No, but it's becoming part of it now," said Lucy. "I called you about something completely different. But I'm interested Ben. I'm interested in who you've been seeing, as you put it. It seems to have the scent of an affair to me. Have you been having an affair?"

"Well, hardly an affair, but yes I have been seeing someone a bit," he said.

"Please explain Ben. At what point does just seeing a bit someone become an affair? Do you go round to this woman and watch her? That's more spectator sport than affair, I grant you. Does seeing someone become an affair with a kiss, or is it a grubby grope in a car, or must it be a dirty week end away Ben? You tell me, because I wouldn't know and I think I'd like to know. I'd like to know what you've been up to."

"Well, yes, we have been away for nights, but it never meant anything...."

"So emotion-free sex doesn't constitute an affair. Is that it Ben? Did you pay her for this 'seeing for a bit' or was it a non-commercial arrangement?"

"Well, yes. No, of course not. I mean, it meant nothing and I was lost. Confused. You were so wrapped up in your father, I felt shut out. Let's face it, this wasn't exactly an emotional heaven, was it? I seemed to be able to do nothing right, and hardly felt welcome in my own home. So perhaps Sally..." Ben hesitated before going on. "That's her name. She's at the office. Perhaps I felt she'd give me what was missing here, I don't know...." Ben faltered and fell silent.

"So your affair's my fault, is that it Ben?" Lucy's anger was beginning to mount, despite her resolve and promise to herself that she would remain calm when she confronted Ben about her conversation with the Matron.

"No, that's not what I meant," said Ben. "Don't

start turning it on me...."

"That's rich, Ben, after what you've just said. You've as much said it's my fault you threw yourself into this woman's arms because I wasn't giving you the attention you wanted. Well poor bloody you. For your information, Ben, the world doesn't revolve around you. It never has, despite your belief that it does, and blaming me because you couldn't keep your bloody trousers up is just more cowardice. When are you going to learn to take responsibility? Your grubby little affair was a choice you made Ben, no one else. No one forced you into it." Lucy was shouting, her indignation at the inequity of Ben's comment consuming her.

For a moment silence fell like a wet blanket on the room, which gave Lucy time to calm herself.

"Anyway," she said, "that all seems pretty irrelevant to me now. I'm not sure I care anymore. I've just spoken to the Matron at Mount Pleasant. Anything there you might want to discuss?"

Ben frowned, momentarily at a loss as to what Lucy was talking about. Suddenly, for the second time in ten minutes, his blood ran cold as he remembered the conversation he'd had with the Matron about George's drip and his refusal to give permission for it. The blood drained from his face and he stood silent, staring at Lucy, hoping that by remaining silent he could avoid incriminating himself. Perhaps she was referring to something else he had not remembered. His lies were beginning to weave a maze in which he was getting lost.

"I've settled the bill there so I'm not sure what you mean. What's there to discuss?"

"Really Ben? Is that the best you can do? Try a little honesty for once. You refused permission for Dad to have a drip. Playing God were you, or was that a clinical judgment?"

"She rang me in the middle of a busy day and wanted to know if they could give George some drip or something. She said it wouldn't make any difference in the long run, that he was dying anyway but the drip thing would just extend his suffering. I saw no point in dragging out an appalling existence that he wasn't even conscious of and would never have wanted. I mean, you'd put a poor animal down that was in that state." Ben didn't feel his words carried much conviction and fell silent again.

"Is that how it was, Ben?" Lucy said. "Putting

Dad down because he was an inconvenience to you? And who said you could play this God of yours?" Lucy had regained her calmness now, the words she had rehearsed in her mind while she had waited for Ben to get home from the office coming with a fluid ease that surprised her.

"Of course I wasn't playing God," said Ben indignantly. "That's ridiculous. A decision had to be made and I made it with George's best interest in mind, that's all."

"From what I heard, they weren't asking for a decision, they were asking for permission. And you refused it. That sounds more like your best interests than Dad's to me. I can't believe you could be so callous. So unfeeling. Whatever happened to compassion? Was this permission so urgent you couldn't have asked to speak to me first? Or did you think I'd spoil it for you and give it, that I might have said yes? Was that it?"

"Of course not," Ben said. "It wasn't my fault they couldn't get hold of you..."

"Like it wasn't your fault you had your little affair," Lucy interrupted. "Why is it never your fault

Ben? Are the rest of us all so imperfect in the blinding glare of your perfection?"

Ben was silent, lost for a reply. Feeling trapped and cornered he desperately wanted to escape the house, to end this nightmare in which he felt enmeshed.

"And how many other little dalliances and affairs have you had?" she asked, the questions now emerging and lining up to be asked as the shock of the revelation subsided.

"None," Ben said, knowing his lie must show in his reddening face. "Anyway, it wasn't an affair as such," he added lamely. "It…"

"It really doesn't matter what we each call it Ben, it comes to the same thing. It's called being unfaithful, and it is typical of you to grade its severity. It may not mean much to you but it's everything to me. You broke your word. Do you remember Ben - to have and to hold, to be faithful, to honour? Which part of 'I promise' didn't you mean or feel you had to keep? We promised to support each other, to be faithful to each other and I have more than done that. I have never stopped you chasing the dream of the career that is so important to you, because I knew it was, no matter how much I wanted you to be here more with us, a present, fully engaged father and husband, not a casual visitor expecting us to be grateful for the crumbs of your time. I seem to have a bachelor with a family for a husband. You know, you haven't even apologised. You've just tried to justify yourself and to blame me."

"Of course I'm sorry," Ben said

"Too late Ben. Would you have said that if I hadn't asked? You know, you were right when you came in," Lucy said. "It is over. I can't live with you anymore. Not like this. You've changed, and I'm not sure I like the new you. I need some space so perhaps you can find somewhere else to stay for a while. I need to think."

The memory of the words made Lucy wince as she put down her book and rolled over on her towel on the sand to lie on her front. Reaching behind, she undid the strap of her bikini top and lay her cheek on her crossed arms. She closed her eyes, the evening sun falling from the west onto her face, warming it. Perhaps, she thought, one day I'll work out where it all went wrong with Ben. Until the moment in the kitchen, there didn't seem to be one cataclysmic moment that brought it all to a final denouement. Whilst the revelation of his affair and selfish decision about her father had been a form of catalyst, spurring her into a decision, it had been more in the way of drifting, moving apart whilst running separate lives. Perhaps we both contributed to that, she thought. Me focusing on Dad and just getting through the day with the children, and Ben on his bloody job, status and position. But I didn't stray, no matter the temptation. He did and that hurt. Perhaps it was the breaking of her trust that was the most significant casualty from his affairs, which she now knew were not limited to that one event that he had mistakenly blurted out to her.

"Would you like some sun cream on those shoulders?"

The interruption brought her back to the present and she lifted her head slightly and smiled. Emma had been brought back and was playing nearby in the sand with a small group of children.

"Yes please," Lucy said, and lay her head back on her arms. James squirted the cream onto her shoulders and started spreading it slowly, gently massaging the taught muscles in her neck. She closed her eyes and luxuriated in his strong hands working the tension out of her as they strayed from her neck and shoulders and down her back.

CHAPTER 21

Ben's small three bedroom flat was at the top of an old house in a quiet street in Islington. It had been advertised in the local paper as the ideal home for the young family just starting out, and in a way he felt he was just starting out again. It had been strange at first, living on his own, and in such a small apartment. He missed the daily rhythms of family life. The children had stayed with Lucy, and whilst he was able to see them regularly, and they came to spend the night with him in the spare bedrooms, there was a sense of artificiality about the arrangements.

In the first few weeks he had found himself forcing an air of jollity when he was with the children, ever eager that they should be happy, their time filled and never with anything boring. They had rushed to Regent's Park to see the animals in the zoo, taken the train to the sea, and generally followed the itinerary Ben had drawn up for each of their visits, until it eventually became clear to him that often the children would prefer just to stay in the apartment and watch the television, or play in the small garden behind the house that those in the flats were able to share. Their time with him took on a less frenetic pace, and he came to enjoy the quiet moments of normality with them.

In the beginning, in those early months after he and Lucy separated, the children asked the inevitable question as to when he was going to come home, but in time they seemed to accept their two centre lives, at least on the surface. Emma was the more straightforward and settled into the bedroom Ben had prepared for her. Sebastian was more reserved, and somehow seemed in need of reassurance about things that might affect his life. He became agitated if Ben was late to collect him, or if plans had to be changed. His self-confidence deserted him and he became introverted and quiet.

The evenings alone in the flat were contemplative moments for Ben. He knew Lucy was lost to him, and the best he could expect was a civil relationship for the sake of the children. He questioned whether he had ever really won her, so was she ever there to lose? Perhaps, he felt, a man never truly wrests a woman away from the bond with her father or a first love. Maybe that strand of love a girl has for her father is a stronger tether than one any husband can create, and asking her to choose between the two is asking too much, and he had asked Lucy to choose. Ben was painfully aware that James had come back into Lucy's life, and the fact that he seemed to make her happy was a piquant reminder of his own inability to do so. Despite the permanence of their separation he still felt the acidic pangs of jealousy. He wondered if Lucy had always secretly wished she had stayed with James, married him instead of Ben and had his children.

Ben found the first few months after he had moved out very difficult. Marriage had become a comfortable jacket, fitting easily on the shoulders and under the arms, pockets filled with familiar objects. On his own in a bare-walled rented flat, living on furniture the Charity shops had probably rejected as unsellable, every faded cushion and uncomfortable chair was a reminder of what he was missing. In truth, to begin with he had probably drunk a little too much and spent too much time on his own, but the soporific affect of the alcohol dulled the memory and he had little stomach for company that would entail questions and advice that he didn't feel strong enough to take. Many friends he and Lucy had shared were strangely unavailable, busy at week ends and seemingly unable to return calls. The sense of rejection added to his sense of isolation but in that solitude he found time to reflect on his values and on the true value of friendships that turned out to be so shallow..

One afternoon at the office just after Christmas, he had been looking at a newly launched magazine the media department had sent to him as a potential platform for some press work that needed to go out, and he had spotted an article about the growing community of single people and how that community was benefiting from a new breed of service businesses that catered for single person's own particular needs. He marvelled at the entrepreneurship in finding a business opportunity in other people's misery. Singles holidays, clubs and dating agencies were all mentioned, but what caught his eye was a paragraph on skiing for the older single. For some unaccountable reason, the article seemed to shake him from his torpor, and he had picked up the phone and called one of the travel companies that had placed an advertisement accompanying the article and made a booking.

The week in the Swiss mountains revived his spirits. The members of the party he joined each had their own reasons for being there, their own history that isolated them from other people's busy lives. There seemed to be an unspoken agreement between them that they each leave their respective stories at home and live in the moment. The past and the future were left in different dimensions, and the group threw themselves into the present, ignoring the past they could not change and not worrying about a future that had not yet arrived. The respite from the thoughts that constantly invaded his mind brought Ben a welcome relief.

Now, as he sat in the evening sun in the window of his flat, a book on his lap, he looked across the roofs of the surrounding houses and realised he had not looked at the words in front of him for some time. Suddenly restless, he closed the book, placed it on the table next to him and picked up the keys that lay next to it. Closing the window he left the flat and walked out into the street, turning towards the busy thoroughfare nearby. He strolled along the bustling pavements with his hands thrust into his trouser pockets, a light sweater around his shoulders, its sleeves crossed at his throat like a scarf against the cool Spring evening breeze that ruffled his hair as he walked into it.

He passed cafes whose tables spilled onto the street, each table encircled by the cheerfully raucous young, out enjoying the late summer light. Tomorrow was Saturday, and he would collect the children after breakfast for their first weekend with him after their holiday in the sun. They would tell him about their time away, and he could feel the warmth of them sitting with him on the flat's lumpy sofa. Then he would take them out for a pizza supper. Suddenly that moment couldn't come soon enough. Tomorrow was his new dawn, bringing with it hope, change and perhaps for once, some insightful wisdom.

Printed in Great Britain
by Amazon